WILD WHISPERS

RYAN JO SUMMERS

I

Season Moriarty gripped the steering wheel, feeling herself tighten with tension. According to the sign she just passed, she was almost there. It felt like she'd been driving forever, but it was only an hour since she refueled and left Riverton. The sign she passed was one of the first indications of life beyond the patches of dried grass and bare trees. Their ghostly silhouettes did nothing to comfort her. Reflecting, she had to admit these western highways had a habit of appearing never-ending if one wasn't used to such wide-open spaces. She felt more at home in the rolling green grass of Kentucky.

At least the roads were in good condition considering the early January weather. She was thankful for the good fortune of avoiding severe storms during her long trek from Florida to Wyoming. Why hadn't she just taken a plane? At the time, the drive seemed like a good idea. Blowing out a shaky breath, she patted the steering wheel. Only two more miles to go and she would be there. Heritage Farms.

And possibly the start of her new future. Or at the very least, a job interview.

Seeing an advertisement last month for a head trainer at Heritage Farms, famed birth place of some of the greatest record breakers of the turf, she'd written. Preparing her resume, credentials, and references all in a tidy little package, she sent it out into the postal world with a prayer and a kiss. She appreciated the old-fashioned charm of someone who still preferred snail mail paper over digital downloads and emails with pasted-in documents. Considering the reputation of Heritage Farms, and the elusive owner, she expected an old-fashioned gentleman.

The owner, Ty Masters, had written back, requesting she come for the weekend. Since there were a number of qualified applicants, he was offering everyone a free weekend vacation at the farm in exchange for an interview. One lucky applicant would end the vacation with a new job contract. Either way, Season surmised, just spending the weekend at Heritage Farms was quite an honor by itself. It was history and fame come to life.

Taking her mind off the fact she was quickly approaching her destination, Season thought about the reclusive owner of the farm. What she, or anyone else, knew about Mr. Masters would barely fill a bucket. He had been born to wealthy English parents. He was rumored to be the black sheep of the family, always seeming to have different ideas than anyone else. The fact that he preferred to live in the wide-open spaces of Wyoming and fly his racehorses to the tracks east and west supported this. Most all other racehorse farms were kept relatively close to the tracks themselves.

When Ty Masters' parents died, he took his share of the vast inheritance and came to America with one foundation stallion. With that single stallion, he worked hard and gradually built the world famous and respected Heritage Farms.

People seemed to know more about the incredible horses that came from the farm and their record-breaking feats than they did about the man who started it all. Every once in a while, he would allow a few snapshots of himself from within the winners' circle, hiding his face behind something and always refusing to comment. It was if he preferred remaining a mystery to the fans and keeping the spotlight on his horses instead. Season liked how he gave more credit to his jockey and horses. It showed he didn't possess an inflated ego like some racehorse owners she knew. A few acted like they had gone out and ran around the track themselves. Mr. Masters earned a bonus point in her opinion.

However, it struck her as odd that he would choose to name his farm Heritage when he clearly wanted nothing to do with his own. Rumors flying around the tracks say he left brothers and a wife in England.

Well, none of that mattered now, she decided as she turned her small pickup truck onto a dirt road labeled Heritage Way. The driveway? One step closer at least. All that mattered was she do well at this interview and get that job. She needed this job, so she had to do better than the other applicants. Absently she wondered who they were. Anyone she might know? The racing world could be a small world too.

Topping a small hill, Heritage Farms spilled into view, giving her the first look at history come alive. Driving past pastures closed in with white planked fences, they looked out of place in the wilds of Wyoming. Miles of white fences stretching across acres of green grass was what you expected to see on the horse farms in Florida, not way out here. Nonetheless, horses grazed lazily in the pastures, soaking up the late afternoon sunshine, not caring if it were Florida or Wyoming sunshine. It was all the same to a horse.

Stopping the truck, she looked them over carefully; a few raised their heads to peer curiously at her before resuming their grazing. She liked what she saw in their confirmation, and she stepped back on the gas, resuming her slow descent down the long, winding driveway.

Several white, crisp outbuildings scattered the landscape. An oval training track lay in the distance. Further to one side, she saw a sprawling white, two-level house. Stately pillars flanked the long balcony. A wistful sigh escaped her. It would be nice to live in such a lovely home.

Driving under the iron arch with a horse statue standing atop a circle, she grinned at the letters *HF* inside. She'd finally made it! She was here! Braking to a stop beside five other dusty and travel worn vehicles, she let out a pent-up breath. One hurdle successfully completed.

Stepping out, she leisurely stretched, sucking in a big lungful of cool mountain air and took in the views of the snowy mountains high in the distance. The air smelled fresh and clean. So different. So good. She bent over to touch her toes, then reached up over her head, and eased the kinks out. It felt good to stretch and feel her muscles expand. Twisting her torso each direction, she continued surveying her majestic surroundings.

It was beautiful here to say the least. Exhilaration chased away her road weariness.

"Very nice. May I see that again?"

A deep male voice behind her made her jump. Whirling, she spotted a tall man leaning causally against an equally tall chestnut horse. He stared at her, smug amusement lighting blue eyes. He towered over her five feet five inches. A well-worn, almost battered cowboy hat covered his head, but a few defiant locks of dusty blonde hair still managed to peek out from under it. A mustache sat under his nose, looking like a comfy caterpillar. Full lips curled up into a mocking grin.

A few soiled patches of straw clung to his faded denim jacket and his form-fitting blue jeans. If he were showered and in cleaner clothes, he might appear handsome. If he were not wearing that mocking smile. He had one of those familiar kind of faces, like she had seen him somewhere before. Nothing came immediately to mind though. It was doubtful. He had most likely never left the Wyoming area in his life.

"That was the best thing I have seen all day," he drawled slowly. "Care to repeat it?"

A male chauvinist. Suddenly, she felt no amount of soap could ever make this man appear handsome. In her line of work, male chauvinists were an occupational hazard. Still, they always made her skin crawl.

"Sorry, only one to a customer and that was for the horse," she said, mustering as much patience and charm as possible. "Could you please tell me where the trainer's interviews are being held?"

The mocking smile instantly vanished like a wisp of smoke. The man ducked his head, his hat shading his eyes. "Inside the house, after supper," he murmured. Pulling the horse's lead shank, he quickly headed for one of the barns, seemingly not able to get away from her quick enough now.

Shrugging, Season wondered what got into him. Well, whatever it was, at least he was gone now. Good riddance. She always got along well with the stable hands, but if she got this job he might be the exception. She grabbed her duffel bags from the truck, and headed up the flagstone path leading to the elegant house.

Sensing someone was watching her, she glanced over her shoulder. The parking yard was empty. The blond man with the chestnut was gone. Somewhere a horse snorted. Quiet blanketed the area.

"All right, Season, get a grip," she told herself softly. "You made it. You're here now. Don't lose it just because you ran into a chauvinistic jerk right away. You can handle this."

Finishing her pep talk, she mounted the stone steps to the brown wooden door. Knocking, she wondered if the illustrious Mr. Masters would personally greet her. Just in case, she put on the brightest, best smile she could, her breath held, shoulders straight, and ready for anything.

Within a few minutes the door swung open and a pimply faced teen-age boy stood there.

"You seriously lost or something?" he asked, clearly surprised to see her. He popped a bubble with his gum, chewing noisily.

"No. I'm here to interview for the trainer's position." Rattled, Season worked to recover. Did Mr. Masters have a teen-age son? She couldn't make the image work in her mind. It did not go with the reputation he made of himself. No one ever spoke of a child—an heir to the mighty Heritage legacy.

The boy's face dropped. "The trainer's position?" he repeated, as if he hadn't heard right. "Well, the rest are over in the library room I guess." He jerked a thumb behind him as he motioned her in and then started walking past her, back outside.

"Wait! Who are you?" she spun and called out quickly.

"I'm Ernie. I deliver Mr. Masters' weekly groceries," he said, waving his hand behind him and leaving her standing at the foyer of the house.

Hoping it was okay to traipse around the house, looking for the library, she wondered why the host hadn't yet put in an appearance. And the delivery boy answered the door? How odd.

Following the sounds of male voices, she came to a huge room, lined wall to wall with books. A giant stone fireplace dominated one wall, with a fire cheerily snapping. Cleverly placed chairs invited people to sit and relax. The crackling fire filled the room with the scent of pine, mixing with the smell of old books. Five men, all middle-aged, sat around, smoking and joking, telling stories and resting.

Glancing at them, she did not recognize any. All dressed the same, in faded western shirts, blue jeans and cowboy hats, they instantly reminded Season of the stable hand out in the yard. How quaint. Dropping her duffel bags, she loudly cleared her throat, announcing her presence.

"You guys all here for the interviews too?" she asked cheerfully when they looked up.

"You a horse trainer?" one asked boldly, drawing from his cigarette, doubt written on the deep lines of his face.

"Yes, of course." Season stepped into the room, her friendly smile fading as she noticed their collective looks of surprise. Much the same as the teen-age boy at the door.

"What did I say?" she asked any of them, feeling a chill slithering up her spine. Whatever was going on around here, she was starting not to like it much at all. And where was the missing host, Mr. Masters? The inviting fire and pine scent of the room faded away, replaced by the startled and suspicious glares from the men. She needed somewhere else to go and wait for Masters.

Hearing sounds coming from another room, she followed the noise, hoping the next person she encountered would be more helpful, or be her weekend host. Hopefully he wouldn't be upset with her exploring around the house.

At the end of the hall, she stepped into a kitchen, so huge it looked like the cook could feed an army. Shiny clean and modern, it was out of place with the rustic decor she'd noticed so far. A long shiny counter top stretched from end to end, two ovens were stacked by the twin stoves and a jumbo fridge and freezer sat along another wall. Three bar stools lined one side of the long counter. An industrial sized coffee machine and several cups rested on one end. A small table and three more chairs sat nestled near the coffee machine. Fresh fruit sat in a bowl on the table and another on the counter.

A heavy set, burly man with a white apron tied daintily around his wide waist was putting groceries away. He was, without exception, the largest man she had ever seen. Seemingly unbalanced, his small, bald head sat upon a fat, short neck and broad shoulders.

Clearing her throat again, she crossed the kitchen's threshold. The man turned around slowly, a chewed up, unlit cigar dangling from his mouth. Small, dark eyes checked her over, surprised flickering in them.

"Yeah?" he snarled irritably, the noise ending in something of a grunt.

Oh Mercy, they just kept getting stranger and stranger. Convinced she'd never make it to the interview anyway, she pasted on a pale smile. "I'm Season Moriarty, and I'm here for the trainer's interview." This time she was more prepared for the same look of surprise that crossed his pudgy face.

Recovering quickly, he pulled out his cigar, stuck his mammoth hand out to her, smiled broadly and introducing himself as Moose, cook of Heritage Farms.

"Pleased to meet you, Ms. Moriarty," he said, taking his gigantic hand and dwarfing hers, giving it a solid pump. A grateful sigh of relief escaped Season as she met his friendly grin.

Moose took her around the lower level of the house, showing her the room she would use for the weekend, the study where Mr. Masters would conduct interviews, and added that supper was served at six. Rounding out the tour he added that Mr. Masters would begin interviews promptly at seven and did not like to be kept waiting.

Supper was an uncomfortable affair. With only three bar stools or three chairs to choose from, Season was stuck at the small table with the other men staring curiously at her. She ignored the hushed murmurs until she'd finished her meal and had enough of the men. Marching into the library, she picked the most comfortable chair, near the snapping fire. The Grandfather clock assured her she still had plenty of time before seven and she'd just bet the men would reassemble back in the library.

Shortly after the men strolled in, lighting cigars and pouring drinks from the bar, she rose. She could finish her waiting time by making sure she was totally polished. Selecting a not-so-faded pair of blue jeans and an ivory and peach checkered sweater, she surveyed herself in the full-length mirror. Nice. Both professional and western looking at the same time without either look being too much. Removing all traces of makeup, she completed the professional look by pulling her unruly brown curls into a single thick braid trailing down her back.

Five minutes before seven, she congregated with the other applicants outside the study door. Smoke and travel dust still clung to them, making her glad she took the extra few minutes for a fast shower. Five times she heard a deep masculine voice coming from behind the heavy oak door, calling out a name and nothing more. Five times one of the men entered, disappearing into the depths of the dark room beyond. Each one returned approximately twenty minutes later, looking shell shocked and worn.

Like a mighty clap of thunder, Season's name was the last one called. Drawing an uneven breath, she closed her eyes for a moment, pulling from within herself, and then strolled into the room.

It was dark inside, largely due to the dark paneled walls, dark carpeting and heavy drapery. It was a man's room. It was a giant of a room. A true primeval man cave. The fire blazing in the stone fireplace did nothing to dispel the dim lighting. Suddenly she was eager to meet the man.

"Close the door," the ominous voice ordered.

Doing so, she turned back, stopping dead as her eyes adjusted to the low light and she recognized the man behind the desk. She felt her mouth hanging open, first in surprise, then disbelief and horror. No, it couldn't be.

"If you leave your mouth open too long, a bug will fly in," the voice warned harshly. "Who the devil are you?"

"Season Moriarty." The words tumbled from her tongue as dread filled her, churning in her stomach. Only barely did she acknowledge the heavy English accent.

Ty Masters, the world-famous racer and breeder, was the very same male chauvinist with the chestnut horse she'd met earlier in the yard.

His cowboy hat was off now, lying on the corner of the tidy desk. A thick, clean unruly heap of dusty blonde curls covered his head. Gone were the dirty clothes. He smelled fresh and clean and extremely male and wearing a blue checkered flannel shirt with the top two buttons left undone, showing off a chest lightly peppered with curly hair. She had no doubts he would be wearing hip hugging jeans and boots behind that massive desk. What startled her more was that he actually could be handsome after all. The blue checkered shirt brought out the blue of his eyes.

"That's impossible!" he snarled, dismissing her with an impatient wave. "I have an interview with Season Moriarty for a horse trainer's position. I have no time for bloody jokes, woman. Be gone."

"I am Season Moriarty," she repeated tartly, sensing his anger. He must have thought one of the other men brought her along as a companion. "I have an interview with you. You wrote me back in Florida, asking me to come here for the weekend and to give me an interview," she paused, emphasizing her next few words as though speaking to a dim-witted child. "A job as chief racehorse trainer."

Coolly, he appraised her like a yearling colt at an auction. Leaning back a little in his chair, lifting the two front legs, he took his time. One blond eyebrow lifted as a sardonic grin crept over his face. His eyes, now freed from the obstruction of the hat's brim, were the bluest shade Season had ever seen. Deep blue like the bottomless lake or the clearest sky after a storm.

Forcing herself not to bend from his steady glare, she reeled in her temper. He was the boss; she had to play by his rules if she wanted the job.

Pasting a bittersweet smile on her lips, she waited until his inspection was done. Would he get up to check her teeth next? She was beginning to wonder.

"You are Season Moriarty?" he finally spoke, his voice and eyes daring her somehow.

Nodding in curt confirmation, she gladly proved him wrong, "Yes, I am."

"Season," he muttered, bringing the chair back down, shaking his head. "How was I supposed to know Season would end up being a woman," he said to no one in general. "All future advertisements will need to specify photos be included with applications."

Okay, she would overlook how sexist that sounded, and continue to fight for this job. Leaning back a little, she intended to fight hard. "It is a feminine name," Season countered. Yes, a little unusual perhaps, but not worth the attention it seemed to be getting at the moment. What difference did her gender make? She'd been a trainer for several years.

"It sounds like a man's name. As in son of the seas or something," he said, giving her a dark look of accusation.

She started to feel a ball of worry forming in her stomach. Just what was he driving at?

"Sorry to prove you wrong, but Season is my name, has always been my name and has nothing to do with sons or seas. And you can obviously see I am a woman." She hesitated briefly, a light dawning in her mind, making her stomach do a sick little roll. "What exactly does my name have to do with this interview?"

"Everything!" he snapped. Grabbing some papers, he shuffled them around. "Now, I'm very busy so let's just end this and—"

Season blinked in astonishment. He was dismissing her? "Are you saying I'm not qualified solely because I am female?" she demanded of him, feeling her temper rising. Not caring about making a professional impression anymore, she stepped up close to the desk, daring him to look away from her.

"You said it, not me," Ty Masters murmured, staring directly into her eyes, unflinching.

Now she understood why everyone was so puzzled as to her presence. It all made sense now. Why hadn't she picked up on it quicker? Fury, hot and raw, rose up within her, heating her like lava. She stood ramrod straight, using every ounce of self-control not to slap him. She blinked, chasing the red away that swam before her. She could probably claim sexual harassment, but she wanted this job. Dammit, she deserved this job.

Slapping her hands down flat on the desk instead, scattering papers, she leveled her stare into his cool blue pools, noticing with some satisfaction a tiny tick begin working in his jaw.

"My name and my gender are of no concern to you or at this interview," she spoke clearly and distinctly. "My abilities and credentials, however, are." Her gaze fell on a sheet of paper. Her reference page. "Now, if you will be so kind as to review my resume, you will see my qualifications are superior and my references are top notch. They adequately prove I'm capable of doing the job you are asking."

Willing it to happen, she held her breath, concentrating, waiting until he did as she ordered. He was going to look at her application if it killed her. And him.

⁂

Suddenly powerless, unable to stop himself, Ty felt himself grabbing the papers and seeing the words before his eyes. He really didn't need to, he already knew what they said. One thing had been clear from the very moment he received the application package; Season Moriarty was the best person for the position.

Both father and grandfather were world renowned horse trainers. Surely they had passed along some family secrets for gaining speed from a horse. Season's experience and past records were more than adequate. Everything he was looking for in a trainer was right here in black and white. He had already intended on hiring this person if the interview went half as good as the application looked. But he never dreamed Season Moriarty would turn out to be a woman!

It wasn't that he didn't like women. He liked them a lot. Just not working with his horses or living on his place. He knew from past experiences that women on his ranch always equaled disaster, trouble he didn't need. Men got into fights over each other's girlfriends, men and women fought over endless things, and it usually ended with the woman leaving and the men all mad at each other. It created friction, distrust, and bad work habits whenever the men had women around. And likewise, prohibiting women to be on the ranch encouraged life to operate smooth and harmoniously, which pleased both Ty, the men, and his horses.

Logically, he had reached the only reasonable explanation: women did not belong on a racehorse ranch. Especially this woman. From the second he saw her turn into the driveway, park and start easing out kinks, his warning lights started flashing and screeching in his mind. Her jeans hugged her long legs, giving the impression she was muscular beneath that medium frame. Her shirt stretched over her lovely bust and the sun shone on her brown hair, burning it to an auburn that matched the chestnut mare he had been leading. At the time, he'd assumed she was a traveling companion of one of the applicants here to watch the horses run for the weekend. Eyeing her now, he realized how terrible an assumption he had made.

He had liked her hair better when it was loose, all wavy and curly, making his fingers itch to touch it, play with it, twirling some around his fingertips. She looked more professional now. Her green eyes, green as the Emerald Isle her family hailed from, had been soft and friendly before, now they were hard, blazing into him, like blazing lights of fire. And making him feel more than a little uncomfortable. Quite an unusual experience.

Wait a minute. Suddenly he wondered why he was the one feeling uncomfortable here. He was the one in control. He was the master. People followed his orders without question. His word was law. Always.

So why did he even care that she was furious? Why did he suddenly feel like a naughty schoolboy? Why was he even continuing this interview? He would give the job to one of the men outside.

So why didn't he?

"Do I have the job or not?" she demanded, her patience just about spent, her green gaze never wavering from his cool glare.

Inwardly, he sighed, feeling something deep inside him collapsing. Realizing he had somehow lost total control of the situation, he also saw he was about to break his number one rule. And worse yet, he was completely unable to stop himself. What just happened? What had she done to him?

"The trainer is to reside here," he heard himself say, the words coming out by themselves. "That person is expected to fly with the horses to the tracks, stay with them for the duration of their final training and race schedule."

"Okay," Season said evenly, eyes boring deeply into his, until he suspected she might crawl into his lap. The thought—and images—both frightened and thrilled him. Shaking his head, he cleared his throat before continuing.

"Everybody is expected to do their share. The trainer is in charge of training, obviously, and to oversee the studs for breeding. Their opinion is wanted for selected breeding partners. Of the horses," he added, swallowing a hard lump and clearing his throat again. "But that person may also be called upon to help feed the stock or do whatever else is required." His eyes lit up dangerously. "Even I have been known to muck out a stall or two," he challenged, taking back a little bit of control from this situation.

"Fine," she agreed crisply. "I can muck stalls with the best of them. I've been mucking stalls since I could barely lift the fork. I have been brushing and grooming since I needed a bucket to reach their backs."

More images popped into his mind, of a brown-haired wisp of a girl standing on an upturned bucket to brush a horse's broad back, or heaving mightily at a pitchfork to muck a pony's stall. That lump in his throat slid south and settled in the pit of his stomach, churning and making a mess of Moose's fine dinner. How could he still manage to convince her not to take the position?

"We are currently racing three horses. One three-year-old colt and a three-year-old filly. I hope to have another two-year-old colt ready for his first start in a few months." He paused, and then added, "Do you believe you can handle all this?" Here was where she could back out gracefully and make an exit easier for both of them. He nearly closed his eyes in prayer as he waited for her response, feeling as though his entire life depended on her answer.

❂

Meeting his challenging gaze Season sensed the currents of electricity coming from him. She also sensed the questions burning in his mind. Giving in and hiring her was costing him a lot, more than he would ever reveal.

"Of course," she said sweetly, flashing a smile, taking a small step away. Was it her imagination or did he sink a little behind that massive desk?

Feeling his surprise, she felt a brief thrill of victory. It took a bit of effort but now she had a job!

"You might as well come meet your new charges," he said, not looking, or sounding, overly thrilled. Standing up, he waited for her to move to the door first. "Do I need to remind you these animals are worth thousands and millions of dollars? They are not cart hags," he warned softly.

"Of course not. I have trained a few racehorses before," she reminded him.

"You alone are solely responsible for their health, their happiness and," he paused, "their performance on the tracks." Shouldering past her, he spoke briefly to the men in the library and then wordlessly lead the way outside. Quietly, Season followed her new boss into one of the white barns she'd seen earlier.

"I shall introduce you to our foundation stallion," Ty announced, pride heavy in his voice. He escorted her to the last stall in the row of about twenty. It was the largest stall, sturdy and well-constructed, as was the entire barn. A black head peered over as Ty whispered softly and Season felt a chill creeping up her spine as she approached.

She automatically knew who this creature was. Here was the king of Heritage Farms. Black Warrior. With utmost reverence, she cautiously approached his stall to look him over.

He was a full eighteen hands high plus a little more, huge, jet black and meaner than a cornered wildcat. Looking closer, she noticed the streamlined body, wide nostrils and well-developed shoulders all great racehorses needed. She felt the fire burning in his soul, the fire of pure hatred. This horse, quickly approaching the ripe age of thirty-two was evil, mean and totally unpredictable. But Season knew this was also the horse Ty Masters had gambled his inheritance and life on. This was the one thing he brought from England and gambled everything on this single animal's speed and competitive spirit. Looking at Heritage Farms now, clearly it had been a good gamble.

"His dame was destroyed when he was just a weanling," Ty offered, gazing affectionately at the old stallion. "Folks said she was a killer. Funny thing is folks said the same thing about him and he never killed anyone."

"Not for lack of trying from what I've heard," Season pointed out. The horse's evil deeds were legendary around the tracks. It seemed Ty Masters was the only person who could handle the huge horse with immunity. "I'll safely say he's dangerous."

"He needs a gentle voice and a firm hand," Ty argued. "In the right hands, he is as gentle as a pet lion." Ty's mouth quirked slightly. That was the most polite way to describe Black Warrior.

"This way." Motioning for her to follow, they left the dimness of the barn, stepping out into the cool Wyoming dusk. Ty headed for some distant fence, Season having to take two steps to match one of his giant swinging strides.

Ty slammed to a halt at the gate of a white fence, whistling sharply. Scanning the dark field, Season saw nothing but the outlined silhouette of some trees. Then she heard the echoing beat of pounding hooves and a smile flashed over Ty's face.

Following his gaze to the horizon, she watched a large black horse galloping into sight from the night cover. Sliding to a stop before them, he blew air from his nostrils, tossing his head and whinnying.

"This is our main racer, Sky Hunter." Ty reached out, affectionately patting the horse's glossy neck. "He is sired by Black Warrior."

If Black Warrior was king, here was the young prince. He was every bit as large as his mighty sire, coal black with four white socks and a striking white blaze racing down his face. He lightly tossed his mane, prancing sideways, unsure what to make of Season. He snorted and blew her direction a few times, looking to Ty for reassurance.

Season saw the same unpredictable wild look in his eyes as she'd noticed in his sire's back in the barn. She reached out to pat him, drawing back when he laced his ears flat, pretending to nip her. Snorting, he pranced away, ears back and head shaking.

"He is no pet," Ty pointed out. "He is powerful and needs to be handled just right." As if to prove his own immunity, he reached a hand out and waited calmly.

Soon Sky Hunter returned, stretched his neck out, sniffing loudly. Taking a step closer, he stomped his foot once, sampling Ty's upturned palm, looking for goodies. Within a mere minute, Ty rubbed his hand along the horse's white blaze, sliding Season a leveled look.

"See, it is all in the handling."

"I'm also new to him. He undoubtedly has known you since he was foaled." Was he implying she wasn't capable of physically handling a large and powerful horse? She'd surprised other men before and she was sure Mr. Masters was going to be in for a surprise soon too. "I will have him eating out of my hand before long."

Sky Hunter snorted once, and as if to prove her wrong, reached out to nip her.

Instinctively, she jumped back, feeling her face grow warm. Glad for the pale moonlight around them, she watched as Sky Hunter curled his lips back in what looked to be a horsey laugh, twist and take off across the field, blending into the night with only his hoof beats echoing behind him.

"It appears our main star feels differently," Ty said slowly, folding his arms along the fence rail.

"Clearly you and Sky Hunter share the same opinions. If you ask me, it's the waste of a perfectly good horse."

Ty blinked in stunned silence.

Season wished she could take the words back, and knew Master's surprise was because no one dared speak to him like that. Except she just had. And he did not immediately bellow out 'You're fired', so she drew in a deep breath and pressed on before the shock on his face was gone. "I assume there are other horses to view?"

"Of course." Galvanized, he strode off in the direction of another barn, leaving her trotting to keep up.

They toured the entire farm by ten o' clock. Season saw the breeding barn, the mare barn, the foaling barn, the weanling barn. She inspected the training track and other points of interest. She saw the airplane hangar where Ty housed the plane for the horses and the adjoining runway.

She met Richmond, the youngster she was to school for his first break in the spring. He was a high stepping blood bay cold. Lacking the cruel spirit of Black Warrior and Sky Hunter, he slowly sniffed her over, finally deciding she was alright. She also met Winter's Dawn, a nice chestnut filly, sired by Black Warrior too. Ty held high hopes for her as a racer. She liked the track, having raced twice and placed well. Ty stressed the right training could coax the last bit of speed out of her. The desire was there, he said, she just needed the skills.

The last horse she met was a stable pony named Doodlebug, a delightful mixture of Welsh and Shetland pony. He had the honor of being Sky Hunter's travel buddy. Barely over twelve hands and covered in white and gray patches, Doodlebug took an immediate liking to Season, sidling up against her and begging for a scratch.

"I see you finally found someone you can properly handle," Ty pointed out, watching the pony make cozy with Season. "I'm afraid Sky Hunter will not be so easy to make friends with. Doodlebug is a friend with everyone he sees." He said the words as if they left a bad taste in his mouth.

Season was struck with the feeling Ty Master had few real, trustworthy friendships. He seemed like a man who could be friendly on the outside, to a point, but managed effectively to keep all people at arm's length. At least he gave her the strong impression he did not want her too close. But she suspected it extended to more people than just her. A sadness filled her at the thought of anyone wanting to be alone.

Measuring her words carefully, Season met his visual stare. "Actually, Doodlebug is the smarter one. He plans ahead to the day he will need someone to lean on." She entwined her fingers into the pony's mane, waiting for his response. He was starting to remind her of a powder keg. If she were not careful, she wouldn't have to worry about having the job.

He forced his gaze away from her, steadily looking out toward the door, as if considering bolting for the exit. *Do I make you that uncomfortable, Mr. Masters?* She nearly asked the question but stopped herself, searching for a better one.

"Don't you ever need somebody?" she asked lightly, still scratching under the pony's mane.

"I try not to," he bit out, stalking away, leaving her alone in the dark with the pony noisily searching her pockets for more treats.

Well! She blew out a breath. She had a challenging new job, a beautiful place to live, and a new boss. And, unless she was mistaken, the battle lines were clearly drawn.

⚜

It was unusually warm for Wyoming and the pale moonlight shown bright, cutting through the trees with alabaster rays. Watching Ty's backside as he strode angrily away, Season felt her nerves stringing out like a worn guitar. Knowing no sleep would come to her any time soon, she decided to explore her new home instead. She could use the time alone in the moonlight.

The air was quiet and cool, only a steady breeze blowing across the snowcapped fields, fed by the colder air flowing down from the snowy peaks surrounding the farm. Night birds called to her, beckoning her down past the barns and into the distant fields, away from humanity and horses. Brushing the snow from a rock, she sat down. This space was quiet, serene and tranquil. Just what she needed.

Spreading her arms wide, she closed her eyes, chanting softly. The night winds spoke to her, whispering, filling her with soothing emotions and gentle thoughts, erasing the earlier strains. Her chanting growing faster and louder, she lifted her arms wider and higher, reaching up toward the shining moon. She felt whole, connected, invigorated. As if she were the only person in the world.

❧ 2 ❧

Watching from the dark shadows of the trees, Ty silently viewed the strange scene unfolding before him. She looked like a gypsy in a trance, reaching up and chanting. He knew she couldn't notice him. So just what was she doing? The night was still, he could hear her singing, her voice carrying to him a soft lilting, whispering song. It was like nothing he ever heard before. Enchanting.

He wasn't really following her, he told himself as he watched the odd little scene. He owed it to his farm and its inhabitants to know a little about his new employee. So he had to go see what she did when she thought she was alone.

Rubbish. When she didn't return to the house, he became worried and went in search of her, hoping she wasn't lost already. Or had decided to quit. Following fresh tracks leading away from the farm, he wasn't sure what to expect. The last thing he thought he would find was her sitting on a rock, bathed in pale moonlight, singing her heart out, and looking so darn pretty. Leaning back on his haunches, blending into the night, he listened to her whispering songs—just watching the show.

❦

U sing the Sight inherited from her Celtic Druid mother, Season sensed she was being watched. Even without the gift of the Sight, she knew it was Ty Masters spying from the shadows to her left. Lowering her arms, she wondered what he would think of her actions and how much had he seen. Not more than a few minutes she decided. Crossing her arms over her chest, she waited, her breathing regular now that she'd regained a good inner sense of control.

Out of the dark stepped three figures. They stood before her, bathed in the moonlight rays. Season's gaze briefly flickered to the center figure before settling on the two figures flanking him.

They were the most enormous canine brutes she'd ever seen. Brownish yellow, they must weigh well over a hundred pounds each, their jaws dripping saliva as they stared at her with challenging yellow eyes. Alert, they waited for the slightest cue from their master, their only movement was an occasional ear twitching back, waiting for the command and an eager licking of their jowls.

Suddenly the night became noticeably less peaceful. Electricity charged the air. The night birds were suddenly gone, flapping away into the night.

"Do these two creatures belong to you?" Season asked innocently, thinking they looked almost demonic in the moonlight, but sensing they were no threat to her.

In one singular motion from Ty, both dogs sat, their huge heads level with his hips. Curling his lips back in a taunting smile, Ty rested one hand on his hip, inches from the one dog's skull. "I doubt anyone lurking about my property at such an hour is innocently enjoying the view," he said. "So what are you doing way out here at such at miserable time?"

Flipping her braid out of the way, she took her time answering him. "After you left me so hastily earlier I decided to go for a stroll," she said evenly. "I seemed to have developed a stale feeling and hoped to use the pleasant evening air to get rid of it."

৩১৩

H e frowned. Did she just call him stale? "Till after midnight?" he insisted.

"I lost track of time." She flipped her braid seductively again. "Is that a crime?"

"No," he allowed, gesturing to the giant dogs. "These mastiffs roam the property at night to ensure no wandering night owl decides to lift a horse or two. You might want to limit your strolls to either earlier hours or stay closer to the house."

"Perhaps you might want to introduce me to your canine pals so we shall have no further incidents like tonight. Just in case I need more fresh air in the future," she added drily.

Catching her subtle hint, knowing she was baiting him, he found it oddly amusing. He couldn't stop the grin twitching at his lips. Both at her attitude, which was beyond anything he could begin to understand and because of the dogs. The mastiffs were professionally trained guard dogs and wouldn't readily accept strangers. He could introduce them, of course, but it was highly unlikely they would accept her as part of the Heritage Farms family for quite some time.

"Absolutely," he agreed. "Quite right. This is Rex." He pointed to the slightly smaller dog to his left. "And this is Bruce," he added, pointing to the slightly larger dog to his right.

"Rex and Bruce," Season repeated softly, kneeling down, slipping off the rock in a fluid motion, putting herself at eye level with the big brutes. She stretched her hand out, palm forward, toward them. Inviting them closer, she softly repeated their names.

At Ty's motion, they stepped forward, noisily sniffling and snuffling, sounding much like the horses did earlier. Remaining motionless, she talked to them in a low, lulling whisper.

Apparently satisfied, they both wagged their tails. Bruce went so far as to give her hand a slobbery kiss.

"Good boys," she said, standing up and giving each dog a pat on his soft, broad head.

Ty felt his mouth hanging open. No one ever got along with the dogs. Not in the four years he had owned them. Two cooks and several hired workers had left because they were scared to death of the big dogs. So how could this mere slip of a woman make actual friends in just a few minutes? Did she cast a spell on them with those bewitching green eyes?

"You do realize anyone who trains horses would have an understanding of how guard dogs are trained as well?" Season said, losing the fight to control the smile twitching at the corners of her mouth.

"Of course I knew that!" he snarled. Confusion swept over him like cold air. That foreign feeling knocked him off balance. He gripped a nearby tree trunk to steady himself. "You might want to consider retiring soon. Morning comes early and it will be a very busy day for you." Motioning for the dogs to heel, he silently faded into the inky blackness.

⟡

Sinking back to the rock, Season wrapped her arms around herself, a triumphant smile on her lips. She'd won this battle, but who would win the war?

Next morning Season rose with the first sun rays. Slipping into the shower, she ran last's night's episode over in her mind. No doubt Ty would still be upset. She had waited an hour, until she saw the house lights go out before she slipped in and crawled into bed. Setting her alarm, she planned on being up early, ready to work.

So far, so good. The water was warm and it felt good as it pulsated over her skin. She took her time, humming a tune, enjoying the simple pleasure of feeling good.

The tension of the last few months melted away, sliding down the drain with the bath water. Last night had cleansed her mind, now she was cleansing her body. Turning the water off, she felt refreshed, ready for another round with life.

Stepping out of the bath, she dried off, stroking her skin gently. Digging around, she found the largest towel available and wrapped it around herself. It was pathetically small and only barely managed to cover her vital areas. Oh well, it wasn't like she planned to meet anyone before she was dressed.

Brushing her wet hair, she pulled it into a ponytail where it would dry into a riot of curls. Done, staring at her reflection in the mirror, she had to admit she was impressed. Her cheeks were brighter, she was thinner from a few months ago, and she had a healthier look than back in Florida.

And now she had a new job, full of promising potential. And battle lines.

"Another chapter," Season murmured, repeating something her mother

22

would say, when something new was about to begin. Readjusting the still-too-small towel, she opened the door to her room, slamming to a halt.

Ty was sitting in a chair, casually flipping through a magazine.

"Don't you ever knock?" Season demanded. Clutching the towel tightly to her chest, she held her ground, cheeks flaming as red as her tiny cloth. "It's quite simple really, I should think you could learn it if you tried it once or twice."

"I was—" Ty stopped, working his jaw as though his tongue suddenly turning to rubber. Clearing his throat, he tossed the magazine aside, stood up and brushed his palms along his jeans, as if sweaty or dirty. "I was extending the hand of friendship by seeing if you needed a hand moving upstairs." He got the words out, slowly and with effort, but they sounded neutral and in control. Something he certainly did not feel at the moment.

"No, I can manage just fine," Season assured him, swinging one arm at her two bags and clutched the terry cloth again. "As you can see, I'm already packed and just need to get dressed. So if you'll kindly—"

"Perhaps you would like to know where your new room is?" Ty asked lightly, cutting her off.

"Yes, of course, that would be nice."

He took one step closer to her, halting as she tightened her hold on the towel, offering her a slight grin. A light danced in his blue eyes.

"It is upstairs, last door on the left," his voice, already deceptively soft, dropped to a whisper. "Right next to mine."

Season felt a cold chill slithering up her spine, making her shiver. Next to his? Impossible! Surely there was another room in this vast house she could have instead. Anywhere but next to him.

He chuckled at her obvious dislike of the situation. Her expression clearly gave her thoughts away.

"You need not worry, Ms. Moriarty," he said softly, allowing himself a decidedly un-gentleman-like examine of her towel clad body, his expression dark. "I prefer my women more—well, you can figure that out for yourself," he said, voice trailing off. He turned on his heel and swept out of the room.

Letting her breath out in a whoosh of anger, Season stalked to the door and slammed it loudly. Turning the lock, she stomped back to the bed, throwing herself down with clenched fists. She knew exactly what thoughts were lingering behind those bedroom eyes. The nerve of that man!

As if she was some mindless doll on personal display just for him! Ha! He might be used to mindless Barbie dolls who swooned and fell at his feet, but she was certainly not one of them. She was completely immune to his few feeble attempts to charm her. And this gallant attempt was a flat failure. He may be her employer, but he wasn't her master and he would soon be learning that fact. The sooner the better!

Grinding her teeth in frustration, she decided on the best way to teach him. Dressing quickly, she pulled a pair of jeans, tee shirt and beige flannel out of her duffel bag. Finished, she next headed for the kitchen. She might be new, but she knew an ally when she sensed one.

"Morning, Moose," she greeted, sliding onto a bar stool.

"Morning, Miss," Moose greeted, turning from the griddle, smiling and showing a few gaps were teeth used to be. Reaching a thickset arm out, he grabbed a plate from above him, filled it with wonderful smelling foods and handed it to Season. Accepting it, she stared at the heaping piles of potatoes, sausage and generous helping of biscuits and gravy. Oh my!

"Thanks," she said, taking a fork and trying a bite. It was delicious as it looked and smelled. "Where is everybody?"

"Everyone else eats in the dining room," he replied, motioning in the general direction of a large room she recalled from her tour yesterday. "I eat in here and the master eats alone in his study. He never eats with the hired help."

Taking a sip of the coffee Moose handed over, she wrinkled her nose. Both at the strength of the wicked brew and at Ty's typical attitude. "I suppose he thinks he's too good to associate with hired help," she said.

"No, he's just the master," Moose replied, stirring the pot of sausage gravy.

"That's what he thinks," Season muttered under her breath, moving off the bar stool.

"You might want to eat in here with me," Moose stopped her. "Those folks in there might be a bit rough on you at first, being a new comer and all."

"Why is it such a surprise to everyone that I'm a trainer?" Season asked, sliding back onto the bar stool and taking a sip of coffee again.

Moose frowned, halting midway at filling his own plate. "Well, now, the master isn't well known for having women around or hiring them to work. It can be a shock to some."

"But I'm a competent trainer and I have held a license for fifteen years. That must count for something around here." She commented around another mouthful of food. Goodness, Moose was a great cook!

"Yeah, it does," Moose bobbed his head, taking a big bite. "But it takes time to win folks over. Don't worry about it any. Make them come to you, Miss." He paused, locking eyes directly over their plates. "And that goes for our beloved master too. He'll come around to seeing your terms someday."

Shocked, she blinked. What did he mean? Before she could ask, a buzzer rang from under the counter, making her jump.

"Ah, the master himself wants me," Moose said, winking at her, stuffing a huge forkful of dripping gravy into his mouth and walked away, chewing noisily.

Ty had a buzzer running from his study to the kitchen? Did he have video cameras in each room too? She glanced up at the kitchen's corners, but didn't see any. She was beginning to wonder about this new employer of hers. Particular and overbearing were just some of his unusual traits. What else lurked beneath his surface? Within minutes Moose shuffled back into the room, smiling to himself.

"So what did our fearless leader want?" Season asked, unable to stop herself. "Did he need someone to butter his toast?"

"No." Moose grinned. "He asked if you were ready to move upstairs yet and I said you were still eating breakfast. He said to give him a knock when you were ready for his help."

A knock. How cute. She surely would love to give him a knock, right over that head of his. Well, apparently, he intended on helping her whether it was warranted or not. Whatever made him happy. He was the boss.

"Great," she muttered, stuffing the last biscuit in her mouth. "Welcome to the neighborhood I guess. Great breakfast, Moose. Thank you." Handing her plate over, she drained the last of the coffee and passed the mug over too. "Here goes nothing."

Ty was waiting patiently for her outside the door of her room. Arms folded across his chest, one foot propped against the wall, with his eyes half closed. He looked to be half asleep. He reminded her of those slow starting racehorses, the kind that lounged at the gate till the field already started.

Then, exploding into action, they usually passed the field and finished pretty well. But those were horses, and this was Ty Masters, every single inch a man. An aggravating, odd man.

"I thought I was supposed to give you a knock when I was ready," she pointed out mildly, refraining from adding the rest of her thoughts.

"I'm not used to being kept waiting."

She frowned. Was he calling her slow? "This really isn't necessary," she insisted, stepping into the room. "I barely have enough for one person to carry, let along two people."

"House rules." He scooped up her twin duffel bags, and headed for the door, looking back over his shoulder at her when he realized she wasn't following. "Is there something nailing you to the floor?"

"No," she snapped, following, though she wasn't sure if she were following her belongings or the man. He led her up a long flight of steps and down an even longer hall, past four heavy paneled wooden doors. Each step made breakfast slosh around her stomach.

"This is the lavatory. We shall be sharing the shower unless you wish to traipse downstairs each day."

Wouldn't he just love that? The sick feeling grew in her stomach.

"Maybe the boss should consider buying larger towels for his staff."

"They work well enough for a man."

"Fine. I'll manage."

"I am sure you will," he muttered softly. "This is my room and here is your room." Pulling a key out of his jeans, he handed it over.

Accepting the key, Season's mind whirled. The way the rooms were set up, she had to pass his door each time she arrived or left hers. Or went to the bathroom.

"What about those rooms? Can't I have one of them instead?" she asked, pointing to the rooms they had already passed.

"No. They are used for storage, probably quite musty by now." He grinned before continuing. "Moose has his own room off the kitchen downstairs and everyone else has apartments or rooms over the barns. You and I are the only ones up here. Don't you feel lucky?"

Oh yeah, lucky as a duck on the opening day of hunting season. Was this a deliberate attempt to get her to quit? Well, too bad if it was. He would find out soon enough. She shouldered past him, throwing the door open, checking out her new room.

Ty followed, setting the bags down just inside the door. "Like I said before, you need not worry about me. I have excellent self-control."

Something in his eye made her stop, something about his vibrations. Reading past them, Season felt her cheeks growing warm. The unspoken question was there, under his breath, but silent.

"Don't worry," she retorted. "I have no problems with my self-control either. Unlike some people, I don't let cheap packaging and a pretty smile fool me. I'm more interested in what is really under all the glitter and wrapper."

"Well put," Ty murmured, a glint shining in his eyes. Touching a finger to his forehead, he spun around, heading for the stairs. Season soon heard his footsteps fading into the distance downstairs.

The man really was impossible. Thinking of all sorts of nasty names for him, she took a few moments to sit down on the bed, closing her eyes and drawing in several deep, calming breaths. Getting her emotions under control, she opened her eyes, looking around the room.

Actually, it wasn't too bad. Practical without being frilly, done up in neutral colors of peach and brown. Who did the designing? Surely not Masters. He must have hired some professional to come in, decorating and mixing patterns and colors into pleasant tones anyone would like. There was the double bed she still sat on, long dresser, walk in closet, small writing desk and two overstuffed chairs flanking a cozy fireplace. A small stack of firewood rested beside it, ready to be lit. All the comforts of home and then some.

Walking over to the large window, she drew back the blinds and was surprised to see an attached balcony. Unlocking the French windows, she stepped out into the crisp morning air, and drew in a few breaths. The view was magnificent, overlooking the paddock where Sky Hunter and a few other horses roamed. Mountains rose majestically in the distance, dressed in their white caps. Turning to her right, her smile faded. Ty had an identical balcony not ten feet away. Why, they could sit and stare at each other from their balconies!

It looked like he planned on keeping her covered from all angles. What he didn't know yet was she was a hard one to follow. He would learn that soon enough. A tart smile tugged at her lips as she turned back to the paddocks. She had ways of dealing with this situation that he could never dream of.

Back inside, unpacking her few belongings, she put them away, barely putting a dent in the huge amounts of storage space. Heading for the stallion barn, she made a slight detour through the kitchen for some apples first, filling her jacket pockets with the tasty treats.

She wanted to see Sky Hunter, but decided to save him for later. First, she would get to know some of the other horses, starting with Richmond and Winter's Dawn, and perhaps Black Warrior, the sire of all three racers. She also wanted to learn more about their individual dames. Last night Ty had shown her a small office above the stallion barn that was hers to work in. Now that she was alone was the perfect time to check it out.

Sky Hunter was running through the paddock, when she finally made it to see him, stretching his legs and racing the wind. Leaning against the fence, Season rested one boot on the bottom rail and her elbows on the top, content just to watch him for a few minutes. Tossing his head, he gloried in his freedom and speed, squealing in sheer happiness to run in the mid-morning sunshine. He went in giant, sweeping circles, giving the impression the paddock was too small for his great speed.

Watching him, Season felt he would be a great racer. If only she could tame his wild heart.

Crawling through the fence railings, she slowly walked across the snowy field, snow crunching under her boots. Seeing her, Sky Hunter stopped, and came to a skittish halt, prancing and tossing his head. Snorting, he pawed the ground and stomped once.

"Hello, Hunter," she said softly, ignoring his aggressive display. "Look what I have for you." Holding out one apple, she offered it to him. He stomped again, snow flying out from under his hoof. Not good. She gave a slight shake of her head. If he was to be a racehorse of any merit, he needed to get used to being around new people without all this fuss and nervousness.

He pretended to charge her, ears laced back and teeth bared. She stood her ground, still offering the sweet apple. When she refused to move, he stood still, blowing through his nose, sniffing the fruit. Wordlessly, Season waited. He snorted and shied away, but moved back again, curious about the apple and her. Finally, he sampled a bite, crunching. The juice ran down

Season's palm but she waited until he took the rest of it, licking the juices with his soft tongue.

Slowly easing her hand up along his neck, she felt its warmth, furry with a winter coat. As soon as her hand landed on him, the colt shuddered, ready to bolt again. Closing her eyes, she whispered to him, creating a connection between her and him, asking him for access to himself. He slowly stilled, lowering his head to her shoulder in surrender.

Touching him, she felt a rush of speed, of energy, a desire to run. She felt a desire to compete and to win, a desire fueled by something deep down inside the big horse.

An image flashed through her mind, a packed grandstand, a large field of horses, and this one black stallion with the white feet sweeping easily under the wire first. It vanished before she could identify the track but she knew one thing—this horse was going to win big.

Snorting, Sky Hunter pretended another nip at her arm as he moved away.

"Uh no, none of that stuff, fella," she scolded lightly, knowing the connection was broken for now, but good ground work had just been made. "You are as foul tempered and stubborn as your owner is." Taking a step forward, she reached for his halter, anticipating he would shy away again.

Half an hour later she could take his halter, lead him in a circle, and touch him anywhere on his body. He let her lift his feet and check his mouth. He still decided for how long each exercise would last and voiced his displeasure but she knew that would ease in time as he grew accustomed to daily work. All it took was a few apples to start. Too bad that wasn't the cure for dealing with Ty.

"Very good," a voice said, coming from behind her. A familiar deep voice. "You won Sky Hunter over much faster than I thought possible for you."

Closing her eyes, she bit back a groan. Surely she hadn't accidentally conjured him up just by thinking about him, had she? No, most likely he was stalking her, spying. Releasing her hold on the horse, he snorted, racing off to the far end of his enclosure, black tail flying like a proud banner.

"Look, you hired me to train your horses. That horse in particular," she said as she climbed over the fence. "How can you expect me to get to know him if you are constantly hovering over my shoulder, getting in the way?"

He looked all innocent, taken aback by her directness. Holding his palms out to her, he flashed her a winning smile. "I wasn't in your way as you were petting and feeding him. I wasn't in your way while you led him around and played with him. You did not even know I was here until a minute ago. So how am I hovering?"

She considered driving her heel into his boot and then decided against it.

"What do you want?" she asked bluntly.

"What do you think of his future?" he asked, nodding out to the stallion in the paddock.

Better than yours. Controlling the temptation to say that, she bit her tongue. She was struck by the idea he wasn't really interested in talking about the horse but seemed on another mission.

"I'd say he has a good shot at the Derby. I wouldn't rule out the Triple Crown right now."

His eyebrows lifted in surprise. "I see. You do not think small, do you?" Leaning against the fence, foot propped up and arms crossed over his chest, his eyes sparkled like the blue sky above them. And just as bright. They momentarily made Season forget she resented his intrusion to her work.

"And what do you think of Winter's Dawn and Richmond? Are they Triple Crown winners as well?"

Of course, his droll question quickly reminded her. She had him with that question though. He was testing her methods, her ideas. Okay she could play this little game. Shrugging, she leaned against the fence, imitating his posture.

"It's too early to tell with Richmond. He has to get his feet wet and compete with real horses before we can tell if he can even make it to a serious race. Winter's Dawn has the desire to run, but lacks the competitive spirit of her sire. And her half-brother," she added dryly. "She needs to be taught why she needs to win, not just run. Right now, it's a social event with her. But in time I think they'll all be flying around the tracks."

"Really?" Again, he lazily lifted one eyebrow. "That ought to be a real magical family secret. I have never seen a horse fly before."

"Then won't you be surprised?" she said, spinning around and sauntering for the barn, leaving Ty standing at the fence all alone.

W atching her stride away, Ty felt that familiar knot tightening in his belly. It formed when she walked out of the shower this morning. Hearing her enter, he'd looked up from the magazine, feeling his eyes grow wide and his heart race. He was powerless to stop his gaze as it traveled from her tart, red mouth pulled into an 'O' of shock, to the bright red towel stretched across the creamy tops of her breasts then dipping beyond her trim waist to her almost exposed thighs. And legs. Oh, her legs went on forever, smooth and shapely. A knot of desire suddenly and unexpectedly formed in the pit of his stomach, cutting off his breath.

She was well built, perfectly proportioned and easily the most-lovely creature he had ever seen. The towel barely managed to cover her, leaving little to his imagination. What was covered made his imagination fly into sudden overdrive.

And ever since, he'd remained mesmerized by this woman and bewildered by her actions. She was constantly on his mind in just the short time she'd been on the farm. Her temper intrigued him and her beauty taunted him. He barely slept last night, knowing he was going to move her upstairs with him in the morning. Moose had been more than a little surprised at that announcement. No one ever stayed upstairs near him, as he valued his privacy. He still did not know what made him want her that close to him.

Unconsciously, unable to stop himself, he felt drawn to wherever she happened to be. No doubt she thought he was spying on her, but he couldn't help himself. He had to see what she was up to. All morning he watched her go from horse to horse, finally to Sky Hunter, passing out apples and getting acquainted.

He was used to weak, passive women; females who gave in with no fight just to please him. Always agreeing with him, never daring to say no. Cheap packages and pretty smiles, he thought with a sardonic smile of his own, thinking back to her earlier words.

Clearly this little pepper pot did not particularly like him and preferred just to work with the horses. She had no problems telling him no and would probably tell him to go straight to Hades if she felt he deserved it. A part of him was amused and fascinated. Excitement pumped through him each time he saw her, thrilled at the idea of sparing words with her again.

Yet, another part of him was almost...scared. Was that the word? He was never scared. Yet there was something about her that made him do things so out of character. Why had he ever hired her? What made him override his good sense and number one rule to do what he vowed never to do? Any woman on the place was bound to bring trouble. He would bet this one packed trouble in her luggage. If she were already affecting him so strangely, what was going to happen when the rest of the men all met her?

Heavens, it could be disastrous.

Letting out a long, deep sigh, he turned back to Sky Hunter galloping in the paddock. She was a woman of mystery. He would never know how she won Sky Hunter over so easy or so fast. It was more than apples. There was more to it. But what? Like the mastiffs from last night.

The image of the big horse just standing still with his massive head hanging inches from her shoulder and her petting him made them appear as old friends, just resting on each other. Impossibly odd.

And she sounded so confident when she said he was Derby and Triple Crown material. It was as if the horse himself had told her so, which was rubbish. Sure, his sire won the Crown twice, won the Belmont once and his dame raced quite well, even taking the Oaks. But that did not mean the son had the same abilities. So why was she so confident when he himself wasn't so sure? And he felt guilty for lacking faith in such a promising colt.

Ever since she arrived at his farm, he hadn't had a normal thought in his mind.

Well, she was a woman of mystery. And he never could refuse a good mystery.

3

Monday morning dawned noticeably cooler and overcast, dark clouds threatening to storm, and erasing any traces of the unseasonably warmer weekend Heritage Farms had enjoyed. Ignoring both the drop in temperature and storm warning, Season was hard at work before most of the others rolled out of their beds. She and Moose shared a pleasant breakfast alone. Now, seated behind the second-hand desk in her small upstairs office at the back of the stallion barn, she was meticulously going over reports left by her predecessor.

They included track times for Sky Hunter, Winter's Dawn and others who had been tried out for speed. Deciphering the scribbled notes, she frowned at the remarks labeling Sky Hunter as an unpredictable and unmanageable brute who should be blacklisted and destroyed. The same person referred to Winter's Dawn as a lazy hag with no future on the track and doubtful as a brood mare. She might make a suitable trail or stock horse though, the notes suggested. Other notes were similar for more horses she recalled meeting around the place.

Obviously, this guy, and she had to assume the previous head trainer was a man, had no idea what these horses were really capable of. Anger rippled through her as she read the cruel comments. Did Ty know of his former trainer's low opinions of his treasured horses? Probably not. Or perhaps that was why he was no longer here. Either way, clearly this guy did not want to put any time or effort into working with a horse, to coach it along. What a waste. She saw a lot of potential in them.

Wadding up the cruel comments, she recorded the old track times on a fresh sheet, leaving lots of room for added times. Faster times. As the sunlight came filtering in through the tiny window far above her head, she had the desk pretty well cleaned out. The guys had also been a pig, in addition to being short sighted. She found scores of old cigarette wrappers, candy bar wrappers, junk mail, broken pencil stubs, and all sorts of debris that need to be trashed. Satisfied at last, she looped the stopwatch over her neck, scooped up the clipboard and pencil, and whistled a merry tune as she headed out into the cold air.

In the first paddock, Eddie, the primary jockey, was warming up Sky Hunter, posting him in tight circles and then letting him frisk about a few moments. Spotting Season approaching, he reined the black horse to a standstill.

Stepping up beside him, she favored the young jockey with a smile, appreciating he was one of the few males who were giving her a chance here. Reaching for Sky Hunter's bridle, she settled the big horse, stopping his anxious pawing with a few murmured words at his twitching ear.

"Okay, Eddie, let's see what this fella has. He seems frisky enough now." Turning to the track in the distance, she pointed as she spoke. "Breeze him over the first half, holding him back. But after you round that last turn, give him his head. Got it?"

He nodded his understanding. "He's a handful," he agreed as the horse whinnied and sidestepped suddenly.

Season yanked hard on his reins, correcting his little protest. He was in desperate need of manners. Leading him through the plowed path and over to the starting chute, she felt more dismay to see how he fought the loading chute as well.

"Did he do this at the track races too?" she asked Eddie. Her heart sank at his silent nod, both of them knowing it was yet another strike against his future racing campaign. Finally, the colt loaded, squealing and balking all the way. Ears back, he was poised for flight.

"Ready?" Season asked Eddie.

At the jockey's nod, she released them and started the stopwatch simultaneously. Leaning over the railing, foot poised on the bottom rail, she watched every move the big colt and man made. Sky Hunter fought the bit, not wanting to be told how to run. His big strides pounded the track, but he wanted to run his way. Just like his owner.

After they rounded the far turn, heading for home, Eddie loosened the reins and Sky Hunter instantly broke out with giant strides that swallowed the ground. Pushing his nose forward, he stretched his neck out low, even with the ground. As he went pounding past her, Season clicked the watch. Looking at it, she let out an involuntary whistle. Incredible, considering he was held back the first half and he was running on a track covered with hard packed snow. Walking over to where Eddie was trying to bring the horse back to a walk, she waved the clipboard in the air.

"Just over one and three quarter minutes," she exclaimed happily. "Can you imagine what he would do if he could ever run his own race?"

"Yeah," Eddie panted breathlessly, working the reins. "But I'd like to imagine him running more and not fighting so much. You'd think he'd get tired from all that fighting he does."

No, she supposed, he would never tire out with all that hot, hateful blood of Black Warrior running through him. Nor would he ever entirely quit fighting everyone around him.

She watched him now, resisting the cooling walk. Again, she had to wonder if Ty suspected this also. He must, having raced the colt's sire in the past. Watching Sky Hunter now was like reading news reports on Black Warrior back then. The old stallion had been hell on wheels when he campaigned.

Next, they practiced with Winter's Dawn and finally Richmond. Each horse ran well, bettering their times from previous practice runs. Yet Sky Hunter remained the obvious swiftest of the three. A fact that did not surprise Season.

"Let's try something different before we wrap it up," Season suggested. "Richmond wants to run in this wind and Sky Hunter's passion is to be first. Let's ride them together, with you on Richmond, and see what happens when they are both challenged."

Mounting up on Sky Hunter, Season connected to the big horse, felt his desire to fly. It was so strong she wanted to give in to it. Images filled her mind as she rested a hand against his shoulder, making a fast connection with him. Glancing over at Eddie, she waited for his nod. In a single motion, she started the stopwatch and kicked the black horse forward.

For the first quarter mile, Sky Hunter held a sizable lead over the bay colt, but by the half mile mark, Richmond was coming on strong, having found his gait. Eddie urged him along, asking for more speed, pushing him to close in on the black horse. After the final turn, Sky Hunter leaped forward with a burst of speed, leaving Richmond several lengths behind. Season settled back, letting her mount finish the race in his own style when suddenly he let out a squeal, jumping forward and shifting gaits.

Nearly unseated, Season almost dropped the reins as she struggled to regain her position. Taking advantage of her preoccupation, Sky Hunter took the bit in his teeth, sailing easily over the low outside railing and taking off across the snow-covered field.

Riding low over his neck, mane and wind whipping her face, Season listened to the colt. She rested both hands on either side of his neck, concentrating on keeping the lines of communication open. Feeling the raw power and muscles driving beneath her, she felt like she was riding a rocket. The trees sped by in a blur and the wind brought tears to her eyes. Unbroken snow flew from under the horse's driving hooves. He responded to her silent permission with even more speed.

Sky Hunter's powerful strides increased as he went faster, completely out of control and gaining momentum, and loving every second of it. She could feel his delight and glory in his freedom. Surely they were going as fast as a freight train by now? The wind grabbed his mane and lashed her with it, cutting into her cheeks. His legs were like pistons on a race car.

Finally, she felt his stride shorten and his speed diminishing. She stopped the stopwatch, eager to look at it later.

Dismounting as he came to a reluctant stop, she offered to calm him, petting and rubbing, speaking soothing little coos to him. Checking him over, touching everywhere on him, she determined he was fine. His legs were solid, he showed no signs of wear, and already his breathing was returning to normal while hers was still racing like the wind. He was only slightly lathered and stomped a foot, saying he was ready to go again. Incredible!

Hearing hoof beats breaking through the snow, she turned, seeing Ty galloping up bareback on Black Warrior. Bracing herself, she saw his face, curled in anger, looking every bit as ferocious as the fiery stallion he rode.

"You bloody idiot!" he roared, dropping off the horse's back and stalking over to her, unmindful of the knee-deep snow. "What the devil was that stunt all about? Didn't you realize what you might have done to this colt?" Fury turned his face bright red. Standing before her, he glared, breath heaving and waiting for some sort of explanation.

She had one fleeting impulse to shrink from his thunderous glare. Enraged, he was an impressive sight. But he still was no match for her. Steeling herself, she faced him square. "Something spooked him as we made that final turn," she explained calmly. "I lost the reins and just now got them back. I have checked him out and he is perfectly fine." A tiny lie she knew.

"What the devil set him off?" Already he was dismissing her, running his hands over the colt, checking for himself.

"I don't know. Maybe a piece of paper in the wind spooked him or he imagined Richmond was a bear chasing him." She shrugged. "You know horses."

Finishing his inspection of the horse, he stood up, wiping his hands on his jeans. "I told you he was a lot of horse. You said you could handle him," he reminded her, eyes and tone full of challenge.

"I can," she argued, her level gaze meeting his searing eyes.

"It bloody well didn't look like it!" Ty exploded, his face turning from red to purple. "He jumped the fence like he was a steeplechaser!"

"Yelling isn't going to help this horse," she insisted calmly. "He's upset enough as it is without your verbal explosions." Her point was proven as Sky Hunter pulled on the reins, side stepping and giving a snort, then shaking his head and rolling his eyes for good measure. Season could have hugged the horse. *What a good boy you are,* she whispered to him. She owed him a carrot.

"Neither is letting him run wild and end up hurting himself. We are trying to build up his racing career, not end it."

She bit back a groan, concentrating on keeping the colt calm. "You know as well as I do that horses spook. They spook at scraps of paper blowing in the wind and they spook at nothing at all. You can't keep a horse from spooking all the time."

"It's the rider's job to control the horse if he bolts," Ty insisted, only marginally calmer. "If the rider is capable of it, that is."

Drawing in a deep, inner breath, she focused on the horse beside her, ignoring the rays of anger still radiating off Ty. "Look, the horse is fine, no harm done, so let's chalk it up to an imaginary monster in his head and let it go. He needs to be properly cooled down now."

Ty stared at her, a blistering flame burning in his eyes and a dark frown on his lips.

"You are the trainer," he reminded thickly. "It is your job to control the horse. So see that you do it. And," he paused, wagging one finger toward her. "You had better pray no harm comes to this colt due to this little escapade of yours."

"Of course," she said evenly, tugging on Sky Hunter's reins. Walking slowly, she began the long trek through the snowy path to the barn where he would be brushed, checked over again and finally stalled. Right now, she had to cool herself off as well. Ty Masters was a force!

Eddie met them half way back, leading Richmond. "Are you okay? I've never seen Masters so mad. Wow!" He let out a low whistle.

"Yeah, the old boy does have a temper, that's for sure," Season agreed, their horses dropping into tandem steps. "He'll get over it eventually," she continued. "I'm fine and so is the horse."

"It sure looked like a wild ride. He was flying. I'm not even sure his hooves ever touched the ground. All I saw was a cloud of white powder flying behind you two."

"Eddie, how far do you think it was from where he took the railing to where he slowed down?"

Stopping, he mentally measured the distance. "I'd say it would be a mile roughly. Why?"

She held the stop watch out to him. "I started this when we left the chutes together and stopped it when he slowed down out there, about two miles later."

Eddie squinted at the time, another low whistled escaping him. "Oh, my word."

"Yeah, that's what I thought when I glanced at it. This horse is fast, but let's not tell anyone just how fast yet."

"Didn't you tell Masters?"

"No, I'll tell him when the time is right."

Ty rode by on Black Warrior, casting dark glances at both of them. Eddie cringed like a scolded pup but Season stoutly marched on with her horse. Kicking the old stallion, Ty loped away, ramrod straight on his back. Season had to admit he looked good sitting on a horse. He looked more like an old time cowboy than a wealthy English racehorse owner. She had to wonder which role he felt the better fit with. He seemed to wear them both with equal comfort.

After the horses were cooled, groomed and put away in their stalls, they worked a little more with Winter's Dawn at various distances. Season was quick to see the filly didn't like snow packed on her hooves. Giving Eddie what was left of the day off, she retreated to her tiny office to record her first day's times. Smiling happily, she recorded Sky Hunter's wild run, underlining it with red ink. If he could do that on the tracks...

Satisfied, she filed her paperwork, content the horses were capable of winning big.

Moose stopped her in the hallway, concern in his dark eyes. "What happened to you, Miss?"

"Can you keep a secret?" she asked, feeling a little like a ten year old on the school playground.

He nodded, looking a little insulted by the question.

"Sky Hunter had a great run." She gripped his meaty forearm. "No, he had a super run. He even jumped the track fence and ran across a snowy field." Excited, she filled him in on the whole story, still feeling the rush of the adrenaline from the wild ride.

"That horse is the spawn of the devil for sure. Beats me how you can take to him like that," Moose said grimly. "And how mad was the Master when he finally caught up with you?"

"On a scale of one to ten? About a fifty, I think. Maybe more." She gave him a lop-sided smile.

He slowly returned the smile, looking at her thoughtfully. "I do believe you are the only person who has never been intimidated by him," Moose said slowly.

Season lifted her shoulder in a shrug. "He is just a man like any other man. Why make the choice to let him intimidate you just because he thinks he should be able to?"

Giving her another long look, he finally shrugged to himself, laying a hand on her shoulder. "Come to the kitchen and I'll fix you a light snack and get you some medicine for those scratches. You must be hungry by now."

Grateful for the brotherly concern, Season let him propel her to the kitchen where she washed up and applied a tube of medicinal balm to her scratches while he prepared a sandwich and cut up some fruit. He also brewed a strong cup of tea and set it all before her.

"That should tide you over until supper time," he decided.

Feeling better with the tea and food in her, she handed back the plate and cup, easing off the bar stool. "I think I'll go take a bath before supper. Maybe ease these aching muscles. It seems it's all caught up with me."

Picking out a change of clothes, she headed for the peace of the shared bathroom across the hall. Showering first, she removed the day's dirt and horse smell before refilling the tub with fresh water. Pouring in a cap full of bath oils, she slowly slid in, enveloping herself beneath the foamy warmth.

Leaning back, she submerged as much of herself under the creamy bubbles, inhaling deep breaths of the exotic flowery aroma. Closing her eyes, she felt the aches slowly leaving her body. Pleasant thoughts of tropical islands filled her mind. She was so tired. Pictures formed in her mind.

Lush palm trees, warm sandy beaches, bright blue ocean teeming with colorful fish, big fragrant flowers, sunshine, magnolia and coconuts, slapping waves, calling birds, a cascading waterfall...

"Well, well. The original sleeping beauty."

A deep voice suddenly rocked her ears, driving the images and sleep from her mind.

Eyes flying open in alarm, she saw two long legs standing beside her. Horrified, dread lodged in her heart, she looked up to where they met, stretching to a lean waist girded in a brown belt, up a taut stomach, and finally she gazed further up to see his eyes crinkling in merriment. Oh God!

"Sorry to wake you," he said, not sounding the least bit sorry. "This was quite an unexpected surprise."

Season fidgeting under the water. How could he just stand there with his hands on his hips and stare? How much could he see through the bubbles? Oh mercy! Entirely too much.

"A gentleman would hand me a towel and leave the room," she pointed out when it appeared he had no intentions of leaving.

"I'm no gentleman." His grin deepened at his husky assurance.

"Obviously," she spat back, feeling her face grow warmer than the bath water. "I'm sure you wouldn't like me to come barging in while you were in the middle of a bath," she offered, trying to reason with him. Did he even take baths? Her mind wandered off for a split second, following that thought. "No. You would expect me to knock first," she pointed out, more to bring her own thoughts back to the matter at hand.

"I'm not accustomed to knocking in my own house. And especially not in my own bathroom."

Okay, she was going to clobber him. She just knew it. As soon as she was dressed, she was going to clobber him with something very big. Or better yet, turn him into a toad. Yes, that was even better. He would make a fine toad for a while. Might humble him a little bit.

"A towel please, Mr. Masters," she asked stiffly, holding out a dripping hand.

Ty looked around casually, found a small towel and innocently handed it out, a good three feet beyond her reach.

She gave him a cold look. "A little closer would be nice."

He moved a foot closer. Convinced she was going to cast that spell and turn him into a toad, she shot him a look of pure detest. Damn him! He was enjoying this. Entirely way too much. Okay, she reasoned, she couldn't reach up for risk of exposing more of herself, but she could reach out and across.

Shooting her wet hand out, she grabbed the leg of his jeans just behind the knee and yanked. Caught unprepared, he dropped the towel within her reach. Snatching it up, she plastered it across her chest.

Unable to catch his balance, Ty felt himself falling, plunging both hands into the tub. His fingers grazed her thigh.

"Mr. Masters!" Leaping out of the tub, Season haphazardly draped the towel around her, hoping everything important was covered. Resentment flared within her as she watched Ty right himself, shaking off the clinging bubbles.

"In future, Mr. Masters, I suggest you knock at all closed doors or else you might find yourself somewhere you don't want to be!"

"Forgive me," Ty said softly. He almost looked contrite.

"Humph!" Grabbing up her pile of clothes, she stormed from the room, pushing a hand out to make the door slam behind her.

W hat a little pepper pot! Ty stared at the closed door and heaved a giant sigh. Wow! He hadn't expected any of that when he ambled into the bathroom a few minutes ago. Yes, admittedly, he should have left the second he smelled her bubble bath and knew she was inside, or better yet, knock and have her turn him away. It was what a gentleman would have done.

But then he would have missed all this. As she lay sleeping, covered in bubbles, so peaceful, his heart was busy doing all sorts of strange tricks. Forgotten was the anger and fear from earlier in the day, replaced by emotions totally foreign to him. Knots of desire were knitting themselves all over his insides. He just had to see more of her. He could no sooner walk away than a moth could avoid a flame.

Except he hadn't bargained for her little trick to knock him off balance and he sure hadn't expected falling into the tub. But he also wasn't complaining right now either. Looking at the tub, he reached over to pull the plug. He still felt her creamy soft leg in his fingertips. And heard her sharp intake of breath before she verbally launched into him. Taking another towel, he dried his wet sleeves. Listening to the sound of gurgling water, his mind filled up with thoughts of her.

Feeling like an idiot, he realized the picture he must make, standing in the middle of the bathroom, arms full of soapy water up to his elbows and a sappy smile pasted on his face. But the picture was nothing compared to the images racing through his mind like runaway wild horses.

Forget all his talk and nonsense about having great self-control. When it came to Season Moriarty, his self-control went out the window, escaping into the night.

A growing throb gnawed at him as his thoughts took form. She was a lot of woman to handle, but he liked that. He found the concept quite intriguing. She was mysterious, despised him, and had a temper to match his. Oh, what a combustible combination they could make. Messing with her was like playing with lit dynamite. And he was surprised to find he was loving every second of it.

Retreating to her room, Season slammed that door too for good measure. Pacing the large floor in looping circles, she felt like a caged panther. Anger boiling, she clenched and unclenched her fists as thoughts rolled through her mind like dark thunderclouds.

He could become a toad. That would be easy. She could cast ill fortune upon him. She could do a number of things that would vindicate her and make her feel oh so good. For a few minutes anyhow. But her powers were not supposed to be used that way.

Her mother had made her promise years ago not to use her gifts for personal gain or satisfaction. Her gifts were a blessing, she'd said, not to be used just because.

But her mother had never met Mr. Ty Masters either.

Throwing herself across the bed, she wailed softly. She would probably regret it if she did something bad to Ty. Later of course, not right away. It would feel too good initially. But later, she would feel the guilt from a misuse of The Gift. And that was an unpardonable crime.

"All I can say is that man is mighty lucky," she gritted out. "Right now, he could be a toad."

If she were going to continue living and working at the farm, and living next door to him, she was going to have to get a better grip on herself and her inner source. She was blessed to have the job, more or less. Now she had to get her priorities in order.

Lying on the bed, she forced herself to reevaluate the situations of the day. She knew the horses had improved their times today over their old times under the old trainer. However, Ty did not know that. All he knew was Sky Hunter's wild bolt. And in all fairness to him, she probably hadn't handled that situation all too well.

She knew the colt was safe. She knew it was his time to fly. The time was right. She could never explain to him her connection to the horse at that moment or the reason she allowed the runaway ride in the first place. Had he been willing to listen, he would have never understood anyway. Hence the little white lie about losing the reins.

Truth be told, she supposed he had a right to be upset at what he considered to be a threat to his valuable horse. Credit for that one, she ruefully decided. But that did not give him the right to enter a shared bathroom without knocking and then stand there, acting like a moron. While she couldn't use her Gift to vindicate herself, she could certainly enjoy a little self-indulging pout for a while. It might teach him a lesson.

Feeling better, she slipped on clean jeans and a heavy sweater. Wrapping her wet hair into a bun and covering it with a cap, she slipped downstairs. She heard Moose in the kitchen, the men noisily eating in the dining room and suspected Ty was in his study eating dinner.

Except she wasn't hungry right now.

Padding softly to the door, she pulled on her coat, boots and gloves, then slipped out the door into the cold night air. After the last hour, she needed to be alone with the moonlight and the wind. Leaving the lighted porch and lighted barns behind her, she plowed through the unbroken snow. Aware Ty's mastiffs might be on guard patrol tonight, she decided to risk it. She knew she could handle the dogs just fine alone.

The snow crunched under her feet, making her smile. She loved the snow. She loved the look and sound and feel of it. It was one of the things she missed while living in Florida. Snow was one of Mother Nature's most pure gifts. Like sunshine or raindrops or moon glow. Untainted and innocent.

Finally, when the house and barns were but a faint glow in the distance, she stopped. Leaning against a tree, she looked up to the sky, counting the stars twinkling down at her. Waiting, she heard her mother's advice calling to her from the stars. She'd done well not to turn her boss into a toad.

Season grinned at that. Her mother cautioned her to keep her stormy temper from rising. *Just like your father*, she clucked.

"Right, Mother. With Masters stalking my every move and behaving like a hormone driven moron. The man has no scruples," she spoke into the cold emptiness of the night.

An image shone before her. Ty was pacing his room, running a hand through his hair repetitively. He strode over to the balcony and stepped out. Peering into the darkness, he seemed to be looking for something. He looked worried. He checked his watch and frowned, returning to his room again. Pacing the floor a few times, he went to the inside door and cast it open, looking down the hall to the stairs.

He was looking and waiting for her, she realized. Somehow, he knew she was outside right now, far from the house and he was worried about her. Concern etched his brow as he waited anxiously for her return.

Incredulously, she struggled with trying to make sense of the images just provided. Why would he care if she was outside right now?

No answer came to her. Instead, she felt the tiny nudge telling her to return to her room.

"Thanks, Mother," she whispered upward, pulling herself heavily away from the tree. "I will try to keep my patience better and my promise to you."

She chuckled as she heard that warm, familiar laugh carried on the wind, brushing her cheek softly. Suddenly she did not feel so all alone. She trekked back to the house. Quietly entering, she slipped off her outer wear and passed through the kitchen. She spotted a plate on the counter, covered loosely with a napkin. Lifting the linen, she realized someone thoughtfully left supper out for her. Moose? Or Ty?

Feeling hungry now, she sat at the table and ate the meal, washing it down with a big glass of milk. Rinsing the dishes, she left them in the sink and quietly stole up the stairs. Ty's door was ajar and the light was lit. It was quiet inside so he was probably not pacing. Perhaps he was outside on the balcony again. It was the perfect time to slip past and into her room. He would hear her close the door, know she was back safely and not have to speak to her. It would also save her trying to explain what she was doing outside late at night—again.

Closing her door just loudly enough to be heard, she undressed and climbed into bed. An image of Ty turning off his light and going to bed came to her. Mystified, she wondered why it mattered so much to him whether she was in the house or outside in the snow.

৩৫৩

Early the next morning Season beat the sun up. Hungry, she headed downstairs, finding Moose already in the kitchen, turning French toast and cutting fresh fruit. The smell of brewing coffee stirred her stomach.

"Good morning, Moose. Smells great in here," she greeted, sliding onto her favorite bar stool.

"Uh huh," Moose nodded, shaking water from a bunch of red grapes. "What's your favorite fruit?" he asked, pointing to a tray already laden with citrus, apples, bananas, and more.

45

"I guess grapes and bananas." She watched as he draped the fruits around a stack of toast and passed it over with a decanter of syrup.

"Sure was a lot of slamming going on upstairs last night," he commented nonchalantly, pouring the coffee and handing over a butter container. Turning away, he reached for another plate.

"Slamming?" Had he heard her and Ty's altercation from down here? What must he be thinking? "Did you hear slamming?" she hedged, playing with her food, unable to take a bite.

"A door or two. You and the Master working everything out okay up there?"

"Oh yeah. We're working it out just fine. He thinks he's the master and I don't."

Moose laughed, a hearty, booming sound that reminded Season of Santa Claus. "Change is good," he said. "For everyone."

"Hey, look, I'm sorry if we kept you up last night," Season began.

Moose waved her away, dismissing the apology as he flipped more toast. "Change is always good. Don't ever be sorry to bring change."

After breakfast, Season disappeared to her office, seated at the desk and warmed by the early morning sunbeams streaming through the window. Several sheets of paper and a few racing schedules lay before her and she absently studied them. As the sun's rays fell on her back, she dropped her pen, rubbed her neck and closed her eyes, and let the liquid warmth penetrate her body.

৩৵৩

Ty slowly entered the stallion barn, listening to the restless pawing of the confined stallions, eager for their breakfast and morning release. Sucking in a deep breath of cool mountain air, heavily laced with horses, hay and manure, he made his way to the back, pausing to pat any head poking out along his route. Stopping at Sky Hunter's stall, he found the colt looking restless and eager for a run. Satisfied the colt suffered no ill effects from yesterday, he moved on to the end stall. His favorite stall.

Leaning against Black Warrior's door, he affectionately stroked the old stallion, wondering if he should go upstairs to Season's office. He knew she

46

was already up there. Would she resent his interruption or would she welcome him in? What was she doing up there?

Indecision wore at him. It was hard to tell what sort of greeting, if any, he would receive.

Still stroking the old horse, he let out a long sigh. He would never know until he tried. Stepping away from the stall, he quietly made his way up the wooden steps, cringing as they creaked and groaned. At the top, he rested his hand on the railing, his heart suddenly skipping several beats.

The sun's rays shone on her hair, lighting it afire with brilliant colors of red, richer than a fiery chestnut. She looked like a ripe peach, ready for picking. His heart suddenly kick-started with a painful boom. Almost as soon as he cast eyes on her, memorizing the scene for future memories, she turned around, her expression not one of welcome.

"Up early I see," he commented, stepping into the room, suddenly feeling out of place. He surveyed the papers stacked on her desk. "Is it always your policy to keep such an untidy desk? However do you find anything?"

"I use a magnet," Season replied dryly. "Clearly you never saw it before. Is there something special you wanted?"

He paced the room twice before answering her. He brushed a few wisps of hay off his jacket. "Actually, yes. I have been thinking. In light of your difficulties with Sky Hunter, I was thinking you need some assistance."

"I have Eddie for assistance."

"I was referring more to another trainer. Someone perhaps older and more capable of handling Sky Hunter. Perhaps one of the men from the weekend."

Season's eyes narrowed. "I thought we already discussed that."

Ty's gaze held her in that challenging glare he was beginning to wear a lot since she came around.

"Look," she said flatly, letting out a low breath. "I can handle that horse. There is more to the story of him bolting than you saw yesterday. At this point you just have to trust me."

Ty took two giant strides to the desk and slammed his palms down, scattering papers.

"Trust you?" he repeated, his voice a raspy growl. "Trust you with a colt worth millions? That isn't some old cart hag. It is a bloody thoroughbred!"

"I'm well aware of the horse's worth," Season calmly stated. "I'm also well aware of his abilities, possibly more so than you are."

Ty leaned dangerously close to her, and he could smell the coffee and sweet syrup in her breath. "And what precisely does that mean?"

She stood up, leaning forward, meeting him half way across the desk. "It means an assistant, or a baby sitter, which is really what you are implying, is unnecessary."

"So do you plan on letting the colt bolt every time he takes it into his head to? What if he decides to break a leg or snap a bone? Then what do you suggest we do?"

"There will be no more wild bolts."

"How do you know that?" he demanded, stepping back two paces, his back almost at the far wall.

"I just told you there will not be."

"And I'm supposed to be happy with that explanation just because you said so?" Ty moved back another step, against the far wall, crossing his arms over his chest, regarding her. "You seem to require someone to keep a watchful eye on you," he finally said, his voice soft. "You are my employee and I say you shall have an assistant. I will post the ad immediately." Spinning on his heels, he marched for the railing leading back downstairs.

"Wait a second," Season called, halting him on the first step. "There is a reason I let him bolt like that." Standing up, she carried a piece of paper over to him. "Maybe this isn't the job for me after all if you will not allow me a measure of trust to do my job. So, before you hire another trainer and before I go, let me say a few words in my defense." She waved the page at him.

"These are the times from yesterday on all the horses that ran. As you will see, they each bettered their times from the previous idiot you had training them. Now I have thrown away the comments he had to say about them so you will have to dig through the trash can over there if you really want to know what he thought of your precious horses. It wasn't nice." Pausing, she dragged her finger down the columns of numbers, drawing Ty's eyes to a particular set of figures.

"Lastly, Mr. Masters, you will want to know Sky Hunter ran almost two miles unrestrained in just over two and a quarter minutes. That is after he had been posting all morning."

Ty's jaw dropped. Snatching the paper from Season's fingers, he scanned the columns for himself, muttering under his breath.

"I'd like to see an assistant do that," she said in tart satisfaction when he raised bewildered eyes to her. "So, am I fired?"

"I would have to be out of my bloody mind to let go any trainer who can get that kind of speed from a horse." Dropping the page, he thumped down the steps, the paper fluttering to the floor.

4

Hearing his retreat down the corridor below, Season wobbled back to her desk, sinking down, exhausted. It didn't sound like she was fired but it wasn't an open arms invitation to stay either. Ty also hadn't said whether he still planned on hiring a baby sitter or not.

Apparently, Ty intended on keeping Season guessing about his intentions. He spent the next couple of days avoiding her. Still uncertain as to his plans, she decided to enjoy the break from his constant presence and concentrate more on her work. She and Eddie ran the horses each day, always keeping full control of Sky Hunter.

Three days later, she filled out the paperwork, feeling bittersweet. It was racing applications to enter Sky Hunter in some upcoming preliminary races. She felt excitement and confidence in his ability, however, to get him entered meant approaching Ty to gain his signature. How miserable an experience would this become? He'd done his best to avoid her, and rumors were he had been in a foul temper lately.

"Hi, Moose," she greeted, breezing into the kitchen, absently noticing the heavy aromas hanging in the room. Moose stood at the stove, stirring spoon in his hand. "Where's Ty?"

"In his study. But I wouldn't be going in there if I were you," he warned.

"Believe me, I don't want to. But I really don't have much choice," she said, rattling the pages in her hand. "Why?"

Moose shook his head. "The master's been in a bad mood. Worse than normal, even for him. Worse than yesterday even. Just grunts and snarls each time he walks by. I was hoping one of his favorite dishes would soften him up some."

Curious, she leaned over the counter. "Uh huh. Just what is his favorite dish anyway?"

"Prime rib and Yorkshire pudding. Usually puts him in a better mood when he's feeling sour." Moose eyed her paperwork. "Does that have to be tonight? Can't it wait?"

She had already put it off way too long as it was. The deadline was only days away. "Not really." She hesitated. Could it wait one more day? "Are you sure he'd be in a better mood tomorrow? We had some words a couple days ago and that's probably why he's acting like such a brat now."

"Words?" Moose lifted one dark eyebrow. "You aren't quitting, are you?"

She shrugged. "Only if he persists with this nonsensical idea of his to hire a baby sitter for me. But then again, he might be getting ready to give me the ax."

"Doubt it."

Moose seemed so confident, Season was taken aback. "Why are you so sure? I'm not."

Moose looked at her over the counter, his small eyes steadily locked on hers, his expression serious. "Because he has finally woken up. He won't be wanting to lose that feeling now."

Stunned, Season slid off the bar stool, not able to think of anything else to say. Awoke to what? Managing a stiff nod, she headed for Ty's study, her steps slow and reluctant. Clearly, Moose had some initiative abilities too. Raising her hand to knock at the heavy door, she was startled to see she was actually shaking.

"Get a grip," she muttered under her breath, feeling every heavy, slow thud of her heart. Rapping twice, she waited.

"Come," came a snarled invitation, sounding anything but warm and friendly.

Pushing the door open, she kept the papers in front of her like some sort of puny shield from him. Ty lifted his head, glanced at her and ducked back to the towering piles of paperwork littering his desk. And he complained about her desk? His looked like the paper fairy just finished having a sneezing fit.

"What?" It wasn't a question, it sounded more like a barking command.

"Sky Hunter is ready for the Santa Anita Stakes next month. These are the races I would like to see him entered in. Four in total." Stepping to the desk, she slid the pages on top of the piles already there.

He took the papers, looking them over and ignoring her. Finally, he lifted his blue gaze to hers.

"Why these? He would be up against older, more experienced horses in one of them. And another one is a longer race too, over a mile. And four races for his first set of the season? Isn't that asking a lot of him?"

"Because he is ready and because he can handle it," she stated confidently. Standing straight, she waited, feeling much like a cadet before a drill sergeant. The emotions rolling off him almost overwhelmed her, making her weak. She tried to block the flow between them.

"So you are still thinking he is Triple Crown material?"

"Yes," she said and nodded. "This is his year to shine."

He favored her with a smile that could have meant anything. "And what makes you so sure of that?" he asked, tapping his fingers on the papers, his smile not quite reaching his eyes.

Faltering, she wondered how she could possibly explain to him how she was so sure. How she could feel it coming from the horse. Because he showed her when they connected? Because she could see it? Enough so that she would stake her life on the certainty that this horse was ready for serious racing. Suddenly, she felt deflated. There was no way she could get him to understand.

"I just am," she said finally. "Woman's intuition," she suggested lightly, knowing he would never buy into that. Indeed, his skepticism was immediately clear.

"Uh huh. Well, consider him entered in them all anyway," he said, his tone and expression neutral. "Is there anything else?"

Okay, should she ask the question burning in her mind or let it ride for now? Indecision pawed at her. Of all his churning thoughts she could see none gave her a clear picture of this one singular question. Could she bear to know the truth? Could she bear not to know?

Oh well, one never got far in life without asking questions.

"Yes, there is one more thing." She took a breath, plunging in. "Are you still intent on hiring a baby sitter?"

His eyes narrowed, another thin smile slashing across his face. The kind that could mean anything, but certainly meant something. "How do you say it? Let us just say the jury is still out on that one yet."

Hardly an answer. Nodding, she turned, spinning on her heels and marching to the door. Outside, she expelled a long breath and returned to the kitchen. She poured herself a cup of coffee, needing the caffeine boost. Perching on a bar stool again, elbows on the counter, chin resting on her knuckles, she quietly watched Moose prepare their supper.

"How did it go?" Moose asked.

"As good as can be expected. He can be as ambiguous as anything I've ever heard. Or should that be not heard instead? Oh whatever." Giving up, she uttered a frustrated moan.

Moose considered that. "Maybe because he doesn't know the answer himself yet."

Good theory. After supper, she retired to the library, curling up in a huge chair by the fire, with a blanket tossed over her and a paperback novel she found on the miles of shelves. The fire crackled and snapped, filling the room with sounds and smells so warm and friendly and relaxing. Moose's meal had been delicious, leaving her full and content. Pushing thoughts of Ty's ambiguous behavior from her mind, she tried to get into the story in her hand.

The warmth spread through the room, covering her like an extra blanket. The story spun along, drawing her in, the snapping fire adding to the background noise. The scent of burning pine filled the room. She felt a yawn pulling at her mouth. If she closed her eyes for just a second, it would do no harm ...

🪷

"Season! Come quick! We need you down to the foaling barn." Ty stood before her, hand on her shoulder, shaking it. "Season!"

She must have dozed off. The book lay on the floor. "Wha-what?" she muttered, shaking the sleepy fog from her mind.

"I need you. Cloudy Lass is foaling and it isn't going well at all." Worry filled his voice. Like cold water, his concern splashed over to her, waking her instantly. Swinging her feet to the floor, she felt his warm hand gripping hers, anxiously helping her up.

"What's she doing?" she asked as he towed her toward the door, all but shoving her coat and boots at her.

"She has been in labor too long. Contracting steadily, but no foal. She is in pain."

Season's heart sank. Heading out the door, she pushed her arms into the sleeves of her coat as the cold gust of mountain air slammed into her. This mare was foaling late and in trouble. *Not good.*

Most the mares had already foaled. She'd been to the foaling barn recently, looking in at the tiny, wobbly babies next to their moms. But foals were not her job. She was responsible for the stallions and the racers, not the babies. Nonetheless who could ignore a precious baby creature once in a while? And when a mare and foal were in trouble, it was all hands on deck. She'd been told Cloudy Lass was known for having bad deliveries. This was to be her last chance at being a mother.

Following Ty into the brightly lit foaling barn, she felt the blast of instant warmth from the heaters. She also immediately felt the heavy tension in the room, hanging like smoke. It was as if all the other mares were feeling Cloudy Lass's difficulties. Ty led her to a roomy stall where a lovely gray mare paced anxiously. Cactus, the foaling man, crouched in the corner, watching her every move. He shot Season a brief worried, strained nod.

"Boss, she blew in her water, but still ignored the food. She just keeps pacing, pawing at the straw, and crying out at the contractions."

"Will she lie down?" Season asked, stepping up to the mare, and catching her halter, pausing her steps.

"She tried a few times and got right back up again."

"Whoa, girl, it's all right." Season touched both palms to the mare, feeling her quivering beneath her touch. Contractions rippled through her, tearing a scared and painful whinny from the mare. Leaving one hand on the halter, she spoke soft and low to the mare, moving alongside her shoulder. Running one hand along her abdomen and flank, she felt the shivers. Clearly, the mare was in great distress. Tremors of pain raced through her in union with the mare's.

"How long has she been like this?" she asked.

"Few hours already. Called the vet and he's on his way but he's been delayed. Be here as soon as he can. Other two vets are out of town, I guess, and he's covering for all three of them," Cactus explained.

Great. Both the mare and foal will be dead before he makes it out here.

"Okay, Lassie girl, can we get you to lie down, please?"

Coaching, she tried to lure the mare to the bed of straw. After pawing a few times, Cloudy Lass lowered herself with a giant moan. Almost immediately another contraction rippled through her, making her cry out and try struggling to her feet. Season bit back the pain as it tore through her own body, clenching her teeth until it passed.

"Whoa there, just stay there, girl." Cooing softly, Season tried to make the panicked mare lie still. She thrashed with her hooves as the pain moved through her, shaking her head and neck in protest. Season moved her palms along the mare's flank again, taking care to avoid the flailing hooves.

"I'm no vet, but I think the foal is too big and I'm fairly sure it's backward too," she called over her shoulder to the men. Right now, she didn't need to be a vet to see and feel the problem.

"Bloody hell," Ty muttered. He dropping down in the straw, and fisted his hands around the stalks.

Cactus swore softly, kicking at the straw and jabbing his hands into his pockets.

Normally it was a death sentence to the foal and most likely for the mare are well. Unless the vet arrived soon with his equipment, they would probably lose both horses. Season felt Ty's pain as much as she felt the mare's. It ripped and tore at her like a wild animal, screaming in anger and frustration and fright.

Pushing her emotions under control she concentrated on the mare. Stroking the gray neck, wet with lather, she whispered soft words, calming and soothing. Whispering prayers and chants, she never stopped caressing along her gray neck. Gradually the mare stopped kicking her hooves and stilled, lifting her head as the contractions rippled over her body. Sweat lathered her body and she grunted a few times, adding a few painful whinnies which echoed through the barn like eerie ghosts.

"Easy, Lassie girl, almost done now," she cooed, chanting more and stroking along her flank as she worked to guide the foal out.

"It's coming," she called. "Get ready." She moved both palms along the flank to the mare's buttocks, encouraging the foal to move along its birth canal, pulling it along beneath her hands. "I can feel it!"

Ty knelt next to her in the straw, his face unreadable as he stared at her.

Season continued stroking along the birth canal. It was moving beneath her palms. Closing her eyes, concentrating all her energies to moving the foal closer to the outside world.

"Now," she breathed, opening her eyes as the foal's back end slid into Ty's waiting hands.

"Damn. Breech," he confirmed, holding the back half of the still foal.

Another contraction shuddered through Cloudy Lass and Season as she moved her palms right by the foal. Soon the back legs, ribs and shoulders passed through to Ty's waiting grip.

"One more time, Lassie girl," Season pleaded.

Within seconds the mare let out a shrill whinny and the foal's head popped out. Season let out a heavy breath. Ty laid the foal out in the straw, grabbing a towel Cactus handed over, rubbing the wet sack away from its mouth and nose. It was larger than a normal newborn but it still looked so tiny compared to its mother.

"Damn. It isn't moving!" Ty cried, rubbing the towel harder. Cactus suctioned liquid from its mouth and nose and Ty rubbed ferociously along the tiny foal's ribcage, his teeth set in determination.

"It is dead," he said finally, dropping back into the straw, dropping the towel next to him. Cactus moved to the mare, who lay breathing heavy, trying to move her head back to check her baby. Ty sat and stared at the dead foal, disappointment written all over his face. Despair. Crushed. It was palatable.

Inhaling a slow, deep breath, Season briskly rubbed her hands together, moving back to the head of the foal. Sitting down, she cradled the small head in her lap and rubbed along its tiny chest. Closing her eyes, she blocked out Ty and Cactus and the mare, feeling only the still little baby in her lap.

Live, little one, breathe life into your lungs, please.

Chanting and praying softly under her breath, she willed the foal to take a breath of life giving air. Yet it lay still and cold and wet on her legs. Using her palms, warmed and pulsating, to massage the tiny chest, she rubbed her fingertips over the heart and lungs. Tirelessly, she repeated the circles, whispering for the foal to live.

"Season, it's no use. It's gone," Ty's voice reached her, sounding so broken, so tired. "Let us go now. We can only hope the vet gets here in time to save the mare. Season?"

Blocking out the sad weariness of his voice, she continued making circles over the cold, lifeless body. Endless little circles massaging the heart and lungs. Over and over again. *Breathe, little one, breathe.* Again, and again.

Suddenly a rattling gasp filled the stall. The foal kicked, raising its head to draw in a breath. Its huge brown eyes looked around the stall and fuzzy whiskers twitched against Season's hand.

"Ohmygosh! It's alive!" Cactus exclaimed, hand over his heart. "I thought it was a goner for sure."

"Not yet, my friend," Season said, still drawing circles over the foal. "Breathe, little one, you aren't done yet." The foal greedily sucked in a few more breaths of air, offering a pitiful little whinny. Its mom answered with a tired whinny of her own.

"Come on, baby." Season supported the foal as she manipulated the legs to a standing position. "Get your legs under you, honey."

Holding the foal in a standing position, she looked over at Ty, who was spellbound, staring at her and the foal in complete and utter amazement. "Ty, could you get another towel and start drying this little baby?" she asked, breaking into his daze.

Blinking, he jumped, startled by her voice. Wordlessly, he felt for another towel and began rubbing the foal, never taking his eyes off Season. His wide-eyed stare told her all she needed to know. She'd just blown his mind. Doubtlessly there would be an explanation or two due, but she wasn't done here yet.

She moved to the mare, touching her lathered neck. "Sweetheart, don't you think it's time you get up to help your baby?" she asked the horse, coaxing the mare to rise by gently and bodily pushing against her. With another whinny, stronger now, the horse climbed to her feet, shaking the straw from her coat and turning to see her baby. Nuzzling it, she pushed Ty out of the way, starting to lick the baby all over with her own soft tongue. The foal happily twitched its bushy tail.

Season moved away, leaning back against the wall, watching the show unfold in front of her. It was a brown foal with two white socks and a tiny snip of white on its muzzle.

"Cute little thing. Looks like it will make it," she said to the men. Suddenly she felt so exhausted. "The mare looks better too, stronger than before."

The mare nuzzled and licked her baby, looking stronger every minute. The foal took a few wobbly steps, shaking its fuzzy tail, looking for dinner. Season knew it would find the milk bar and suckle soon. She felt good. She had helped give and sustain life in what might have otherwise been a tragic disaster. Now, she was tired, drained and her head was throbbing. The Gift sure could be taxing. Casting a look over at Ty, she tried to prepare herself for the look of total disbelief and suspicion etched on his face.

"It's done, Ty. They'll be okay," she said softly. Glancing at Cactus, he looked equally bewildered.

"H-h-how?" Ty sputtered.

Shrugging, she lifted her shoulders. "Can't explain it. Just the way it goes. How come you came to get me for this? I'm not responsible for foaling." Always good to change the question with another one.

He blinked slowly, as if trying to remember why. "Moose. I ran in to phone the vet again and Moose was there. He said to fetch you instead. Why?"

Why? Again, Season had the sense that Moose was more intuitive than she or anyone else suspected. And he must have known or guessed something of her capabilities. She shrugged again, not knowing how to answer Ty.

Suddenly, his jaw dropped as a guarded, suspicious look stamped itself across his face. He scooted a foot or two away from her. "What are you? Are you some sort of witch or something?"

"No, I'm hardly a witch." She could have almost laughed at the suggestion had he not looked so serious by it. Actually, she supposed, it was close though not in the same classification. "Why don't we go get some coffee and I'll try to explain?" And just how was she going to explain what he just witnessed? *Clearly, he was thinking the worse already.*

He remained motionless at her suggestion, distrust on his face.

"I really could go for a cup of coffee," she hinted, trying to galvanize him from his shock. True enough, coffee would be good as she still felt the draining effects of her earlier actions. If she were a witch, she could just snap her fingers and voila! Behold a cup of coffee. It did not work that way with her. She could give life but if she wanted coffee, she had to make the trip for it. Climbing to her feet, she held her hand out to Ty, offering a way up. "I'll explain it all inside." *Sort of.*

Shooting her a look of pure distrust, he got to his feet alone, pushing aside her offer of assistance and marched to the stall door. Cactus barely noticed them leaving, so intent on watching mom and baby getting to know each other, a look of awe and disbelief still on his face. Smiling at the peaceful scene of mare and foal, Season pulled on her coat, trotting after Ty into the cold air outside.

The house was empty, a few lamps lit along the hallways. Ty dropped his coat in the foyer, ignoring the hook on the wall, wordlessly heading for the kitchen, his back straight and tension radiating from him like steam from a radiator.

Season quietly pulled out two coffee mugs and reheated leftover coffee. Pouring it, she tried to think how best to explain. Clearly, he was still thinking the worse and after what he had just witnessed, she couldn't blame him. Would he even go so far as to fire her for what he witnessed? She kind of doubted it. But if he did not particularly trust her before, this wasn't going to help. *Okay, here goes nothing.*

Setting the mugs on the table, she sat down opposite him, hair behind her, arms folded in front of her. Ty cradled the warm mug in his palms, steam rising from the top, the fragrant scent filling the air between them. He eyed her warily. Waiting. She searched for the best answer.

"Are you a witch?" he finally asked, breaking the ice.

"No. Again." she said. "I'm more of a druid."

He blinked. "A who?"

"Druid. An ancient Celtic religion. I'm kind of like a fae or faerie."

He shook his head. "What?"

She sighed. She really was terrible at these explanations. Another good reason not to tell anyone about her skills. "Okay, I inherited it from my folks, who inherited it from their folks and so on down their respective lines. Mom was a seer, she could see into the future, she'd have images or visions. Like a fae. And Dad communicated with animals and other things. It was almost magical how he could know what they were thinking or feeling. It sure helped his and Granddaddy's successes as trainers. They were druids in that they could give life. Just like you saw now." She gave him with a shrug. "So I inherited the Sight from my mom and the Gift from my Dad. Lucky me," she finished with a lop-sided smile.

He never moved or blinked. He just stared at her, hands curled around the mug, not drinking, as if it offered some protection between him and her. "So you aren't a witch?" he finally asked.

Shaking her head, she stilled a laugh at the comparison. It was so typical she supposed. "No. Witches are more into black arts and stuff, learning their craft from anywhere. Faes and druids inherit it from their family, learning how to hone it from their parents. Plus I can't use my Gifts for personal gain. Only for good services." She gave him another tentative smile. "Otherwise, if I were a witch, I would have turned you into a toad last night."

That made him blink. "Pardon me?"

"When you broke into the bathroom and tried that little stunt of yours, I really wanted to turn you into a toad. But I decided not to. A witch probably would have anyway."

He shook his head, baffled. "Guess I'm glad for that," he said slowly. "Why didn't you ... er ... do that?"

She shrugged, amused at his faltering question. "Misuse of the Gift. Unpardonable sin." She grinned.

"Why? Would thunderbolts from heaven strike you dead if you had?"

"No." She laughed outright at his suggestion. "No, it's just I learned it's not acceptable to do that kind of stuff. No real harm would come to me, but I know it's not right."

"Again, glad to know that. I think," he said, uncurling his hands from the mug and pushing it away. "So I thank you that I'm not a toad now. Could you warn me if you ever decided to do that? Turn me into something?" He grimaced at the request.

"Sure, what do you prefer? A toad or maybe a mammal?" she asked lightly.

"I prefer to be a man." He jabbed a finger to his chest. "This man. Me."

"Oh, okay. I'll keep that in mind."

He stared at her, questions burning in his eyes. "So what else can you do? Other than turn men into toads and bring dead foals to life?" He paused, inhaling a sharp breath. "You made that foal come out, didn't you?" He paled at her silent nod, swallowing hard. "What else can you do?"

"Oh, lots of stuff." Thinking, she pushed her mug away and started listing items on her fingers. "I am attuned to nature so I'm one with the animals. How do you really think I won the mastiffs over so easily? And Sky Hunter? With the Sight of the fae, I can sometimes get visions of things about to happen or images of things that are happening now. Even from a distance. It's kind of cool, actually.

"And with the Gift of the druids, I can cure, heal, and weld powers over the elements and nature. I can make the sun shine for a little while or maybe work up a small thunderstorm. Light a campfire with two snaps of the fingers," she added, winking, snapping two fingers. A flame sparked to life from her fingertips.

Ty blinked, astonished. "So you can see Sky Hunter winning the Triple Crown? Is that how you are so sure he can? Or will you just snap your fingers and make him win? Or burst into flames?"

"No, I can't just make him win. I can only train him to run and win like any other trainer and horse. But I sense he has the potential to go that far. The day he jumped the fence he told me he was ready for an all-out run. I sensed there was no danger and saw no danger ahead so I let him go."

"Uh huh." He frowned at her words. Casting his eyes around the room he searched for answers, as if they were written on the walls. Finding none, he returned his gaze to Season. "So now what?"

"What do you mean?" she asked, finally taking a sip of the tepid coffee, then pushing it away with a grimace.

"Where do we go from here?"

"Where do you want to go?"

A sparkle glinted in his eyes, flashing for the briefest second and then it was gone. He shook his head, clearing all thoughts. "Can you read minds too?" he asked her, a new wariness on his face.

"Uh, sometimes I can get vibrations or emotions or feelings," she hedged. "Why?"

"No reason," he said, dismissing the topic. "So if I forgo the assistant, or baby sitter idea, will you stay on here?"

A smile crept over her face. Did he really mean it? Yes, he did. "You bet. Deal." Shoving her hand across the table, she offered it to Ty. Frowning, he hesitated.

"I won't do anything," she promised with a little groan. "You have to learn some trust if I'm going to stay."

Gingerly he took her hand, giving it a fast little pump.

"Welcome to the team," he said, eyes glinting again for a brief moment before vanishing. "And please do not turn me into a toad or anything."

She could see his genuine concern in her abilities and how she might reduce him to an animal and how it warred with quieter interests sparking in his mind. She pondered whether to assure him she would never do such a thing, even in anger, or let a little fear help him behave. Admittedly, the latter was a bit tempting.

Thinking of Moose's vague comments from before, she let the conversation end.

<h1 style="text-align:center">❧ 5 ❧</h1>

Ty seemed content to avoid Season as much as possible after their little chat, which suited her just fine. She felt freer to work now, being able to better concentrate on the horses or while pouring over data in her office or curled up alone by the fire in the library after everyone else retired to their own spaces. When not busy doing that, she was happy to just hang out in the stallion barn, watching the big horses munching their hay and getting to know them better.

This was a frequent thing of hers once the February storms started blowing through, blanketing the farm with several inches of fresh snow with each new storm and temporarily shutting most operations down until they were dug out once again. The horses stomped and snorted under their confinement, eager to run in the pastures and paddocks again when kept too long indoors. Season waited just as eagerly as the horses while men drove tractors and plows, opening up paths.

All the horses were taking to her, each at their own pace. Even fiery Sky Hunter and the mighty Black Warrior were softening up a little bit, thanks to a lot of patience and even more apples and carrots. Even so, she was careful to never let her guard down, risking a painful bite. Ty's stallions did not lack for courage or fire, and she had to admire them for that. Coupled with the sensible and steadfast personalities of the mares, no wonder his racehorses were legendary.

Occasionally, as Eddie and she breezed the horses, Ty would appear at track side, silently watching for a moment. Resting one leg on the railings, he made an imposing silhouette, always managing to take Season's breath away, despite being able to sense his apprehension from whatever distance he was. Dressed in jeans and denim coat, the rugged sight of him made her pulse jump and heart beat fast. Though his hat shielded his eyes, she felt his currents of curiousness and wariness.

Once their eyes connected, he quickly ducked out of sight.

It was to be expected, she reasoned. People tended to avoid what they did not understand. Telling herself to enjoy this respite from his constant irritating attitude, she still felt a tiny jab of disappointment each time he appeared and silently disappeared a few minutes later. Each visit left her feeling unsettled.

Every once in a while, when she was on the balcony or resting by the fireplace, she caught him paroling with the mastiffs, riding Black Warrior. The sight of him atop the old stallion bathed in the moonlight always caused something inside her to burn warmly. Heat kindled like stoking a fire; burning interest she could do nothing about.

Life seemed to have settled into a semi-comfortable, if not predictable, pattern. After the final meal, when all the other workers left the main house and Moose retired to his room, Season was left alone in hers, reading a book in bed, and listening to Ty next door. The floor squeaked rhythmically as he performed his nightly push-ups or some other heart pumping calisthenics. She pictured his muscular body stretching and straining, breaking out into a sweat, not unlike a racehorse pushing mightily for the finish line. The images of his extending muscles and heavy panting stoked that heat, making her extra blankets unnecessary.

Actually, she yielded just once to the temptation, used her ability, and visited his room without his being able to notice her. Silently, she leaned against the wall that separated their rooms, watching him working out, as her heart beat in tattoo to his. Suddenly he paused, lifting his head as though sensing her. Carefully he sniffed, like a dog searching the air for a scent. Quickly she slipped back to her room, the images staying with her each night after that. If he knew she could transcend solid matter, he'd really think she was a witch. Except now she had the impressions in her mind of his bulging muscles.

After the lights went out, the big house seemed eerie and lonely. She considered getting a cat for company. Not one of the half wild barn cats, but a real house cat for her. Someone furry and warm to take to bed and keep her wandering thoughts away from Ty. She could get a solid black cat, one with wicked orange eyes. Seeing that prowling around upstairs would really goad him. She might go so far as to tell him it used to be one of the stable hands.

Retiring to the library one particularly cold and snowy evening, she pulled a hardcover book off the shelf, settled on the sofa by the snapping fire and attempted to give the impression of reading the words. Every few minutes she dutifully turned the page, even though the letters blurred before her eyes.

What was it with Ty? When he was bugging her, and shadowing her every move, she hated it, and resented his lack of trust. When he threatened to hire a baby sitter, she was insulted and furious. When he tried to annoy her, it infuriated her. And now, having shown him a side of herself most people can never accept, he has run in the other direction. So instead of being happy, and relieved, she was finding it more difficult to accept. Why? What about him left her feeling so unsettled inside? She wanted to shake him up as much as he had managed to shake her world up.

This was supposed to be the dream job of a lifetime, where she could just focus on the horses, and not deal with a man. She turned the page with a derisive snort. What happened?

His behavior challenged her thinking in ways no man ever had before. His presence left her feeling things she never had before. She read the wariness in his eyes the rare moments they met. And how could she forget the unspoken challenges in those baby blues before she revealed herself? But when he would flash her a rare, soft, fleeting smile it warmed her inside out like sunshine. His moods were as endless and almost hypnotized her.

She could count the reasons she wanted to turn him into a toad and end up running out of fingers and toes. But when she spied him propped up against the fence or riding astride a horse or marching across the floor, her blood boiled in weird ways. She felt funny inside. He could goad her by the mere dare in his eyes and then toss her that passing smile, melting her insides like jelly. But mostly now he just looked wary and moved away, leaving her feeling deflated as an old balloon.

What was it with him? Why did he affect her so? Frustration mounting, she turned another page, wishing someone would turn the heat down.

"Sure is warm in here, isn't it?"

Jumping, she slammed the book shut with a loud thud. Looking upright, she cranked her head all the way up to see Moose towering over her, an innocent smile on his face.

"Huh?" she managed dimly. How long had he been standing there? And why hadn't she noticed his arrival? She was losing it.

He grinned even more, showing his toothless gap. "I was just thinking it was warm in here. The fire is too hot," he said, gesturing a huge hand to the fireplace. "I think we should let it burn down a little before adding more fuel."

"Oh yeah, right. Good idea," she agreed automatically.

"Sometimes, when things are a little too hot, it's best to let them simmer and cool down a little," he pointed out slowly. "They might just burn themselves out, given enough time."

Staring at him, she analyzed his words. Somehow, there had to be a cryptic message in there. But what did she know about such things? Surely he was referring to her and Ty perhaps?

"Okay, thanks for the tip, I'll keep it in mind." She shrugged, looking for the connection. Moose turned to walk away. She stopped him at the archway. "Moose?"

"Yeah?" he asked, turning back, an amused smile still on his face.

"How?" she asked simply, knowing he would understand.

He jerked a thumb at the closed book. "You just spent half an hour reading a book you don't even like. And it's upside down."

"Oh." Feeling her cheeks growing warm, she studied the book still in her hands. Sure enough, he was right on both counts. Lifting her gaze, she saw she was alone once more. Surely there was a special place reserved somewhere for that man in the afterlife. She would have to speak to her mother about that someday.

⊗⊗⊗

E arly the next morning, Season took an inventory of her personal toiletries. She was low on some items. So how did one manage to go shopping for feminine stuff when stuck way out here, miles from anywhere, surrounded by men and without a day off in a while? By then, she would be in real trouble.

Okay, the men must have to drive into town regularly for grain and horse related stuff. Except there was no way she was going to ask them to pick up her stuff. No sir. And forget about asking Ty to add it to the weekly groceries. Cringing, she pictured the men pawing through the bags, eyeballing her personal items. Nope, that wouldn't work either. Sighing she adjusted her braid and headed for the stairs. No doubt Moose would have an answer for her dilemma.

Slipping onto her favorite stool a few minutes later, she took the coffee mug he offered. "Hey, Moose, how do the men go about getting their stuff when we're out here every day?"

"Stuff?" he asked, passing over a heavily loaded plate.

"Yeah, shaving cream, deodorant, razor blades, chewing tobacco? That kind of personal stuff."

"Oh," Moose nodded, a small grin on his face. "You mean like tampons and bath oils."

Feeling heat creeping into her cheeks, she crammed a forkful of food into her mouth. "Yeah, something like that."

Moose shook his head. "It's all very low key. Give me your list of personal needs by Wednesday afternoon. I order everything for the farm. Everything arrives in with the weekly groceries. I separate personal items and seal them in plain wrappers with your name on it. It's all kept secure until you come to collect your package. This way no one else knows what anyone else is getting and privacy is kept."

He made a cross over his chest with a stubby finger, grinning. "Your secrets are safe with me."

Remembering Ernie, the delivery boy who greeted her upon her first day at the farm, and the many bags of groceries, she had to admit it was a good system. And now that she thought about it, she did recall later seeing a few of the men walking in and right back out with plain brown bags under their arms. Probably dirty magazines considering the mentality of some of the guys around here, she thought in disgust. But everything was kept private. And it certainly was a benefit to her situation since she was the only female for miles around.

"I also need a list of your allergies to foods and any medications you're allergic to or are taking now," Moose added, breaking into her thoughts. "And any surgeries you might have had, appendix removed, things like that."

"Oh, that's a great idea."

"It was the Master's idea."

She wasn't sure if she should applaud the idea or scoff at it.

"I'll have both lists to you by Wednesday," she promised, handing back the empty plate. She drained the last of the coffee and was halfway to the door when Ty's call froze her in mid stride.

"Glad I caught you," he said as she swung around to face him. "What are your plans for the day?" he asked, his expression neutral. He was fresh from the shower, damp hair curling, freshly shaven, and smelling of musk and woodlands.

Such an innocent question, but it sent ideas unexpectedly spiraling through her mind. Reeling them in, she tried to appear nonchalant, acutely aware Moose was within earshot. Lifting a shoulder in a shrug, she answered. "I was thinking of just breezing the horses and work out a shoeing schedule. The farrier is coming soon and I want new shoes on Sky Hunter before he leaves. Why?"

"Starry Skye is ready for covering. I want you to help with it. Bring Bold Raven to the breeding barn in about twenty minutes," he said, spinning on his heel. He swung away, leaving her no option but to do as he instructed.

"Aye aye, captain," she muttered, giving his retreating back a mock salute. Behind her, she sensed the Moose's amusement.

Bold Raven was a shiny, tall black horse who had raced well and won some big races. He never did get the coveted Triple Crown but he did place well enough to be retired with dignity and was now used as a stud on the farm.

Being a son of Black Warrior and half-brother to Sky Hunter, he also had that fiery temperament and stubborn nature. However, he was slightly easier to handle and more likely to want to please his handler than some members of his family tree. Perhaps that was the mix Ty was trying for. A competitive racing spirit with some common sense thrown in.

When she led the stallion into the breeding barn, the chestnut mare with the big white star on her forehead for which she was named was already tied in place. Ty stood nearby, along with several other men, prepared to help make this match happen.

Immediately Bold Raven's attention was riveted to Starry Skye. Pulling against the lead rope, eagerly, his nostrils expanded, inhaling her scent. Season pulled off his cooler blanket and he rumbled a hearty whinny, pluming his tail and arching his mane, to show off how powerful and handsome he was.

The stallion and the mare knew just what to do. She whinnied joyfully once, allowing him to nibble her arched neck a few times. For countless generations, their species have ensured the production of their kind. Without help from humans, they knew their roles and eagerly got to work.

Season felt a sense of joy as they coupled together. It was wild and wonderful and breathtaking. Briefly they touched noses and then, with a wild shriek, Bold Raven mounted Starry Skye. Watching, Season wished the man-made trappings were removed and the horses were free out on the prairies to complete their courtship. It was raw and powerful to watch.

But with the value of the mare, Ty was taking no chances.

She was fully wrapped in protective coverings so she wouldn't be hurt by the overzealous stallion's teeth or hooves. And her long, lovely tail was wrapped so not to interfere with the stallion's path. Tubes of lubricant and pipettes lay nearby, as did restraining ropes and chains.

It all seemed so ... melodramatic. Or bittersweet. A lovely moment of beauty to watch and share, hampered by man's view of protecting an investment.

Wondering what Ty thought of the mating, she cast a look over at him.

He stood, one foot propped against the wall, arms folded across his chest. No longer watching the horses, he had eyes only for Season. His eyes were dark and heated, piercing out from the shadows of his hat.

She immediately knew what he was thinking. It sprang from him as if he had shouted the words out loud. He wanted her.

Stunned, she forced her gaze away, back to the horses, then back to Ty again. Zipping quickly to the men, she saw they were oblivious to their boss. They were there only to ensure a safe mating of the horses and be ready to jump in immediately if need be. They knew their job and paid neither Ty nor Season a second look.

Looking back to Ty, she met his smoldering gaze, holding it. Her breath caught in her chest. Her heart pounded painfully. Her pulse thudded and raced. His thoughts were raw, put on display for her to easily read. Did he know he was leaving himself open to her? Did he care?

Heat slowly uncoiled from deep within her, taking her by surprise. She had vowed to never feel such passion for a man again. No, she wasn't going down that path again and certainly not with Ty Masters. She shook her head in denial. Still, the heat spread through her body against her will as she darted her eyes from Ty to the horses and back to Ty again. He never flinched. The excited, exuberant passion of the horses only served to add fuel to her own simmering thoughts. Distantly, she remembered Moose's words from last night about fueling a fire.

Suddenly it was very hot inside the barn. She wished she'd dressed lighter. Her sweater and barn coat were too much. As she considered removing her coat, the stallion suddenly finished. Bugling a triumphed snort, he dropped off the mare and stood, his energy spent. He had done his part to ensure the survival of the Black Warrior gene pool.

Eagerly Season rushed forward, grabbing his lead rope and rushing him toward the outside door. The sooner she got him back to his barn, and away from Ty's smoldering vibrations, the better she would feel.

Away from the heated passion she saw in Ty's eyes and mirrored in her own soul. Away from memories and most of all, away from her own weakness.

"What's your hurry?" Ty's voice called after her as she stepped out into the cold air outside the breeding barn. Knowing she couldn't leave the heated stallion in the cold air she clucked him to hurry up. Realizing she had forgotten his cooler blanket, she gave herself a mental kick. Well, there was no going back for it now. Wishing she could hesitate and linger outside in the cool air, she rushed him inside instead, still hearing Ty's voice behind them, ignoring him.

Inside, she threw another cooler blanket on and cross tied him, then took the time to pull off her coat and sweater, tossing them to the nearest bale of hay. Stripping down to just her turtleneck cooled her down a tiny bit. Too bad she couldn't throw a window open as well. The brief respite of cold air felt great. Grabbing a bottle of sheath cleaner, she set about cleaning up the stallion. Placidly, he stood there, wobbling one lazy ear, looking very much like the proverbial guy who just got lucky.

"I shall ask again, what is the rush?" Ty asked, closing the door and lounging in the doorway.

"I ... uh, I just wanted to get him back here and cooled off," Heat touched her face. Goodness! She didn't have any more layers to take off. She wished he had left the door partially open.

Ty slowly nodded, not looking convinced. "Yes, that brisk trot through the cold should have done the trick quick enough. Especially without a blanket on."

She frowned. Was he mocking her?

"I just figured the sooner he was out of there, the sooner the men could get to work on what they needed to do for the mare." It sounded like a good enough excuse. Just as she had post breeding care for him, they had similar stuff to do for her.

He stood there, quiet and patient as he waited for her to finish. Finally, as she brushed the same spot repetitively on the horse's shiny rump, his hand fell over hers, warm.

"There was nothing wrong with what happened back there in the barn, Season," he said softly.

Jerking her hand away from his, she went to the other side of the horse, placing him between them. "I don't know what you are talking about."

"The excitement of watching two horses mating can be quite a turn on," he clarified with a maddening grin.

Knowing her cheeks were blushing, giving her away, she still shook her head in denial, still running the brush over the horse. "I don't know what you mean. I did not get excited by watching the horses."

"All right. You got excited by watching me then."

"No!" She gasped, shocked by his bold statement, bothered by his confident smile. What happened to the wariness she was now used to seeing in his blue eyes?

"I think yes," he persisted, moving around the horse slowly, petting it as he went.

Season stopped grooming and faced him square, aware of the flames in her cheeks. "Is that why you wanted me to help with the breeding? You can't get off with just guys around. You needed a female there other than the mare. Since I was handy, you ordered me to assist. For your personal gratification. Am I right, Mr. Masters?" She shook her fist, and brush, at him.

"No, that wasn't it all," he said, his smile fading as her words grew angrier. "Look, I asked you there—"

"Never mind!" she broke in, cutting him off. "I know why you wanted me there. I know you, remember? I can read you. And you made your thoughts and feelings perfectly loud and clear back there."

Around them the stallions moved about, pawing and snorting, picking up on the anger and tension in their barn.

Ty groaned, taking a step back. "Wait a minute. You are getting this all wrong, Season," he groaned as he held his hands up in defense. "Do not turn me into a toad or anything, please. Just let me explain."

That familiar wariness crept back into his eyes, as if he thought she just might reduce him to an amphibian yet. It was sorely tempting.

"Just leave me alone and I'll leave you as you are. A chauvinistic pig!" Season spat, dropping the brush. She curled up both fists, releasing her palms toward Ty. Cold water shot out from her fingertips, instantly dousing him. His startled yelp gave her a tart satisfaction.

Spinning around, she headed for the door. "Don't forget to put that horse away in his stall!" she tossed over her shoulder. Grabbing her coat and sweater, she chose to slam the door behind her with a wave of her hand. A minute later, standing in the icy air, with the wind swirling around her, did she realize she just ordered her boss around, and sprayed water on him. She bit her lip. Yes, he deserved to get soaked and bossed about, however, she might have crossed a line and could very well be headed to the unemployment line.

Desperately needing a cup of coffee, she stalked into the house, dropped her outer clothes and headed for the kitchen, hoping to find it deserted. Even when Moose was elsewhere, the coffee pot was always on and there was continuously fresh coffee brewing. One of the many little perks of working at Heritage.

With anger still making her back rigid and her steps heavy, she marched past the counter and poured herself a cup. Spying a bottle of whiskey under the counter, she added a splash of it to her coffee—just because.

She was halfway through the cup before Moose shuffled into the room, halting when he spotted her.

"You feeling okay?" he asked, concern in his eyes.

"Yes. Why?" she asked, taking another sip, enjoying the burn of the whiskey mixed with the heat of the coffee.

Moose raised one eyebrow, a bizarre expression for him. If she hadn't been so angry, she might have considered it comical. If she drank enough whiskey, she still might consider it comical.

"All right. I'm not okay," Season admitted. "But at least now I know why he wanted me to help with the breeding."

"Oh." Moose nodded slowly and, picking up a rag, he started wiping the counter top down.

"It's not just part of the job description like he led me to believe. He gets perverse pleasure out of it," she stated, pouring more coffee and adding another big splash of whiskey. Then one more. She wasn't sure if she was more upset at Ty for his blatant actions or at herself for her body and mind's runaway reaction. Both took her by surprise. And both angered her.

"He used me," she announced finally, taking a big swallow of the brew and smacking her lips.

"Sounds like it," Moose agreed, wiping down a new spot on the counter top.

"He has no right!" she insisted.

"No. No, he don't."

"I'm not some mindless sex babe he can use to get his jollies. I demand respect just like any man who works here," she said, slamming her cup down, hiccupping.

Moose moved over to the far end of the counter and started wiping dishes. Silence fell over them as she toyed with her mug and he wiped the dishes, quietly putting them away. A plate clinked against another, echoing loudly. It reminded Season she might have seen the desire in Ty's eyes and read it in his thoughts, but she harbored them within herself just the same. So who was she really so mad at? Herself or him?

"Have you told him any of this yet?" Moose finally asked.

Bringing her head up with a snap, she blinked. Tell mighty Ty to respect her? What a concept. Tell him she might have desires for him, but he was way out of line today? He'd probably die laughing. So tell him what?

"No," she admitted.

"I'll send him to your office," Moose said simply, walking away.

Taking her cue, she wordlessly headed out the door, much of her anger subdued now. Or at least slowly simmering instead. The whiskey was helping.

⊗✧⊗

S till startled with the cold water that unexpectedly showered over him, Ty walked into the house, eager to get changed. Unfortunately, Moose was in the kitchen. Standing tall, he felt his lips tighten.

"Is it raining out, Boss?" Moose asked, looking up from the stove.

Ty shot him a dark glare, refusing to answer, and stalked to the steps.

Moose grinned, wiping down the stove top. "I'll just catch the Master on his trip back downstairs." He spoke into the empty room. "That'll give both the pepper hots a few minutes to cool down."

⊗✧⊗

T aking a direct course for the stallion barn, and her office above it, Season wondered how Moose knew Ty would be gone when she arrived. She found Bold Raven back in his stall, happily munching hay, everything back in its place, and Ty nowhere to be seen.

Going to her desk, she pulled out the shoeing schedule and mindlessly stared at the names on the list. Not five minutes later, a knock sounded at the top of the stairs. Her heart skipped a beat, her chest tightening. How had Moose managed to get him to come here? And so quickly?

Another knock echoed the first, reminding her Ty Masters wasn't long on patience.

"It's open," she called out, choking down the lump in her throat.

Ty stepped in, shrinking her tiny office space. Holding his hat in one hand, he managed to look contrite. An interesting and new look on him, she decided, thinking this might be a little fun yet. Thank goodness, he only thought he knew what she was thinking, and couldn't be absolutely certain.

"Yes?" she asked, looking up from her paperwork, gaining some pleasure for the shoe being on the other foot for a change. He had changed his clothes too.

"Season, I owe you an apology."

She arched an eyebrow. "Go on."

A small sigh escaped him, letting her know how hard this was for him to admit.

"I had no right to embarrass you like I did."

She waited, lips pursed together. His shoulders lifted in a heavy shrug.

"I should have treated you with more respect. You deserve it." he added quickly.

As much fun as this was, she knew he had about exhausted his apology quota. Resting her elbows on the desk, she fixed her gaze level with his, both eyebrows raised, waiting.

"Look, I'm really sorry. Now please don't use your hocus pocus on me again."

Quietly she regarded him, reading him. How much was sincere regret and how much was fear of retribution? There was a glint of wariness in his eyes, but also a look of sheer contrition and a small measure of impatience creeping in as well. Typical Ty.

"It's not hocus pocus," she said finally.

"You know what I mean," he insisted with a wag of his head. Stuffing his hat back on his head, he made for the stairs.

"What made you come here?" she asked, halting him.

Slowly he turned around, facing her. She wished he'd take the hat off again.

He sighed deeply, glancing around the room, looking uncomfortable.

"Like I said, I owed you an apology," he said finally.

"And like I said, it's not hocus pocus," she pointed out. "And you have no reason to be scared."

He shot her a startled look, one that clearly said he didn't believe her.

"I'm not scared," he declared, standing straighter, shrinking the office even more so it felt like a child's dollhouse.

"Look, Ty, I'm not going to do anything that harms any human life. Including yours. But I do expect you to treat me with respect. Not just because you think I'm going to toad you if you don't, but because you should. And to respect me, you have to stop being scared of being within ten feet of me. And also not to think of me as your personal sex babe."

He cracked a fleeting smile, one that did not quite reach his eyes. It stopped her heart for a split second, then caused her tummy to somersault. "I wasn't scared to be in the breeding barn with you," he reminded softly. "Or in the stallion barn below."

"Point taken," she conceded, knowing it was true, just adding to the enigmatic mystery around Ty Masters. "But more of that kind of behavior in the future might get you on a first name basis with Freddy the Frog and his buddies down at the lily pond."

This time her threat did not seem to bother him. Towering over her, his eyes bored into hers, daring her, and challenging her, igniting her from within. "There will be future breedings to cover, babe," he promised, his voice a husky whisper, a ghost of a smile in his eyes. Finished, he stepped to the stairs.

This time, she did not call him back.

৩৩

Two days later, she helped Stan and Eddie load Sky Hunter, Winter's Dawn, and Doodlebug onto the plane for their flight to the racetrack. The plane was a custom built flying machine and she had to admire the thought and quality that had gone into it. Ty spared no expense with his horses or his crew during their cross-country flights.

The plane was a customized cargo jet, with spacious seating forward for two pilots and eight passengers, a television, microwave, and small refrigerator. There was space in the rear for six horses, with padded stalls and lots of room for luggage and tack. A small lavatory was thoughtfully tucked into a corner. Ty said he would have joined them if it were not for some important matters he couldn't avoid. Season was just grateful for the respite.

He joined them on the runway, giving last minute instructions to Stan, their pilot, and the valet and groom who were accompanying Season, Eddie, and the rest of the team. "Make sure that Doodlebug stays next to Sky Hunter for both flights," he ordered. "Bloody pony is the only thing that keeps that stallion from going crazy in the air."

"Why don't you like Doodlebug?" Season suddenly asked, surprising both Ty and the men around them.

Ty blinked, as if he had to think of why. "Because the little beast cozies up to everyone as if they were his long lost friends. He shows no pride."

78

She smiled at that. "I didn't realize horses were supposed to show pride. Besides, what's wrong with making friends easily? Beats acting like a spoiled brat similar to some horses I know."

Hearing snickers coming from the men, Ty cut them a dark scowl. Hastily, they scurried to find something to do. Season moved slowly away to follow them when Ty's arm shot out and grabbed her wrist, halting her.

"Wait a minute," he said, hauling her back to his side. "Before you go off with my prized spoiled brat, I want you to remember one thing."

"Oh, what's that?" she blinked up at him, smelling the coffee and bacon on his breath, liking how it smelled, mixed with his natural clean woodsy, musky scent.

"You had promised me that horse was going to fly."

"Aha. So I did." She glanced at the plane over her shoulder. "And he will. See?" A smile tugged at her lips, giving her away.

"Season," Growling, he pressed her closer. "Flying around a track," he murmured, scant seconds before touching his lips to hers.

Holding her tight, pushing his mouth over hers, he forced himself upon her, surprising her. Her startled intake of breath urged him on, forcing her mouth open. He probed her mouth as his hands roamed her body, going from her arms to her shoulders, and then to cup around her rear. He pulled her body closer to his own and she felt the heat of his skin against hers. He tasted of apples.

For a moment, she resisted, then she relaxed in his arms, melting. She tasted the apples he had for breakfast on his tongue. Heat unfurled deep inside her, awakening a hunger encouraged by his tongue and touch. Unbidden, her fingers reached up and wound into his hair, tugging as a moan escaped her lips. Then she explored, going under his coat and trailing her fingertips along his back. Layers of muscles twitched beneath her touch. She moved to his chest, gripping the mat of hair and flicking a fingernail off each hard nipple. This time he moaned, and sucked at her bottom lip.

Then, from a distant part of her mind, she recalled there were men standing nearby, ready to take off and no doubt watching with open curiosity.

With reluctance and great effort, she pulled herself away, tasting him on her lips. He held her at arm's length, drawing in a few ragged breaths as he licked his own lips. He smiled at her, his blue eyes dark with desire. Heaven help her, but she could kiss him again right now. Suddenly she wished he would hop on that plane and kiss her all the way until it touched down again.

Instead, he took a deep, shaky breath, and released her. "Flying," he whispered next to her ear. He stepped back and immediately she regretted the distance between them.

He waved to the crew and spun around, his strides swinging as he strode toward the house.

Inside the cabin of the plane, Season checked on the horses to see they were comfortable and secure. Giving them each a reassuring pat and a few extra scratches for nervous Sky Hunter, she moved to the seat closest to them and sat down. Buckling her safety belt, she waited for the roar of the engines. All she heard so far were the surprised chuckles of the men and felt the heat burning her cheeks.

Ty had kissed her! Her heart was still racing like a runaway horse, out of control. Disbelief pulsed through her like a raging fire. Ty had held her and he'd kissed her!

And she'd allowed it. More importantly, she actually enjoyed it. One thing was for sure, if they did not get this plane off the ground soon, she might get out of the plane and go find him in the house.

6

Before Sky Hunter was ready to run in the big races, he needed a few small prep races. Races away from the familiar horses and track of Heritage, where he would be competing with real racers and jockeys out to beat him. For Season, the prep races served three good reasons.

One, they offered the big colt a chance to extend himself and practice in the world of real racing where others didn't want to see him succeed. Second, they allowed the public a good view of Ty Master's newest cannonball. And third, they gave Season some much needed time away from Ty Masters. Time and distance she emotionally needed to collect herself. Whatever his reason for not being able to accompany them was just fine by her.

Leaning her head back and closing her eyes, she concentrated on the rumble of the airplane as it taxied and the moist bruising of her lips. The man could kiss!

She barely felt the gradual rising of the plane as it lifted off the ground. Subconsciously she heard the stirring and pawing of the horses as they resettled their weight.

"There, there, babies," she absently murmured to them, her voice a soft and relaxing coo, though the pet word reminded her of Ty's subtle innuendo when he called her 'Babe' in her office, in reference to her pointing out she wasn't his sex babe. Pure defiance. On both their parts.

The airplane leveled out and the horses settled in, patiently waiting for the ride to end. In the cabin space ahead of her, the men occupied themselves with an impromptu card game. The pilot seemed relaxed and confident. Perhaps a nap wasn't such a bad idea Season decided as she wriggled into a comfortable position.

A subtle jolt startled her, shaking her into wakefulness. Drowsy, she still felt Ty's lips pushing against hers, a suggestion of his powerful force

"No, only a dream," she muttered, shaking her head, blinking a few times. The lingering effects of Ty was only a dream. Glancing out the window, she saw they were descending and the landscape of southern California was coming into view.

Running her tongue over her lips one more time, she hoped it would effectively erase all of Ty's lingering memories. She had work to do, serious work, and she couldn't afford to be distracted by one very powerful kiss.

The plane slid to a perfect landing a short distance from the barns. A van was already waiting to truck the horses and people to the receiving barn. Their hotel rooms were booked and a rental car would be waiting at the track for their use while at the races. Season had to admit it, Ty did take very good care of his employees.

The horses, the men, and she would want for nothing while they were at the track.

Once they were safely landed, Season took it upon herself to load Sky Hunter into the van. As she suspected, the colt was spooked, glancing over at Doodlebug a number of times, seeking reassurance from the docile pony. Thank goodness, they had the pony to tag-a-long, despite how Ty felt about him.

"It's okay, Sky Boy," Season murmured, rubbing his neck with her palms. She felt his trembling as he held his head high, nostrils flaring as he took in the sights and sounds.

Ears swiveling, catching every little sound, his eyes rolled in the directions of the endless loud clangs and bangs. Stomping a hoof, he showed his displeasure for his new surroundings. A light sweat broke out on his neck, coating the black hair with white foam, already, and he wasn't even loaded into the van yet.

Season swallowed another groan of disappointment. If he was to have a successful racing career, he was going to have to be a lot more settled at new tracks.

Once Sky Hunter was loaded and secured, Doodlebug and Winter's Dawn slid up next to him. The ride to the receiving barn was short and Season rode in the back with the horses, mostly for Sky Hunter's benefit. For their part, Doodlebug took the excitement all in his calm, unruffled stride and Winter's Dawn looked around eagerly, as if wondering and ready for whatever was coming her way next.

"There we go, guys. Your new home for the next few days," she said twenty minutes later, scratching Winter's Dawn under her halter. Each horse had water and some hay and was comfortably bedded down. Now the men and she could take time for themselves and see their new digs. But first, Season needed a few moments to herself.

"Do you want us to wait for you?" Stan called as she headed for the paddock gardens.

"No," she said and waved them away. "Go on. I'll be along in time for dinner."

Hearing them walk away, talking excitedly among themselves, Season paused to breathe in the fresh, warm California air. The russet soil, flowered fragrances hanging heavy in the air, leafy trees native to the Valley; it all filled her senses and poked at her memories.

These were familiar grounds, hollowed grounds. She had raced horses here before. It was here that she cut her teeth with her father and grandfather before that. Here legends raced. Here legends were made and some died.

Part racetrack, part public park, it invited her to linger, breathe deep, view the mountains in the distance, and enjoy the Spanish designs surrounding her. She could feel herself coming alive again, the blood pumping within her, fueling her, energizing her. The warm breezes lifted and played with her hair. Somewhere a couple of birds called out and horses snorted. Finally satisfied, she turned to go. It was good to be back.

Since the men had already left, taking the rental car and her luggage, she flagged down a taxi.

Sliding into the back seat, she gave the driver her destination and settled back to watch the city move around her. Checking into the hotel, she again had to marvel at the way Ty treated his employees. No second rate motel here. Ty Masters treated his workers to a nice, four star inn. She was privileged to have a room all to herself, on the third floor, around the corner from her traveling companions.

Seeing it was still early, she decided to give in to the luxury of a bath. Filling the tub with warm water, she poured in a cap full of strawberry bubble bath, popped a soothing CD in her portable player, piled her hair into a coil on top her head, and slid into the foamy bubbles.

"Too bad I didn't think to pack a few candles too," she complained wistfully, moving her hands under the water, encouraging the bubbles to multiply. Even without the candle light, it still felt heavenly.

Leaning back into the bath pillow, she closed her eyes and opened her mind. The scent of strawberries and sounds of harps and flutes filled the room. Shutting out the rest of the day's agenda, Season let her mind travel, going to a green valley laced with warm sunshine and acres of vibrant wildflowers swaying in the gentle breeze in tune to the flutes.

Picturing a waterfall, rushing down, falling to a river below, she could hear the happy sound of falling water mingling with the relaxing tones of music. A solitary bullfrog croaked a few times, echoed by the chattering of merry birds. In her mind's eye, horses grazed the meadow, stepping between the flowers. She could hear the tearing sounds as their teeth tore off blades of grass.

Mares with foals at their side, and a watchful black stallion, basked in the warm sunshine of their own private oasis. Older colts frisked and played, chasing butterflies. So real seemed her fantasy, Season felt like an intruder to their private oasis. Or was it her oasis and they shared it?

The sudden, unexpected, shrill peal of the telephone broke the spell. The flowered meadow and horses and waterfall all vanished like thieves in the night.

Coming back to reality, Season blinked, separating the here and now from where she had just traveled from. Another impatient peal of the phone made her reluctantly reach for the tub side receiver. Knowing how spooked Sky Hunter got she didn't even bring her cell phone with her.

"Hi. It's Eddie." Her jockey's cheery voice greeted her. "The guys and I are going out for dinner now and wanted to know if you wanted to join us."

"Sure," she agreed. "Can you give me about ten minutes to get dressed?"

Already she was pulling the drain plug with her toe and reaching for a towel with her other hand. Was it that late already?

"Yep. Ten minutes," Eddie agreed. "Downstairs in the lobby."

Nine minutes later Season stepped out from the elevator doors at the lobby level. Scanning the sets of chairs, she spotted Eddie and Stan sitting by a plant barrier. Eddie was laughing at something Stan just said. A joke most likely. Stan considered himself a pilot first and a comedian second.

They were a good bunch of guys though, and she felt herself lucky to have been accepted into their group. Not everyone at Heritage Farms was quick to accept her, including Ty Masters.

Brushing away thoughts of Ty from her mind like a stray cobweb, she smoothed her skirt and adjusted her shirt collar before she approached them. "Hey guys," she greeted. "So where are we going to eat?"

"Since we'll be at the Park tomorrow, we figured we might as well go to a local place tonight.

They piled into their rental car and Stan drove them to his favorite restaurant when he was in town called the 'Whole Caboose'. Later, so full she practically had to roll out of the Caboose, Season pleaded fatigue when the men suggested a nightcap at another of their favorite nightspots. Happy to walk back to the hotel, Season wished them well and started back.

Next morning, Season bounded out of bed, ready and eager to get to the tracks. Showering briefly and dressing, she caught herself humming a cheery little melody. Excitement buzzed within her. Today was going to be a good day, she could just feel it.

Upon arriving at the track, they piled out of the car and spread out, each intent with their own jobs. Season again had to admire how each person jumped in, doing his own chores, knowing their tasks, but willing to help another if needed. It was a good thing to see and even better to be a part of. She had to hand it to Ty once more, he had a good racing team.

The horses had spent a quiet night, which made Season feel better about Sky Hunter. Finally, a point in his favor. Now they were eager to get out of their stalls and move around. Sky Hunter picked at his light breakfast, too busy casting his head out over the stall door at the proceedings going on around him.

Placing a monogrammed saddled cloth in place, she cinched down the saddle on Sky Hunter. Eddie tacked up Doodlebug in much simpler tack.

"Okay, we go to post at one o' clock," Season instructed. "Let's just breeze him now, keeping him under control. Let's not break any records just yet," she added with a smile.

"Keeping this bad boy under control is a record," Eddie quipped, taking up Sky Hunter's reins and leading him out. Robert, another of Season's helpers, took up Doodlebug's reins and fell in step alongside, keeping the track pony next to the black horse at all times.

Season positioned herself at the rail, stopwatch in hand. Robert, mounted now on Doodlebug, lead Eddie and Sky Hunter out onto the track. At Season's nod, they galloped once around the track, plucky little Doodlebug pushing mightily to keep up to the slower pace of the black.

With no other horses nearby, Sky Hunter was content to just frolic along the track with his buddy alongside. They looked almost comical with the sleek black colt and the scruffy patchwork gray pony.

"Certainly, no records at this rate," Season commented to herself, watching the funny little scene.

One o' clock, post parade time, and a warm ocean breeze blew in. Season gave Eddie a leg up in the paddock area, patted his leg and wished him luck. "You'll do fine out there. This guy wants to run, try for a fast break, keep him on the inside, and don't allow him any nonsense."

"Got it." Gathering the reins, Eddie started the black colt toward the track, Doodlebug beside him, keeping him calm with all the noise around them.

At the gate, Doodlebug and Robert fell back, leaving Eddie and the colt on their own. He balked at the starting gate, half rearing and pawing the air. Season groaned as an outrider dodged out of the way. People around her gasped. Finally, the track outrider caught his bridle and, together with two other men, forced him into the chute. If Ty was watching from home, which he promised he'd do, no doubt he was frowning at his colt's bad behavior and seeing it as her failure to control the brute.

At last all six horses were loaded in the gate and the starter set them loose. In one split second, half a dozen horses and riders exploded from the gate as one body, each fighting for the best position. Colors blurred and swirled.

Sky Hunter fell into third position, his nose one step behind the number two horse. Eagerly, Season focused her gaze on the black horse wearing the black and white Heritage Farms colors.

The railing dug into her abdomen and she curled her hands around the top edge. The track was dry, clods of dirt flew up from under the pounding hooves as the horses all strained for the finish. It was a long race. Some of the horses running were older and more experienced than Sky Hunter. Ty had been concerned but she felt confident he was up for it.

He flattened his ears back, nostrils flaring as his strides ate up the ground, sending dirt flying up behind him. Season could almost picture Eddie talking to the horse, knowing his words were being torn away in the wind. At the mile mark, Sky Hunter moved up to second position. Half a mile to take the lead, and keep it. His strides lengthened out as some of the field was tiring, slowing down, not able to keep such speeds for such a long length. Not the black colt. Savagely, he bore down on the lead horse still ahead of him.

Lips pulled back, ears flat to his head, he bared his teeth as he bore down on his opponent. He pressed the other horse close, forcing him into the railing. The truth hit Season like a sledgehammer, shaking her. Instead of focusing on running and winning the race, Sky Hunter was focused on running the other horse down, like a brawl instead of a race.

She could see Eddie fighting the horse, trying to persuade him to pass the other horse. She could see Sky Hunter fighting the bit, tossing his head in anger and defiance. Clearly, he had no interest in passing the horse when he could run it into the rail instead.

They passed the half mile mark, finishing the race as they ran most of it; first and second place. Season checked the time. Just a hair over two minutes and twenty-one seconds. Her horse could have done much better if he had been racing instead of fighting.

Still shaken by the savagery she witnessed, she headed back to the barn, her mind whirling with possibilities. Retiring to her hotel for the night, she wasn't in the room five minutes when the phone rang. With an inward groan, she picked it up, ready for what was to come.

"What the bloody hell happened out there this afternoon?"

"He placed," she said, trying to sound cheerful, dropping onto the bed.

"He could have done much better," Ty pointed out.

"Yes, but he had another agenda out there."

"It sure as hell looked like it!"

"Well, second place isn't so bad. He still finished in the money."

"Damn the money! I have no desire to see him black listed. I thought you could do better than just finish in the money." There was a pause before he added, "I believe you said, and I quote you, you will have him flying around the track. That speed wasn't what I would call flying."

Season blew out a breath. She suspected they could do this all evening.

She closed her eyes, focusing on the breathing on the line. Ty was seated at his desk, feet propped up on the mounds of paperwork. Though he was clearly upset at how his horse ran this afternoon, he still wore a smile on his face. As if he were enjoying this sparing with her. As if he called her deliberately just to argue now.

"Look, Ty, it was his first race of the season and out away from the farm. He was just getting his feet wet. I will work on the other issues he seems to have."

"Issues? Are there more than just this silly little wanton desire to run the other horses down instead of racing against them? What else has my prized spoiled brat been doing out there?"

She could picture his feet hitting the floor as he became serious all of a sudden.

"Well, gee, what do you really expect, Ty, considering Black Warrior's blood runs though him like black oil?" she retorted. "I will work on his savage impulses. And the fact he hates to load in the gate. I already have a couple of ideas. He didn't do it during his morning breeze so I think we can catch this before it gets too serious."

"That is exactly what I hired you for and pay you for."

She let out another long breath. "Winter's Dawn is running tomorrow. I'm sure you will be much more satisfied with her performance."

His reply came out as a throaty purr, making her skin crawl. "I had better be more than satisfied, Season." With that, the line went dead.

Holding the receiver limply for a moment, she slowly returned it to the cradle. His parting comment was laced with more than mere sparking. She clearly sensed the undercurrents hidden behind the threat. The hint of the force of his kiss. She could almost see the twinkling in his blue eyes as he whispered the words and hung up.

Suddenly tired, she dropped her clothes in a pile on the floor, pulled a t-shirt over her head and dropped into bed. Though it was still light outside, she turned her back to the windows, too fatigued to pull the curtain further closed. Laying there, facing the blank wall, she re-ran the race over in her mind. Like counting sheep, she counted galloping horses striving for the finish line. Her final lingering thought as sleep at last claimed her was the throaty purr and sparkling blue eyes of a handsome Wyoming Englishman.

Next morning, the sun's bright rays barely peeked through her window when Season stepped out of the shower. After her restless night, she was ready to get to the track and work Sky Hunter again. She had a few theories about his track rage syndrome and was eager to test them out.

"So did you hear from our mighty master last night?" Eddie asked her during the ride to the track.

"Yes." She nodded.

"I bet he was upset with Sky Hunter's track rage."

"You could say that," she agreed. Most of the men at the farm had experienced his wrath once or twice and they always left a lasting impression, and folks learned fast to stay out of the way. Moose seemed to be the other unfortunate soul who got regular subjection to the infamous Ty Masters temper. However, on this trip, unless someone messed up really bad, all temper tantrums and indignations were going to be directed at Season alone.

"He was a little riled alright," she responded.

Remembering his parting threat that had purred over the line, she still couldn't suppress a shiver.

"That bad, huh?" Eddie misinterpreted her tremor, shaking his head in pity. "Let's hope today goes better."

"Let's hope so," Season agreed, not willing to explain why Ty could make her tremble from hundreds of miles away.

Today they had two races, one for Winter's Dawn and a second one for Sky Hunter and she planned to have better experiences with both of them. The next time Ty Masters called her, he was going to be congratulating her on a job well done.

Even though thunderstorms were in the forecast for the day and Winter's Dawn hated both mud and rain, Season was clinging to her optimism.

"So what's the plan, Boss Lady?" Eddie asked, coming up behind her, using the nickname some of the men had adopted for her.

"When he went after that other horse yesterday, tell me, what was it like?" she asked.

Eddie's laugh was heavy in the air. "Like trying to hold back a tornado. He had that bit in his teeth and just ignored me like I wasn't even on board. I could have been a fly for all the attention he gave me. He just wanted that number nine horse. Raw power like I have never seen or felt. That's what it was like. Why?"

Season was familiar with the colt's raw power. "I think I have the perfect solution for that. But it will require a bit more work on your part. Okay?"

Eddie shrugged good-naturedly. "Hey, when that fool horse gets an idea in his head, I'm just along for the ride anyway. I could be knitting a sweater while I'm on board."

She cracked a smile. "If I'm right, you won't be having to be knitting sweaters for long. Get Winter's Dawn ready please. I need to go find something."

By the time the grandstands were filling up with spectators and the cameras were rolling, Season felt confident in her charges. Knowing Ty would be home, watching the television and studying every move, she relaxed, knowing she was doing the best she could.

Riding Doodlebug alongside Sky Hunter to the paddock, she handed her small packages over to Eddie.

"Just keep it handy and easy to get to," she instructed, placing them into the special glove on his left hand. "Let him do his own thing right now."

"Got it," he nodded, testing the weight of the items. "Ingenious."

"Not really. Just a spin off from another old trainer's trick."

Within minutes the horses loaded and the race started. Sky Hunter's dark blur broke forth from the starting gate and he shot through the air like a cannon. Racing alongside a brown horse, he leveled his head out, snaking it from side to side. He tipped an ear back, as if waiting for Eddie to urge him forward but Eddie seemed content to just sit in the saddle and, as he put it earlier, 'knit a sweater'. Eagerly, the horse grabbed the bit in his teeth and reached out towards the other horse, pushing it against the inside railing.

Knowing his horse was pinned, the other rider was helpless to do much for his mount except to swat his rump with a crop.

Just as Sky Hunter's jaws opened, ready to tear a chunk out of the brown horse's neck, Eddie stirred. Leaning down, he shoved one small package into the gaping, bared jaws of the black horse. The results were instantaneous.

Sky Hunter slammed to a halt, his mouth working frantically and his eyes wide with surprise. Forgetting all about attacking the brown horse, he chewed and rolled the thing in his mouth, trying to dislodge it. The brown horse pulled past him and the rest of the track thundered past, steering around the black horse stopped dead on the track.

Finally, the white object rolled to the ground and Eddie slapped his whip down on Sky Hunter's haunches.

Like a gunshot, the horse jumped to life, streaking down the track after the other racers. As he neared the last ones, he lowered his head, snaking it out and again reaching for their rumps. Just as he reached out for the closest one, Eddie leaned to his left again, a small white item in his gloved hand.

Snatching the bit, Sky Hunter rolled his eyes and surged past the horses like they were walking. He pushed through the field until he came to the leaders. Dodging between the leaders, he swung his head out toward one, jaws open, ready for a bite. Again, Eddie leaned over, white item in hand. Seeing the object of such torture, Sky Hunter leaped forward, passing the leaders and crossing the finish line half a length ahead, his ears plastered hard against his head.

From her position at the gates, Season smiled as she accepted the congratulation from others around her. Her plan had worked well although poor Eddie would have a hard time bringing Sky Hunter to a stop now.

"What was that thing your jockey kept handing down to the horse?" one reporter asked her.

"A potato."

Surprised gasps went up from the group. "What is the significance of a potato?"

She smiled into the camera. "An old trainer's trick for biting horses is a hot potato placed wherever the horse happens to bite. A couple good mouthfuls of burning hot potato soon teaches it not to bite anymore. It's the same principle here except my jockey just had to place the hot potato near the horse's mouth whenever he thought about biting. Only the first one was hot and the second one was just for looks to keep reminding him."

Seeing Eddie had Sky Hunter under control, she walked out to help escort him to the winner's circle, still followed by cameras and reporters.

Many chuckled at her clever hot potato trick. Sky Hunter stomped and snorted, tossing his mane and still working his mouth as if to demonstrate how well the hoax had worked.

Standing there, Season had a quick flash of Ty race through her mind. She saw him seated in his study, feet propped up on the desk as he watched the screen. He was laughing heartily at her idea and how well it had worked. She breathed out a sigh of relief, knowing he was pleased.

Less than two hours later, it was time to take Winter's Dawn back out on the track for her debut race of the season. The clouds were even darker, thunder grumbling in the distance and moisture heavy in the air, filling the air with the scent of rain. Season ground her teeth, wishing they could hurry the race along before the rains came.

Maybe she should just scrub the filly from the day's race. But it was a fact of life for a racehorse to run in all sorts of weather.

"I wish I had great words of wisdom for you," she told Eddie. "If the rain holds off, we'll be okay. But I'm pretty sure we'll be in the wet before she ever finishes the race." A clap of thunder followed her words. Sighing, she patted the filly's already lathered neck. "Just do the best you can. It's her debut so there is lots of time for refinement later on."

Winter's Dawn snorted, shaking her head at the growling thunder and milling horses. She was nervous, white foamy lather covering her body. Season drew in a long breath, placing both hands on either side of the mare's long face.

"Easy, Dawnie," she purred softly. "It's just some old noises. Don't worry so much. You'll be fine." Closing her eyes, she stilled the filly, muttering soft reassurances next to her ear. Winter's Dawn tipped an ear forward to listen to the whispered soft words. Her breathing quieted and she stopped pounding the ground.

Unable to catch what Season was whispering to the filly, Eddie listened, straining in apt attention as his mount grew quieter beneath him. When Season finished and stepped away, he caught her eye.

"I don't know what you said to her, but I guess that's why you are the trainer." He smiled, tipping the edge of his riding crop to his helmet in salute.

Casting another look upward at the sharp crack of thunder, she moved over to the railing for a good view of the race. A few rain droplets sprinkled her shoulders.

"Darn," she muttered, knowing for sure Winter's Dawn was going to have to race in the mud and rain after all. And she would come away hating real races. She should have scrubbed her from the race, except now it was too late. "Drat." She considered higher methods, but at this point it was pretty much useless. She couldn't stop the rain for the duration of a race.

The horses were led into the gates. Winter's Dawn was number three, a good position to start. At least the filly entered the chute easier than Sky Hunter did. Score one for her. However, she still looked nervous as the other horses milled around, uncomfortable with the growing thunder. Not a good day for a horse race.

Just as the starter released them from the gate, a bolt of lightning flashed overhead, simultaneous with the starter's bell. Each filly shot from the gate, all eager to escape the noises and lights over their heads.

Even as Winter's Dawn started in third position, she soon fell to fifth place. Season ground her teeth in frustration, wishing more than ever she'd scratched the filly.

"Too late now," she muttered, feeling her hands curling around the railing.

Winter's Dawn was one of only two chestnut fillies out on the track and easy to spot in the field of racing horses. Eddie dropped his crop down on her haunches, trying to move her along, but she was running scared and not listening.

The skies opened, making the small rain droplets turn into large drops. Soon the track was a pool of sloppy mud.

Winter's Dawn clearly hated it. She hated the mud in her face from the other four horses in front of her. Shaking her head, she tried to slow down, trying to escape.

Eddie dropped his crop a few more times, urging her forward. As they approached the five furlong mark, she was urged up to fourth place, ears laced back and the very picture of equine indignity. Approaching the six furlong mark, she was nose for nose with the number three horse. Season felt herself holding her breath. She might actually finish in the money.

"Just a little more, Dawnie," she whispered. "Come on, just a little more," She felt herself straining, pushing like the filly. She could feel the cold rain pelting her and the sting of the mud in her face, the slippery surface of the track, the solid thud of Eddie's crop. She could feel the filly's heart skipping each time the thunder crashed and lightening streaked overhead. She could smell the fear.

"Almost there, Dawnie. It's almost over. So close now," she breathed into the rain.

Watching the filly sweeping third under the wire, Season expelled the breath she'd been holding. It was over. She had placed in the money. Just barely, but she had placed. Technically, she had run a terrible race, full of flaws, but she ran it scared and she still finished third. Season was happy.

Moving down to the track, she caught Dawn's bridle when Eddie guided the lathered filly over.

"Good job," she praised both the jockey and the filly.

"She sure hates storms," Eddied panted, his breath coming in ragged gasps.

"She does," Season nodded, rubbing the filly's cheek. "You did fine. I'm so proud of you, Dawnie. We'll work on refining the details later on, okay, Sweetie?"

Beneath her hand, the filly was hot, lathered and breathing heavily, but Season could sense her pleasure at the verbal praise and soft stroking. Ignoring the cold rain, she slowly led the way back to the barn where a good rubdown and some warm mash awaited Dawnie.

7

"So couldn't you have used your hocus pocus to stop the rain until after the race?"

Season bit off a sigh, closing her eyes and praying for patience.

"Ty, for the hundredth time, it's not hocus pocus, okay. And it does not work that way. I can't just stop the rain any more than you could."

"Yet you can turn me into a toad or some other animal," Ty pointed out. "Why not just stop the rain for a short bit?"

Don't tempt me, she mentally warned him, thinking he would make a fine toad. Drawing in a long breath, she felt her lungs fill. She squeezed her eyes tight and reminded herself not to do anything rash. "Because I can't," she finally explained, so sorry she ever picked up the phone minutes ago. "Besides, don't you think that constitutes cheating if I did?"

Ty had called her hotel room to congratulate her on the placing of Winter's Dawn and, of course, in typical Ty Masters manner, point out she could have made the filly place even better. When Season had foolishly pointed out the filly did not like running in the mud and that slowed her down, he'd simply suggested she stop the rain, thus eliminating the problem. The man was maddening.

"All right, fine. You can't," Ty said, sounding far from convinced. "So what ideas do you have for the next time she has to run in the mud?"

Why couldn't he have just called up, said congratulation on a job well done and be over with it?

She flipped off the radio, since she couldn't pay attention to it anyway, and drew up a picture of him. He was rough shaven, giving him a rugged look, lounging on the sofa in his study. Long legs clad in tight denim stretched out, one arm pulled back and raised over his tousled hair. The phone cradled against his shoulder, and a wicked smile on his lips.

Her heart skipped a few beats. Did he really look so ruggedly handsome or was her heart playing tricks with her mind? The accuracy of her connected visions was usually pretty dead on.

"Did you hear me?" he demanded when she failed to answer him.

"Yes, I heard you. As it so happens, I was working on that problem, among others, when you called me just now."

"Splendid. What did you work out?"

She smiled into the phone. "Guess you'll just have to watch the races on television to find out for yourself. Good night, Ty."

Hanging the phone back up, she picked up her pencil and stared at the papers before her on the desk. Thanks to him, her mind went completely blank. Oh! That man could get under her skin!

Rolling the pencil between her palms, she tried to force the image of him stretched out on the sofa from her mind. He looked entirely too sexy for her to concentrate on horses right now. She had to erase them and get back to the matters at hand. Sometimes her Gift was also a huge curse as well.

Dredging up pictures of Winter's Dawn barreling through the flying mud, she dragged her thoughts back, the sexy images of Ty lounging on the sofa slowly and reluctantly fading from her mind's eye. Sketches of track patterns and pole positions filled her vision and she waved the fleeting picture away with a long, heavy sigh.

"Horses," she muttered to herself, holding the pencil over the paper. "Horse races." she repeated, grounding herself. It was going to be a long night.

⚜

The blaring of the alarm clock awoke Season the next morning. Pushing herself away from the desk, she dragged a hand through her mussed hair and glared at the clock. Slowly, she forced herself up, stepped over to the alarm and slapped it into silence. Darn thing.

Moaning, she swept up her clothes and headed for the shower. She desperately wished for a cup of Moose's strong brew. Standing under the pulsing water, dreamy visions of Ty filled the room like the rising steam. He'd haunted her dreams after she had accidentally dozed off at the desk. Using the heat of the shower, she forced the haunting pictures out of her mind, filling her thoughts instead with pounding hooves, flying turf, and cheering fans.

Arriving at the track, streaks of sunlight promised to pop through the early morning darkness. At the stalls the horses greeted them with whinnies and curious snuffling for any hidden treats.

"Well gang, we have six hours till post time," she said, slapping her hands together. "Let's not waste them. We'll start with Sky Hunter first."

Watching the black colt shake his head in fury and do battle with the night mist, she hoped she and her team were able to control Ty's little hopeful. Finally, she jotted down his times on her clipboard and waved Eddie in.

Handing the reins over to his hot walker, Eddie panted for breath. "I swear this guy's moods go up and down like a roller coaster."

Sounds like Ty's moods, Season mused, smiling in sympathy at Eddie. "Are you ready for a little stroll on Dawnie?"

Eddie smirked. "After this keg of dynamite, there's no challenge to riding that little tornado.

Five hours later, Season helped Eddie mount Winter's Dawn for her next race.

"No rain this time, but she'll likely to want to hang out with the others, so be prepared to move her along," she advised. "Remind her she's not here to socialize."

"Our belle of the ball," Eddie grinned, nodding as he checked his stirrups. "Got it."

The filly drew fifth position, halfway through the field of ten racers. Season handed the reins over to the loaders and made her way to her place at the railing. She could feel the filly's eagerness to run coursing through the filly's veins, just not the desire to win.

Season bit back a stab of disappointment, knowing Winter's Dawn still did not get it; this wasn't a team sport and she was expected to pass up other racers.

The late winter sun shone bright overhead as the starter released the field.

Winter's Dawn broke out in sixth place, her strides lengthening as she quickly moved up one place, running next to the fourth horse's right flank. Eddie stretched his hand up, dropping his crop down on her flank, urging her to move along. Slowly, as they approached the quarter mile mark, she pushed alongside the fourth-place horse, running in tandem with it, her ears up.

"Drat. She's way out on the outside." Season groaned. "Move her closer to the rail."

At the half mile pole, she was running third and still a good distance out from the inside railing. Chewing her bottom lip, Season gripped the railing, leaning forward, studying every move made on the track.

At the three quarters pole, Winter's Dawn slowly moved up to second place, closer to the railing, her nose at the leader's flank. Season could feel signs of tiring from the filly. It had been a long race for her. She also had no interest in passing the leaders.

With just seconds to go, the finish line looming closer and closer, Eddie simultaneously dropped his crop as Season whispered words of encouragement from track side. Both events galvanized her into action.

She dropped her head and lengthened her stride, nostrils flaring as she pulled abreast of the leading horse. The chestnut filly and the bay horse, neck and neck they raced, matching each other stride for stride. The official clock read 1:37 as they swept under the finish line together.

Holding her breath, Season tasted blood from her lip as she stared at the board. It was a photo finish. *Who won?* Her chest screamed for air, the noise in the crowds making her dizzy. Excitement hung suspended in the stands as everyone waited for the final results.

Suddenly shouts erupted and the air rushed out of her lungs. It was official. The bay horse won the race, beating Winter's Dawn in a very close race.

Shaky, Season made her way past the crowds to her filly on the track. Eddie slowed her down by the time Season walked up.

"Great job. That was close," she praised, reaching for the filly's reins, giving her a pat too.

Winter's Dawn had done well for her debut of the season and now she had areas to work on during her practice runs in the weeks ahead.

Next day clouds once more hung over the track as Sky Hunter walked out for his next race. Ty hadn't called the night following Winter's Dawn photo finish race. Season took it as a mixed blessing. Tomorrow they were all flying back home to Heritage for a short break.

Sky Hunter was in a good mood as he stepped onto the track. Doodlebug pressed against his side and he whinnied, pushing his head playfully into the pony's neck. He acted more like they were strolling through the paddocks at home than minutes from a major horse race. Season handed the reins over to the loader and urged Doodlebug away from the track. Sky Hunter whinnied loudly as his buddy left him, kicking out at the nearest horse. Loaders quickly separated the two, forcing Sky Hunter into the end chute.

It wasn't a position Season liked but maybe by starting out on the outside, he might use up his energy by trying to get to the inside, where his competition was. It was a mile and a quarter long, lots of time to make up distance if he didn't use all the time trying to run down the others. Ty had expressed concern it was a long track, whereas Season saw it as a blessing of sorts. Now they would see who was right.

Eddie's face was set in a grim frown as the starter released the field and the black colt shot out. He quickly swept over the track towards the inside, aligning himself alongside the nearest horse. Lacing his ears back, he bared his teeth and reached out for the straining haunches. Eddie responded immediately, leaning a gloved hand down towards the colt's mouth.

The ruse worked and Sky Hunter swung back, moving away and up on the fourth-place horse. Eddie slapped him and he shot past. His strides lengthened and he lowered himself along the ground, passing by the next two horses, making it look so easy. He pressed alongside the first-place horse, squeezing next to the inside railing.

Picking up the pace, he raced side by side in first position, heads bobbing in unison as they passed the mile mark. Only a quarter mile to go! Season's heart hammered in her chest as she clung to the railing, her knuckles white. She tasted warm blood from her lip. Both the dark colt and the leader raced for the finish, stride for stride as if harnessed together. It was another photo finish.

It was endless, waiting for the results. As one unified sound, the sigh went up from the crowd as the official decision streamed across the board. Sky Hunter had won by the barest fraction of a second. He had won!

That night, back in her room, Season relaxed in bed, flipping through the channels. Nothing could hold her attention for long. The ringing of the phone startled her and she cast a glance at it. It was Ty.

"You did well."

"Thank you," she said, her breath catching unevenly. His grumbly voice sent a wave of warmth washing over her. Images popped through her mind, distracting her.

"But they both could have done better."

"Maybe. But they were both photo finishes."

His chuckle reached through the phone wires, teasing her ears. "Maybe," he echoed her. "Maybe next time they will do better."

"Maybe," Season murmured, her heart racing along as her mind fixed on one image of Ty, a new one, shocking her. He was lying in the bathtub, their shared bathtub, covered in bubbles. The phone cradled between his ear and shoulder and his toes peeking through the suds. Bubbles lapped at his chest. Warm water cocooned him. Suddenly, she needed a cold shower.

"When you get back tomorrow night, there will be a few surprises here," he said.

She wagged her head to clear the image. "Such as?"

He chuckled again, making her toes curl as she pictured him scrubbing his toes. "Guess you will have to wait and see when you return. Good bye, dear Season."

The phone went dead and she stared at it in amazement. It had more effect than a cold shower.

The man was endless in his ways to confuse her sensibilities.

Early the next morning, fog hung like mist in the darkness as the team arrived at the track. All the horses greeted them in their usual fashion. Everything seemed normal. Sky Hunter had one race in the afternoon, a short seven furlong, and then they could pack up and go home for a short break and to whatever surprise Ty had waiting there. He'd been careful not to allow any thoughts to enter his mind last night.

A prickling worry nagged at Season. She glanced around at the track, at the horses and the crews arriving for the day's work. Everything seemed just fine. Nothing out of order. So why the pinprick of worry? The men laughed at another of Stan's corny jokes, just like always.

A few hours later the black colt entered the track for his last race of the week. Clouds hung on the horizon, promising rain before the day's end. He pranced around, eager to run, ears swiveling all around him, taking in all the sights and sounds with wide nostrils and eyes. Eddie took care to keep him away from the other horses, just in case.

Loaders forced him into chute number three, a good position for a seven furlong race.

The bell rang and the horses sprang forward. Sky Hunter got out to a late start. The track was fast, the horses liked it and each stretched out along the turf. Seeing the horses before him, Sky Hunter went crazy, trying to get closer. He swept along the track like a black blur, moving up to the front with amazing speed. Moving past the number three horse, it suddenly stumbled, lurching into Sky Hunter's shoulder, pushing him off balance.

Eddie almost lost his seat, leaning way to the right, dragging on his colt's rein. Sky Hunter's front leg buckled as he tried to catch himself. He swerved way out to the far edge of the track.

Season gasped and gripped the rail, watching in horror. Would they fall? Praying, she pulled herself up straighter, watching as the big colt gathered himself and Eddie righted himself in the saddle. Together, they swerved back toward the inside rail, having lost several precious seconds.

Disaster avoided, Season let out a big breath. Could they make up for lost time? It was a short race, with no extra time given for making up mistakes.

Sky Hunter laced back his ears and grabbed the bit from Eddie, tearing along the track. Within a matter of milliseconds, he passed up two horses, gaining the position he had just held. He swung past the horse that had slammed his shoulder and now moved up on the two leaders. Stretched low to the ground, nose scooping in the air, he nosed past them like a dark phantom, sweeping under the wire first. Cheers erupted from the stands as fans climbed to their feet, applauding the black colt and his comeback.

"That was a great recovery," one reporter said, stuffing a microphone in front of Season's face as she made her way to her horse and rider. "Did you think they were out of it when you saw them both stumble?"

"Eddie is a talented, wonderful jockey and Sky Hunter has lots of heart. I credit both of them for working together for such a quick and effective recovery and a beautiful win."

"What's next for this powerhouse?"

She laughed, liking the phrase. "We are all taking a short break and then back on the road for Kentucky, like everyone else."

"Do you think this colt can place at the Derby?" another reporter asked.

"Don't you?" she asked, smiling at the cameras before giving Sky Hunter's reins a little jingle. "Right now, we have a horse to cool off so excuse us, please."

Two hours later, Doodlebug led the way up the ramp into the airplane. Season secured the horses and made sure their equipment was safely in place. Giving each horse a reassuring pat, she settled herself in the seat closest to them and waited for take-off.

The day had gone perfectly with the single exception of the shoulder slamming incident that ended up working out great. Still she felt that nagging pinprick of worry edging up on her again. Something was going to happen, she was sure of it. Did it have anything to do with the surprise Ty promised was waiting back at Heritage?

Leaning back, she closed her eyes, content in knowing that in a few hours they would be home. Giving in to the weariness that so quickly caught up with her, she let out a long breath, relaxing down into the seat. Shoving the needling worry aside, she relived the last few days. It had felt good to be back at Santa Anita and it now felt good returning back to home a winner.

⚜

Some time later, dozing, she was startled awake by the scream of a horse and yelling voices of the men.

"I can't fight it!" Stan yelled over his shoulder, tension pouring off of him. "Brace yourselves! We're going down!"

Fully alert now, Season leaned against her seat belt. Beside her the horses stomped and snorted. Sky Hunter screamed in terror. Ahead of her, the men talked excitedly, panic heavy in their voices. Suddenly the plane listed to one side.

"Mayday!" Stan yelled into his radio microphone. "Mayday! This is

Heritage Air One. We are experiencing technical troubles. We are going down. Repeat, we are going down. Our position is ...."

Images slammed into Season's mind, blotting out Stan's words. The plane nose diving, plummeting to the ground. Horses fighting to be free. Men screaming in terror. Falling out of control. Twisting metal. Smell of burning flesh. Flames. Heat. Smoke.

Bracing her hands on the armrests, she centered herself, blocking out the images and sounds around her. Squeezing her eyes closed, she focused solely on the airplane. She bolted her feet flat to the floor, feeling the plane pitch beneath her. Wild pitching, from side to side with no control.

Drawing in a deep, steady breath, she felt the plane, catching its rhythm as it listed and pitched again. She sensed Stan's hands tighten as he fought to bring it back under control. She felt the cold air outside as the plane broke through it, through the clouds, rushing to the ground below.

Her breathing slowed down as she focused on picturing the plane leveling out, the engines returning to their normal rumble, the listing to cease.

Fighting the waves of fear at every drop of altitude, she clamped her jaw tight, again seeing the plane straighten out, hearing Stan gain control of the plane.

Her lungs screamed for air, demanding air, but she held tight to the images. The plane dropped altitude again.

Dizzy, she leaned her head back into the seat rest, grit her teeth together, dug her nails into the armrests. The plane lurched one more time, defiantly.

"*No!*" her mind screamed back. "*Level out!*"

Her mind reeling, gradually, she became aware of the sensation of sliding smoothly through the blue sky. She pictured the plane gliding evenly to their destination and arriving gently on the ground unharmed. The view of Heritage filled her mind.

"Oh my gosh!" Stan shouted. "I think I got it back!"

Exhausted, dizzy and faint, Season managed a brief smile as she heard his words.

"That was a close one," Stan said, his breath coming in heavy pants. "But we'll be okay now, I think. I don't know how though, but we'll be okay."

Surrendering to the dizziness engulfing her, Season's last conscious thought was the horses as they calmed down now that the plane was flying straight and smooth. Gratefully, she let the darkness envelope her.

❦

"Season, we made it!"

Excited voices at her ears brought her back. Groggy, she blinked a few times. Eddie's face swam into focus before her.

"Hey, Season, we're here," he gently shook her shoulder. "We made it. We just landed."

He was kneeling in front of her, concern and nervousness etched on his face. Looking at the other men around her, she saw the same strained looks on their faces too. The horses milled fretfully, eager to be off the plane.

The plane crept slowly along the runway. Looking out the window she saw the familiar sights of Heritage. They had made it. Stan had safely brought them home, now taxiing them to a stop.

"I'm okay, Eddie," she assured him, running a hand through her hair.

He smiled. "Pretty anxious there for a few minutes, huh?"

"Yes," she agreed. "So what happened?"

Eddie shook his head. "I don't know. One minute we're doing just great, next minute Stan's yelling mayday and I was sure we were going down. The plane was going all crazy and suddenly it just straightened out. Like magic or something. Stan got it under control and flew us in with no more problems. The whole thing is just plain freaky weird."

She let out a huge sigh as the plane finally taxied to a complete stop. Stan opened the door and daylight rushed in, filling the cabin with light and fresh air.

Gingerly she climbed to her feet and moved to Sky Hunter's stall. Untying his lead rope, she gently eased him backward, whispering softly to him.

"Can you get Doodlebug, please?" she asked Eddie.

Moving down the ramp, he pulled eagerly at his rope, rushing Season along. Reaching the bottom, she spotted Ty hustling toward them.

As he drew nearer, she noticed the worry written all over his face. Slamming to a halt before her, he briefly studied her, paused to run his eyes over the colt, then looked over at the others leaving the plane behind her. He moved up to Stan, the last to leave the plane.

"What the bloody hell happened up there?" he asked.

Season heard part of his explanation, which sounded much like Eddie's had to her. Then she moved out of hearing range. The clip clop of the horse's hooves on the tarmac replaced Stan's explanation. As she led the small group back to the stables, she could feel Ty's eyes burning into her back. Later he would come find her. Right now, she had three horses to care for. After that, a bath and long nap awaited her. Sheer exhaustion was already dragging her down.

❦

An hour later, after the horses had been stripped and brushed out, fed and bedded down, she dropped her travel bag in her room and soaked in a hot bath. Then she allowed herself the indescribable luxury of stretching out on the cool clean sheets of her bed. Just as she drifted off in a peaceful rest, a loud knock at her door nudged her consciousness.

Without waiting for an invitation to enter, Ty swung the door open and strode into the room. Determination and something else—apprehension— stamped on his face as he approached her. Reluctantly, she dragged herself into a sitting position, pooling the blanket around herself.

"That was you? Up there?" Ty asked, pointing a hand toward the ceiling. "That was you, somehow stopping the plane from crashing? Right?" He stood there, hands at his sides, waiting for her answer, eyes drilling into hers and face tight. Silently she nodded.

Exhaling deeply, he dropped into the nearby chair, still eying her warily.

"It's like when you delivered that foal and gave it life, right? You did the same hocus—the same thing then that you did to keep the plane from crashing today?" A warning look from her made him alter his sentence. He raked his hand through his hair.

"Yes, it is the same thing," she assured him quietly.

"But how? The men can't explain it."

"No, I don't expect they ever could explain it. I've already explained it the best I can."

"But this is .... this is simply ... incredible," Ty finished, his voice filled with awe and disbelief. "The men, they are using words like magic and weird and indescribable." He blew out another breath and gave her a long look. "That is you."

She gave him a tight smile. "It's also very tiring physically. It drains me."

Ty blinked. "Oh. That is why you are ... oh," Standing up, his face flushed red. "I shall leave you alone then."

Moving to the door, he paused at the threshold, looking back. "Are you sure you can't tell me what happened up there?"

She gave him another tired smile. "The men already explained what happened and I think you understand the rest. Good night, Ty."

"All right," he said, his voice softer than before. He closed the door, leaving the room in darkness.

With a tired sigh, Season wriggled into a comfortable position, closing her eyes again.

⚜

Ty sat at his desk, staring blindly at the computer screen before him, acutely aware of the woman resting in the room above his head. How the devil had she managed to bring that plane safely down? After hearing each man's account and knowing what little he did of her voodoo powers, he was at a loss to explain it.

But it had happened. Every man had testified they felt sure it was the end for them, even Stan, who was an experienced pilot. And Season herself said she had done it.

One thing was for sure; he almost lost the lives of a good crew of employees, his prized racehorses, and the plane today had it not been for that slip of a woman resting above him right now. She had somehow, in her own magical way, prevented a terrible tragedy.

And, if he were honest, he suspected this wasn't the first time he'd witnessed her doing so. He still had a nagging suspicion about that last race of Sky Hunter's when the colt made such a remarkable recovery. Had she been instrumental in that too? What else was she responsible for? What other coincidences had he failed to contribute to her?

Absently he stared at the screen, now kicked into screen saver mode. What was that stuff called? What had she called her abilities?

Voodoo was wrong. And it wasn't hocus pocus. What the devil did she call it? Shaking his head, he thought back to the night of the foal's birth with Cloudy Lass. The time they sat at the kitchen table and she explained what she could do. What words had she used to name them?

Concentrating, picturing the kitchen in his mind, smelling the barn smell on their clothes, the smell of new birth on their skin, the coffee in the mugs, he focused on her lips and eyes as she had spoken, trying to get him to understand what he didn't want to know then. Except he sure did now.

More afraid than he wanted to admit, he knew he had to figure this out. What had she said?

Fae and druid. Yes, that was what she had said her parents and ancestors were. Faeries. The stuff he'd always assumed were legends and fairytales and utter rubbish.

Tapping the mouse, the stagnate computer sprang to life. Moving his fingertips over the keys, he held his breath, afraid of what he was about to discover.

Two hours later he clicked off the computer, leaned back in his chair and raked a hand through his hair once more, this time leaving the hat on the desktop. Sighing deeply, he stared back at the blank screen. The various pages and sites he read hadn't helped much, but at least he had the basic knowledge of what she had tried to tell him in the kitchen that night.

And it helped to explain the things he'd seen since her arrival at the farm. So many little pieces now fit into the mysterious puzzle. And it explained why he was so quickly becoming so drawn to her.

Even now, after everything he'd just read, most of it he hadn't understood anyway; he was keenly aware of her sleeping above him. And there was no doubt in his mind that she had brought that plane down safely today, among other incredible things.

He sighed again, deep and heavy. She was a mystery. And a challenge. And a bite of worry pinched at his stomach because he knew he could never refuse either one.

Perhaps he should retire for the night, he thought, glancing at the clock, though he doubted he would get much sleep tonight. Rubbing his eyes, he pushed away from the desk, wondering what tomorrow would bring.

❁

Season awoke as the first streaks of sun topped the hills around the farm. Stretching and yawning, she determined she was no worse off from her strenuous experience yesterday with the plane. After a refreshing shower, she found the kitchen abandoned. Helping herself to some coffee and a couple fresh donuts, she headed outside to breathe in the brisk mountain air.

Milling horses caught her attention.

Following the sounds of stomping hooves and snorting, she approached a small group of horses in a nearby corral. She had missed noticing them yesterday. Curious now, she went over for a closer look. A hundred yards from the corral, she stopped, her blood running cold, half a doughnut falling forgotten to the dirt.

These were not thoroughbreds, or even racehorses. These were stock horses. Heavy muscled and stocky; they were not bred for speed. As she lightly rested her hands on the top rail for a closer look, she noted they didn't come over to check her out. Even range horses were curious and friendly with people. This small group was indifferent.

Studying them closer, a chill washed over her as the truth slowly revealed itself to her heart.

These were bucking horses, like the kind used in rodeos. They swam before her as her vision blurred. Suddenly ill, she clenched a hand to her belly and turned away from them, memories assaulting her like fiery darts, piercing her heart and soul.

Almost sobbing, she returned to the house, hearing Moose clanking around in the kitchen as he prepared bowls of food. It was now or never. She had to know.

Forcing herself to be calm, sucking in a deep breath, she slowed her entrance to the kitchen, trying hard to make it look natural.

"Hi. You're up early," Moose greeted her, looking up from mixing a huge bowl of pancake batter. "Heard about your return flight. Sure was something, huh?"

"Yes, it certainly was something," she agreed as she refilled her cup and felt blindly for the nearest bar stool. "Uh, Moose, what can you tell me about those horses in the middle corral? I hadn't noticed them before."

Moose paused in his stirring. "Oh, you mean the bucking broncs the Master had brought in for his practice?"

"Practice?" she croaked, the word lodging in her throat. Fear, or something like it tightened in her stomach. The coffee now felt like a lead ball inside her and she shoved the mug away.

"Yeah," Moose resumed stirring and measuring as he continued his explanation. "Every year the area holds a festival and rodeo. Each year the Master enters the bucking bronco contest to try to ride old Widow Maker. I guess by now it's become personal between them two. So he starts to practice weeks ahead of time for his one shot with old Widow Maker."

"Widow Maker? Is that the name of a horse?"

"Not just any horse, Missy. He's legendary. Famous for never being ridden and for killing a few who tried and hurting a whole bunch of others, including our own beloved Master."

Season watched him pour batter out into the sizzling skillet, letting his words slowly sink in, overriding the fear and dread already etched there from the word *rodeo*. It was a venomous word. "But how did a wealthy thoroughbred racehorse owner get involved in the world of ... of ... of rodeos?" She could barely get the word out of her dry mouth.

Moose glanced up from flipping his cakes and she had to wonder if he noticed how frail she felt. If he did, he gave no indication. "Quite by accident. Kind of silly when you think about it. Some years ago, some fellows in town dared the Master to ride this particular horse, Widow Maker. The Master can never turn down a dare and, of course, he was thrown off within a second or two in front of everyone. Since then the die has been cast with him and that old horse. Like I said, guess it's just personal now."

"Maybe he's died by now," she whispered hopefully. "Died since last year and won't be here."

Moose scoffed. "That kind live on forever, getting meaner and trickier every year. No, that evil beast will be there this year and the Master will try to ride him again. Until one of them finally dies."

Memories shook Season by the shoulders, making her tremble. Muttering a thank you to Moose, she pushed away from the counter.

Fleeing to her room, she pulled a worn photo album from a drawer and sat on the bed with it cradled gently on her lap. Tears quickly built up behind her eyes as she softly caressed the cover, feeling the familiar touch of the fabric. Oh, the memories inside the book, locked between the pages, she thought, as she felt the tiny darts pricking her harder and deeper.

As the first tear slid down her cheeks and splashed the cover, she sucked in a deep breath, lifting it up.

A smiling face greeted her, blue eyes twinkling with merriment and more than a bit of mischief as well. Blonde hair streaked blonder by the sun, tanned face, dimples and the promise of youth. The boy grew from a youngster to a handsome young man in the pages of her pictures. From racing toy trucks in the dirt with her when they were four, riding their first horses, and all along the road through high school. Birthday parties and Christmas celebrations, summer vacations and Thanksgiving feasts; the boy shared so many days and weeks with her. They played together and fought together and double dated together.

The years fell aside as she flipped the pages slowly, remembering each event preserved forever on film as they grew up together. Her heart constricted as she neared the end of the album, knowing what was coming. Shoulders shaking with tears, she let them fall unchecked, the grief as raw and painful today as it was then.

Hot tears fell on faded snapshots of riding bucking horses and bucking bulls. The scenes were all the same—dirt floored rodeo arenas. In some photos he was dirt streaked and smiling after a grand ride and some were snapped at the height of his ride. Horses and bulls changed in each picture, but he always looked the same. Carefree and happy, a promising professional rodeo rider. Except he never fulfilled the promise of a full life. Confident and skilled, her beloved cousin met misfortune in the rodeo area where he made his living; stomped to death before her eyes. Before she could do anything to help him.

Stunned, she sat in the crowds along with so many others on that terrible day and watched Scotty, her best friend since childhood, get squashed beneath eight hundred pounds of enraged horse. The day of Scotty's funeral, she vowed to never watch another rodeo and she'd packed his album away, never to look at it again.

Until today.

❧ 8 ❧

She hated herself, but she had to know. She had to do this. She had to face this. Hands curled into tights fists, her heart hammering, Season crept downstairs, hoping Moose would be in the kitchen. He was, cleaning up a pile of plates.

"You be ready for breakfast now, Missy?" he asked, raising one eyebrow at her approach.

She slid onto a bar stool, hand on her stomach, the churning inside so loud, she wondered how Moose couldn't help but hear.

"You feeling okay?" Moving away from the dirty dishes, he dried his hands and came up beside her, concern on his face. "You don't look so good."

"I ... uh ... don't feel so good. It's ... uh ... sort of personal."

"Are you in—?"

She shook her head quickly. "No, nothing like that, Moose. It's just the rodeo topic upset me a lot. It has a lot of personal history for me."

He nodded, backing up a step. "Guess it's mostly bad history by the looks of you."

"You could say that. Look, Moose, I need to know something. Is Ty really determined to go and ride that horse?"

"Nothing on earth could stop him. We've even thought of drugging him, but he gets suspicious and edgy just before the day so he won't walk into any traps. Wiley as an old lobo wolf. And can you imagine the hell to pay for someone who tried doing that to the Master?"

Better than letting him meet his death. His temper would eventually wear down and at least he would be alive to vent it. Might be worth the price so she filed the idea away. Even if the men were too scared to act upon it, she wasn't.

"Okay, if he is so foolishly determined to do this, is there any chance he might succeed?"

Moose rocked back on his heels, counting off on his fingers. "Let's see. That horse has killed four riders locally so far. Bobby Garrett. Davy Thomson. Frosty Jones. Wes Smith. Wes looked like a crippled pancake afterward and had to have a casket specially made as he couldn't fit in a normal one.

Something cold swirled in Season's stomach and she rubbed her hand over it. "What." She swallowed. "What about the ones who didn't die? Like Ty when they rode before. What happened other than a humiliating fall in public?"

"Oh, the fall for the Master was the biggest part. The injuries were easier to handle than the humility of falling in public."

"Yeah, I get he'd rather die than be publicly humiliated and all that, but other than his pride, what else has he hurt over that stupid horse?"

"Let's see. Last year he broke four ribs and strained his wrist. Two years ago, he got a concussion. Before that it was a broken leg and arm I think." Moose paused, thinking, counting on his fingers. "And before that—"

"Okay, never mind!" Season cried, holding up her hand for him to stop. "I get the idea. So it's not likely he will actually succeed and even less likely he will let it go."

She was torn between sheer anger at the insanity of Ty's idiotic actions and a niggling of concern he could and probably would be seriously hurt. Even killed. And, apparently, he didn't seem to care. Had Scotty ever felt that way before? Had he known he would die? Would he still have ridden that day?

Fresh pain washed over her as she considered, for the first time, that he still might have.

Moose's expression softened as he laid his giant hand gently over hers. "The Master and that horse are cut from the same mold. The horse didn't care who was on his back. He just wanted him off and did what he had to do to succeed. The Master doesn't care what has to happen to himself. He just wants to undo the humiliation."

About to protest, Season hesitated, mulling over Moose's words. He was right. No matter how unreasonable or unsafe Ty's plan was, it was Ty's plan and there was no stopping him.

"You hold some influence with him, Missy, but not on this matter I'm afraid."

Stunned, she stared at him. Influence? Over Ty? None that she had noticed.

"Perhaps you can find another way to solve this yearly problem once and for all, Season. In your own special way."

Speechless, Season nodded, puzzled by his cryptic messages and still processing the horrible history between Ty, a vicious bronc, and her beloved cousin.

Right now, she needed space to be alone and think. "I need to take a ride, Moose," she said quietly, her voice hardly more than a whisper. "I'll be back later on, okay? Thank you for telling me all that. Right now, I just need to get away."

Pausing, she rested a hand on the counter briefly, inches from his. "Please don't tell Ty about this."

Wordlessly, Moose nodded, returning to his cleaning up chores. Season slipped from the house and down to the barns, avoiding the corral holding the broncos. Saddling up a stock horse, she swung aboard and kicked it into a canter, heading for the woods beyond the farm, toward the towering mountain peaks.

The horse plowed through the unbroken snow, white powder flying up beneath its hooves. Steam blew from its nostrils. With Scotty's memories and Moose's words keeping her company, she urged the horse along at a brisk pace.

Finally, she reached a good spot at the edge of the woods, leading up higher into the mountains. Despite the mid-morning hour, the air was sharper and noticeably cooler. Sliding off the horse, she wrapped the reins loosely around a tree trunk and sank onto a nearby rock, brushing the snow away. Crossing her legs, she rested her palms on her knees, closing her eyes, inhaling a slow, deep breath.

Tears welled up within her as Scotty's images from over the years played through her mind like a video slide show. Growing up together, two kids playing in the mud, climbing trees, learning to drive his dad's old pickup, dates with best friends, the prom, summer jobs, graduation, and all their big plans. She worked with racehorses, learning the training secrets of the Moriarty generations. He turned to the rodeo world, bent on conquering bucking horses and bulls.

For years she went to see him, being there to support him, just like he came to her races. They celebrated the victories with each other and comforted one another in the losses. Oh, she missed him so much!

Grief tore at her soul, shaking her shoulders as tears fell from her eyes. Her hands moved to her stomach as she curled into a miserable ball, rocking back and forth on the cold rock.

The cool wind listened to her anguished misery and loneliness, echoing her weeping. Trees bowed their branches. Deep sadness hung heavy in the air. Even her horse hung its head low, as if feeling her weary sorrows.

A sound came to her in the wind, a whisper soft and sweet, breaking through the cold sorrows of her grief. Looking up, she looked around, seeking a face from the whisper.

Gray mist swirled near, whispering softness. She did not feel the cold breeze anymore, just warm caresses of love surrounding her from within the mist. Murmured whispers of shared memories touched her deep inside, down to her heart.

"Scotty?" she asked, dabbing at her tears, sniffling.

"It's me, Seasoned Salt."

It was the pet name Scotty sometimes called her in teasing. Fresh tears washed down her face. Stunned, she glanced around to ensure she was alone.

"Season, please don't cry so. Let it go," the mist whispered to her heart. *"I will always be a part of you now and I will always love you."*

"But I couldn't save you that day," she sobbed again, fresh grief ripping at her soul.

"There was no time to. No one can fault you so stop faulting yourself. I never blamed you."

The mist sounded so much like her beloved cousin, it rocked Season. She wished she could see him and touch him just one more time.

"I'm fine here, Season. I'll be waiting for you. In the meantime, go live your life and don't grieve for me."

Thoughts to argue crowded her mind, to protest, but equally persistent thoughts from the mist overrode them within her heart, silencing her. Finally, she stopped, giving up.

"I will always love you, Season and I will always be a part of you. Now go live a happy life. Do it for me as much as for you, sweet Season."

"I will, Scotty," she promised.

Blinking, the mist was gone, the whispers vanishing, and she was alone in the cold air once more. Yet she felt lighter somehow, freer, the heavy weight of her sorrows and regrets now broken.

Perhaps now she could face Ty's reckless ambitions with Widow Maker.

Wiping the last of her tears away, she gathered up the horse's reins and swung up. Clucking to it, she urged it back along their previous path. Somehow, the day seemed just a little brighter on her return trip. Putting the horse back in its stall, she headed for the house, thinking maybe she could finally handle a little food herself.

Entering the kitchen, she found it deserted. The coffee was fresh so she poured a cup. About to sit down, she noticed the note lying on the counter, held down by a red apple. It was easy to recognize Ty's bold, heavy scrawl.

Season,

Another breeding scheduled today.
Bring Bold Raven to Timely Act at 4:00.
Try to be 'on time', babe.

Ty Masters

She sneered, both at his poor attempt at humor and his reference to calling her Babe.

It was only one now, plenty of time before having to deal with another breeding session. She stared at the note, wondering whether to write her own response back or just crumple it up and leave it for him to see. In the end she did neither. By leaving it alone, he would have to wonder if she had seen it or not. Then at four, she would put in her 'timely appearance' with the stallion.

And if he tried anything this time around, she couldn't be responsible for any further actions. Widow Maker might end up being the least of Ty Masters' troubles.

Still hungry, she poked around the kitchen and slapped together a sandwich to hold her until later. Taking care to clean up after herself, she left nothing behind for Moose to deal with. Grabbing a banana from the fruit bowl as well as the apple and a small package of crackers, she headed out for her office in the barn. There was still time to find Eddie and work her charges before Bold Raven's date.

Two hours later it was time to prepare the stallion for his date. Remembering this time to keep the cooler blanket handy, Season led the horse off to the breeding barn. The waiting scene was much the same as before, a mare ready and waiting, eager to start their quick courtship. Experienced at this, Bold Raven was enthusiastic to do his part. Stepping aside, Season looked over at Ty.

"Am I timely enough for you?" she asked, her tone light, but daring him to mock her.

"I see you got my note. I was beginning to wonder."

For some reason his accent seemed stronger today than she had remembered. The look in his eye was different from before. His thoughts were more guarded this time, eyes sheltered by the brim of his hat. Whatever he might be thinking, he planned to keep it to himself.

A wild shriek drew her eyes to the stallion and mare, again wishing they could be free out in the meadows for their union. But she also knew why it couldn't be. As long as the men were handy, she was free to use this time to help prepare herself mentally on dealing with Ty's upcoming rodeo issue. Noticing the mere thought of a rodeo didn't cause that sharp stab in her heart this time, she sent a mental thank you to Scotty. If she could make this right in her mind, she could deal with it on a daily basis.

Moving her gaze back at Ty, she drew up a picture of him on a bucking horse in a dirt floored arena. A shudder involuntarily slithered over her as a picture of Scotty replaced Ty, but she let it go peacefully and brought Ty back into the scene. She had to make peace with this event if she wanted any peace in her life. Making herself keep her mind locked on the image she drew of Ty riding some unknown horse to a successful ride, she played it over in her mind, rewinding and playing it again.

Not knowing what color Widow Maker was, she made him into a sorrel with four white feet in her pictures. She had to see Ty do this safely in her mind, and keep memories of Scotty in the past, if she wanted to survive the coming weeks.

Finally, able to keep seeing him finish the ride successfully enough times to satisfy her heart and mind, Season let the picture go, mentally tearing it up and throwing it away in her mind's garbage can. Blinking, she was startled to see Ty's curious gaze fixed on her, unspoken questions in his eyes. His guard was lowered now and she sensed a heated passion, but foremost of that was genuine concern.

He seemed about to speak, but unsure what to say. What was she doing?

How could she explain what she had just done? One more thing about her he would see as hocus pocus and not fully understand.

The bugling completion of the horse kept him from having to speak and saved Season from the deep concern shining in his eyes. Throwing the cooler around the horse, she grabbed his lead shank and headed for the door.

"Season, wait up and I shall assist you," Ty called.

This time she did not run off. Still needing to get the stallion back soon, she waited for him and they walked side by side to the barn. Once inside, she stripped the horse as he was cross tying it. Together, they wordlessly shared the work of caring for the horse until he was brushed and back in his stall.

"Are you all right?" Ty asked finally, grabbing her wrist as she secured the stall door bolt.

"Of course," she answered. "Why?"

"You seemed to ... go away back there. Go someplace else..." He paused, giving her a hard look. "Did you leave? I mean, can you leave like that?" Fumbling for the right words, he shook his head.

She smiled, understanding what he was trying to say. "No, I was concentrating on something I had to think very hard about. At no time did I leave myself."

"Could you? If you wanted to?"

"Maybe," she answered vaguely.

He blew out a breath, releasing her wrist. "Season, you boggle me. I'll be honest with you. I want to understand you yet I can't. You are a complete mystery to me."

Still smiling, she started to move away when his arm encircled her waist. Startled, she whirled around, facing him, seeing the smoky heat in his eyes.

"There are other things I want to do to you as well, babe. Things I do understand. As a man."

Pulling her close, he captured her lips in a hard kiss. Her hands moved up to his neck, touching his heated skin, feeling the hard muscles and pulsating of a vein in his neck. Her fingertips slowly slid to his rough chin, leaving tingling trails along his skin.

His hands bunched up her shirt, pressing into her back, sliding up to her shoulders, and finally encircling her hair, his lips never stopping, his tongue equally sparing with hers. Their hips touching, his hard excitement crushing against her. His earthy scent filled her nose as she breathed deep.

She met him boldly kiss for kiss, wrapping her fingertips around his neck, burning him with her own heated response, branding him like a steer.

His fingers wound into her hair, holding her close to him, capturing her.

Finally, breathlessly, they broke apart, panting for air. Exchanging dark, heavy looks under hooded eyes, it was Season who spoke first.

"Let's take a ride, Ty. I want to share something with you. Something very important to me."

Wordlessly, he nodded, questions flaring in his eyes. She pressed two fingers to his lips.

"Go saddle up two horses and I'll meet you in front of the house in a few minutes, okay?"

He nodded, running his tongue over her fingertips before she removed her hand.

She gave him a sweet smile and spun around, leaving him standing in the middle of the barn aisle. He led Black Warrior out of his stall, saddling him up for himself. Picking a docile stock mare from the other barn, he saddled it for Season and was ready when she came out of the house carrying a rolled-up bundle.

Tying it to the back of her saddle, she swung aboard, flashing him that mysterious smile once more and kicking the mare into a lope out of the yard.

⁂

T y followed her, keeping his horse's head at her mare's flank. She led him through snowy paths and he had to suspect if she had carved these in her private hours away from the house. When he was locked away in his study or thought she was busy up in her office, was she really out on horseback riding toward the mountains? It certainly appeared that was where she was leading him now he decided, watching the white peaks growing closer and larger.

Finally, she reined in her mare at the edge of the wooded forest and slid from the saddle, tying its reins. Doing the same with Black Warrior, he noticed fresh horse tracks in the snow and a single pair of small boot tracks not just a few feet away. She had been here quite recently. Today?

"Season ..."

"Shh," she stopped him, holding up a finger as she was untying her bundle. "Come with me and I will explain everything."

Taking the bundle, she led him past the large rock where the foot prints had ended. She led him on through a stand of evergreen trees to a small clearing beyond and spread the blanket down on the snow. Settling down on it, she patted a spot next to her, smiling sweetly up at him, sending sparks knifing through him.

Though it was still daylight, he felt the stillness of this place. The oneness of the forest and of nature. He glanced up, half expecting it to be dark and the moon out. It was if somehow this place, miles from Heritage, moved on a different rule of time.

Here, she was in her element. With the wild and whispering winds. Here, he felt completely out of his element. Here, she was master over him. Swallowing a lump, he joined her on the blanket, accepting the bottle of water she passed over to him. He took a drink and recapped it, waiting and watching, letting her lead the way, keenly aware of her as he had never noticed a woman before.

She took a long drink from her water bottle and set it aside. Then she drew her knees up to her chest and studied him, a thoughtful and sad smile on her face.

"Ty, I have to share something very personal with you. And I have to do this to explain what I was doing back in the barn just a bit ago."

He started to speak, felt the lump in his throat and nodded instead, not sure what she would say next. What could she possibly say? Desires mixed with concern in his heart, both waring for his attention. Her next words, so sadly spoken, decided the path of his thoughts.

"I had a cousin. His name was Scotty. We grew up very close, very fond of one another. We were only a few months apart in age." She paused, inhaling a breath. "After graduation, he started riding bucking bulls and horses. He rode the rodeo circuit. He was very talented and had good success."

He heard the pride in her voice, saw the mist of tears in her eyes, dotting her dark lashes, and knew this was going to turn bad.

"At one particular rodeo, I was in the stands watching. Scotty was riding a wild horse. He finished the ride and jumped off, another successful ride. He'd moved to the next level now. Without warning, the horse turned on Scotty and smashed him into the dirt. My cousin died, crushed under the horse and there was nothing I or anyone could do."

She stopped, wiping at her tears, her voice thick with emotion. He considered hauling her into his arms and kissing away the pain this clearly was causing her to tell him—yet he hesitated. He waited, watching her lashes grow wet with tears and her lips tremble as she fought to keep from breaking down.

"From that day on, I hated anything to do with rodeos, avoiding them. Until today, when I saw the horses in the corral and Moose told me about you and the history with Widow Maker. Don't be mad at Moose, I asked him about it. And then I came out here today, to get away and reconcile my past hatred of rodeos to you riding in one soon. I can't really explain what happened out here for me earlier today, but it led to what I could do in the breeding barn afterward."

His heart suddenly hammered, knowing her special powers somehow played into this. Despite the cold of the snow, his palms were sweaty as he waited, breathless, for the rest of her story.

"I had to paint the picture in my mind of you riding a horse, Widow Maker, successfully in the rodeo. Like a little, short movie. I played it over and over in my mind, making peace with the fact you were going to do this. And after I was done, I tore it up and threw it away in my mind's garbage can." Finished, she ended with another sad smile, waiting.

He blinked, putting the pieces together, trying to connect it all. "So, because you played the little movie in your mind, does that mean I will ride the horse successfully now?"

"No, Ty. Just because I made it so in my mind, it has no impact on what happens later."

That could have been nice, he thought wistfully. "Why tear it up and throw it away? The movie?"

"As a way of making peace with everything that had happened and letting it all go. What happened before is over now, what lies ahead will be."

"I see. Rather enigmatic."

"Maybe. But I wanted to explain to you what I was doing back in the barn."

"Thank you for that," he said slowly, still trying to reconcile her story. A hearty chuckle finally broke from his lips. "I was sort of hoping you were dreaming of me in a different kind of way though. More of a manly way."

She slid him a slow grin. "Maybe there might have been a little of that as well," she teased, licking her lips. "But first, can you satisfy a question or two I have of you?"

"A question of me?" He touched a finger to his chest. "I'm not the mysterious one around here. That's all you, babe."

Ignoring his barb, she forked a hand through her hair. "Tell me about the man behind the mystery. The one that everyone wants to know about."

He laughed, relaxing now, leaning back on his elbows on the blanket. He itched to tangle his fingers in her shimmery hair. "No mystery. Just me."

She lowered herself down across from him, her elbow on the blanket as well. "Not true. You are quite the mystery man, Ty Masters. First, there is the billionaire English racehorse owner. You are never seen with a woman."

"Not true," he said, grinning. "I have been seen with you many times."

She frowned. "You know what I mean. No history. People have to guess, and rumors abound. No one really knows anything about you." She paused. "And I think you actually enjoy that. The mystery part."

He gave her a coy smile, refusing to comment, like he often did in the Winner's Circle when his horses won.

"And there is the Ty Masters, Wyoming rancher. Why don't you raise your thoroughbreds back east like everyone else? Or California. Why Wyoming?"

"Easy to explain that one. I came out here on a trip years ago, fell in love with the land, the wide-open spaces and fresh air. I decided it was only natural to move everything I owned out here instead of staying on at those stuffy eastern farms."

"Stuffy? Coming from you? Uh huh. And then there is Ty Masters the rodeo king. A man willing to risk life and limb, and apparently usually does, just to try and conquer a single horse."

"Not just any horse." He shook his head. "That brute and I have had a long-standing feud for many years now."

"Yeah, it sure sounds like jealousy to me."

"Jealousy? Who? Me jealous of a horse?" He smirked "Not likely."

She smiled. "No, just jealous of being bettered by a horse. And one more part of the Ty Masters mystique."

He leaned in, closing the distance between them. "If you think I have a bit of mystery surrounding me, love, it pales when compared to all the mysteries around you." Lifting a brow, he dared her to deny it. "You bring me way out here, all alone, and I can't help but wonder what else you could have going on in that crafty little mind of yours."

She gave him a wicked smile and waved an arm skyward. The late afternoon sky instantly darkened, the stars suddenly appearing, twinkling merrily down to them. Cuing an unseen orchestra, birds and crickets chimed in. She snapped her fingers at a nearby pile of dried wood and a crackling fire leaped to life. Holding her palm out, she blew a gentle breath out to the trees and a breeze starting whispering sweetly through the pine boughs and branches. Finished, she looked at him, waiting.

He arched a brow, taking in the sudden change of scene. His heart hammered. "You certainly do know how to create a mood."

"Are you going to kiss me or not?" she asked him, her voice husky and deep. She reached out and touched the back of his neck. "It's alright."

He stiffened. "I have never made love to ... someone quite like you, Season."

"I'm still just a woman," she murmured, her eyes smoky with her own desires.

"Not just a woman. You are so ..."

Bringing him to her, she pushed her lips to his, ending his conflict. Molding her body under his, she erased his doubts.

Bolder, he grew hungry, drawing fire from her. He felt as if he was seeing into her soul and touching a fine golden vessel. He felt like a blessed and gifted man. He lay back, taking her with him, so she straddled him. His hands moved up her arms, to tangle in the swinging hair. She peppered him with kisses. A moan escaped him.

"We have entirely too much clothing between us," he lamented between kisses.

"I agree." She reached for the zipper of his jeans.

The wind swept over the pines, gently caressing them. The horses snorted, adding a background melody to the trilling of the birds overhead. Nature's orchestra played its own tune in rhythm to them. Outside their circle, beyond the pines, the sun slowly set. Mixing with the darkness above them, it sent its long rays of orange and red streaking through the trees to lay softly across the couple, blanketing them in warm liquid sunshine. Stardust twinkled off the golden shimmers.

❧ 9 ❧

The plane lifted slowly off the ground, taking them up higher into the blue sky. Season watched Heritage growing smaller through the window, her thoughts heavy. No, they hadn't made love yesterday. They came incredibly close, stopping just before the point of no return. They kissed wildly, cuddled close and ignited hot fires, but they did not make love.

For Season it was both sad and good they hadn't. Admittedly, it was exciting to be alone in the wilderness with Ty, feeling everything he was feeling, and sharing all that she shared with him. To move forward would logically have been the next step for them. Yet she was also glad they hadn't gone further. Romance with Ty would have greatly complicated their delicately balanced working relationship. It was better to be just employer and employee. Mixed with just a touch of friendship at times, when they weren't sparing over some matter. That was enough of a recipe without adding in being lovers too.

And now she was heading off for another race. Right now, she needed to focus all her energies on this horse, not insane passions with his owner. Although she knew she would always treasure that quiet time alone with him in the wilderness.

The plane touched down smoothly and the crew instantly went into action, each busy with their own tasks. Tomorrow was race day, not leaving much time to settle the nervous colt in and prepare him for his race.

"Any last minute instructions?" Eddie asked her the next morning, as she was giving him a leg up. She considered the question, running over a mental list of horses they were competing against.

"Yes, when you get even with High Ransom, push Hunter ahead a few yards just to see if he can keep up with you two. See if Ransom struggles. Then, slow down after a few furlongs. That should tell us if High Ransom will have the energy for a fast finish."

"You think High Ransom is the only threat out there today?" Eddie nodded toward the track.

"Well, the only one worth considering anyway," Season said with a grin.

Eddie broke into a huge smile. "Some might call that conceited."

"No," Season smiled back. "Just confident in our big star." She patted the colt on his neck, feeling his energy, ready to run, eager to run. Needing to run. It was like an addiction to the horse; he had to be out somewhere running wide open, racing the stars if he had only them for company.

Leading Shy Hunter to the start, she gave him another reassuring pat and found her place along the rail, searching for High Ransom. The large honey bay colt was the only one that worried her for the Derby. Though he and Sky Hunter hadn't raced together until now, she had been noticing his own great progress at other races. He was making records of his own and creating a media frenzy following much like Hunter, only without the high maintenance or viciousness. High Ransom was as gentle as a kitten to handle and obedient as a lapdog. It was enough to almost make Season jealous. Almost.

Eagerly, she waited for Eddie to test his endurance today. Sometimes strong leaders fell behind after the final turn, not able to withstand long, hard runs. Testing horses early in a race would tell her how much stamina any particular horse had for a big finish.

Her father swore by testing such as that when he suspected his horse would find itself stuck behind a strong leader. And of course Sky Hunter hated to be stuck behind any horse. Today's race would tell her a lot.

From the start, High Ransom was the clear threat to Sky Hunter. They broke early and battled for first place all along the course.

In the end, she watched Sky Hunter pound down the track in first place by half a nose, and with another new record under his name while High Ransom finished in a good second place showing, also creating a new track record. Happy, she took her place in the Winner's Circle, smiling for the cameras, one hand resting reassuringly on Sky Hunter's lathered neck, acutely aware Ty was at home watching them on TV. She could almost feel as if she were in the room with him, hundreds of miles away.

The plane took them to Kentucky, where they settled Sky Hunter in his stall and left for their own hotel rooms. This time Season remembered to pack a few candles with her bath supplies. She didn't need any special abilities to know a phone call was to be expected soon. She might as well be relaxed while waiting. She drew her bath, lit the candles, put a calming song on the portable player, and slid into the warm bubbles, the hotel phone at her elbow.

Just as her eyelids were heavy and drooping, the ringing of the phone startled her awake.

"Hello. Did I wake you?" Ty asked, his voice a sultry rumble in Season's ear.

"Not really. Well, sort of. I was relaxed." Something slowly knotted around her heart strings.

"You deserve it. He looked great out there. All of you deserve a pat on the back."

"I'll pass that on to the men tomorrow, okay."

"I'm serious, Season. I do appreciate what a wonderful job you people are doing out there with my horses." He hesitated. "I just wanted you to know that. And yes, please tell the men tomorrow as well."

"I will," she promised, aware of something tightening deep inside her. "Is there anything else?"

She could feel the tension coming over the lines. There was something on his mind. Something he wasn't able to say.

"Everything all right back home?" she asked casually.

"Yes, just fine," he assured quickly. A little too quickly. "I will see you all in a few days."

"Good night, Ty."

Hanging up the phone, she had to wonder what he left unspoken. Something that had nothing to do with praising his employees, although the men would appreciate hearing that tomorrow.

In the meantime, she was tired, and he did not feel it important enough to share just yet. She'd let it go.

❦

"Wow, that's the first time I ever heard of the Master calling to give us a pat on the back," Stan said the next morning, a bit stunned as Season relayed Ty's message. Glancing at the men around the hotel's breakfast table, she had to admit they all looked shocked.

"You mean he never calls up with good news?" Granted, she was used to his nasty tempered calls of complaints, but she had expected them to be aimed at her. She also expected good calls for the men who worked so hard.

"Nope. Can't recall a single time," Eddie said, shaking his head and reaching for another piece of toast. "He'd call up the old trainer, rant and rave a bit, but we never heard a good word for our parts."

"Wonder what got into him?" Stan speculated. "Think he got sick or something?"

Eddie gave her a long look before speaking. "I think he's got a bug all right, but I think it has to do with our own sweet Season. That's the change in him."

Stan pulled at his goatee beard. "You're right. The old Master hasn't been the same since you arrived, Season. What did you do to him?"

"Nothing. Honestly," she protested, her cheeks turning warm. "And believe me, I still hear a lot of ranting and raving temper tantrums from him."

❦

Next morning heralded a series of strong thunderstorms for Sky Hunter's first race.

Season was glad the colt didn't mind the mud. He sloshed through it, passing all the horses to an easy win, a cookie cutter version of the last race.

The rain finally stopped for his second race, leaving the track a muddy mess.

"Watch for slick spots out there," Season advised. "Our wonder boy goes so fast, him hitting a slick patch is like us hitting black ice with our cars."

Eddie nodded his understanding. "At least he's a little more manageable out there lately and he isn't trying to kill the other horses." He still kept the glove over his left hand in case the horse needed a hot potato reminder in the middle of a race.

"Yes, he is improving. He's getting the race them idea now instead of run them down idea he used to have. And he's running with better times and winning more too."

"And now he's only like riding a mere hurricane," Eddie quipped.

The race was a short one, with only six horses running. Sky Hunter broke fourth out of the gate, eager to pass up the three leaders. Just into the race, the number two horse slipped on the mud, causing the rider of the number three horse to swerve into Sky Hunter's oncoming path, just grazing his shoulder. Eddie pulled Sky Hunter over to avoid a collision, making him lose his footing on the slippery mud.

Season watched, almost vaulting over the railing. One horse was down, struggling in the mud along with its rider. Another horse was up, standing still, his rider next to him looking disgusted. One horse was still far in the lead and two more came on from the back, moving out to give the still horses and riders a wide berth. Sky Hunter had slipped, he'd lost ground. And seconds. Eddie grimly held the reins, trying to shift his weight to help the colt regain his footing in the slippery slop.

His next lurch forward tilted him in the other direction, like a deer stuck on a patch of ice and unable to get his balance or traction.

Season closed her eyes, picturing the shoes on Sky Hunter's hooves. Feeling how they gripped the slippery track, how they dug in, giving him grip and footing. She shifted her shoulders in rhythm, like a horse would shift his weight as he ran. She felt his strong legs moving through the wet, sloppy mud, more mud splashing his velvet nose. She felt Eddie's hands taking control once more as Hunter gathered himself.

When she opened her eyes, Sky Hunter was running flat out again, making up for his lost time, swiftly closing the gap between him and the leading horse. Mud shone brightly on his chest and legs as he stretched out his neck and nose, Eddie low in the saddle, also covered in mud. They had their balance and rhythm back as they swept first under the finish wire.

"That was a close call," Ty said, his voice coming over the phone later. "I fully expected him to only come out third or fourth in that one."

"The track was bad. All the horses had problems. I'm just glad no one got hurt. Even the horses and riders that went down were fine."

"So tell me, Season, did you have anything to do with that?"

His directness surprised her. "What do you mean? No, everyone was just lucky no one was hurt. It was a bad day for a race."

"No, I meant with Hunter's recovery and victory."

She hesitated. It seemed his questions lately were more pointed than before. More direct. He must be doing some homework.

"Perhaps a little bit," she confessed.

"What did you do? Make another little movie in your mind?"

"Something like that. But it's a little more complicated than just making a movie up."

He seemed about to speak but the line went silent for a minute. "I will see you upon your return tomorrow. Good night."

☙❧

Next morning, feeling like kids when school let out for summer, the crew eagerly boarded the plane to go back home, ready for another break. Season especially was anxious to arrive, a familiar, unwelcome niggling worry pricking at her conscious since Ty's unusual phone call. The plane touched down back at Heritage. Four men waited on the ground to help them unload and handle Sky Hunter and Doodlebug. Ty's absence stood out.

"Where's Ty?" Season asked the closest man to her.

He shrugged, reaching for a tote of equipment. "Don't know. He just sent word for us to come help. Said he wasn't able to make it down here himself."

A cold ripple ran over Season. Ty would never pass up seeing the plane take off or land unless there was a very good reason. It was important enough for him to always clear his calendar from what she understood from Moose. Automatically, her eyes drifted up to the main house, her every sense telling her she needed to be up there. Seeing things were in good hands, she excused herself and trotted up to the house, concern nipping at her the whole way like an irate terrier.

Breezing in, she found Moose in the hallway, looking concerned. The sight halted her.

130

"It's the Master, Missy. He's upstairs in bed. Took a fall off one of those training buckers in the corral early this morning."

Something lurched inside her, and her heart plummeted. That explained things more now. Words raced around her mind as she slowly understood his behavior on the phone last night. He was still practicing with those wretched things but couldn't tell her so. And now ... Tears choked her throat.

"Has he been seen by a doctor yet?" was the only question she managed to get out.

Moose shook his head. "Nope. Refused to go and refused to send for one." He nodded to the stairs. "Go on, Missy. See to him for yourself. Don't let his fierceness chase you away."

Remembering the horror stories Moose had told her about years past, she had to wonder how badly injured he was. Perhaps enough so that he couldn't ride the Widow Maker in a few weeks. She knew it was horrible to think that way and guilt niggled at her conscience. Mounting the stairs, she halted just before his closed door, drawing in a deep breath. Fierceness. Apparently, he didn't make a good patient. That was so typical. Knocking once, she squared her shoulders and swung the door open.

Ty sat on the edge of the bed, clad in only the briefest pair of undershorts. Her breath caught at the sight of him. Firm chest peppered with blond curls, wide shoulders, and bare feet so small, they looked like they belonged on a woman. She immediately loved his small feet.

"Now who doesn't know how to knock?" Ty growled sarcastically, his face drawn and pinched. He grunted softly as he tried to rise, paled and slid back to the edge again, scowling fiercely.

She suspected it was more at his own pain and limitations and not so much at her personally. She fought back a grin, her anger and concern temporarily forgotten. He may look pale and shaky, but there was nothing wrong with his memory or biting tongue.

"Now don't you get snippy with me, Mr. Ty Masters." She strode up to him, hands planted on her hips, glaring down at him. Ignoring his sarcasm, she studied his bruising marks. "I can't believe you. Despite all we talked about and everything about Scotty, you are still determined to ride that stupid horse. You couldn't even tell me on the phone last night you were practicing. And now look at what happened to you..." She paused for a breath. "I hope it hurts."

"It does," he agreed softly, wincing as he shifted to get up.

"Good. Serves you right. Why are you trying to get up? You should be flat on your back."

Ty gave her a silent scowl, dark and thunderous. He tried once more to gain his footing.

Watching him, she could see the obvious pain. "Now maybe you can be more sensible about this nonsense," she pointed out, as he failed and slid back to the bed again. "This is just insane for one stupid horse."

"Only to you," he grunted, lips fixed as he steadily climbed to his feet. "Important to me."

"Great. Now that you are upright, what do you intend to do next? Go plow the back forty acres?"

He grinned slightly at her barb. Swaying, he took a lurching step toward the door. He made it to the wing back chair, two steps away, planting both hands on the edge. She resisted the impulse to steady him. What could she do to bribe him back to bed and make him stay there? Tie him down? Drug him?

She recalled a comment Moose made not long ago. Perhaps a spell wasn't uncalled for? Eying him speculatively, she had to wonder how much hell would there be to pay for later if she did.

"Do not start harboring any insane notions of your own to make me stay in bed," he growled, casting her another dark warning look.

"I would never dream of it," she lied, smiling sweetly. "Even in your weakened condition, I still could never overpower you."

"As I understand it, you do have abilities to rectify situations such as this one."

"Do you mean, can I make you act sensible? No. I can't make people be less stupid, though I wish I could. Imagine the trouble it could save me," she added, watching as he slowly pushed away from the chair, bringing up a pair of dirty blue jeans that had been tossed there earlier.

"No doubt," he grunted, determination stamped on his face to make the next step. And the next. Season watched, unable to ignore what a fine piece of male he was and how slow he was moving. She grew angry with herself as there really wasn't much of anything she could do to help him. Maybe Moose had a bottle of sleeping pills she could force him to take. Extra strength. In the meantime, as she waited for him to do what he planned to do, she could enjoy the view.

Coiled muscles rolled and flexed as he slowly gathered himself. Sweat broke out, coating his face and shoulders in a fine sheen. The bright blue briefs left little to Season's imagination, and she tried not to let her eyes linger there for too long. She did, however, allow herself a good study of his tight derriere when his back was turned. It was a shame he wanted to put the jeans back on.

"Congratulations on Sky Hunter's most recent victories. You and the men make a great team out there," he said, breathlessly, gripping the denim in a tight fist.

Hearing his words, sincerely spoken, startled Season. She dragged her eyes and mind from his exposed physique, lingering for one final second before meeting his blue eyes. Sweat beaded his brow and his face was puckered with exertion.

"Yes, the men were quite amazed to hear you singing their praises. But aside from that, you must not care much for yourself."

"And what makes you say all that?" He lifted one eyebrow in question. He might have looked better she thought if his eyes weren't glassy and his face so drawn and pale.

"First, apparently you aren't well known for praising people for a job well done. Until lately it seems. And second, you are risking your life and the livelihood of everyone and the future of Heritage Farms for a stupid ride on an equally stupid horse. That tells us you don't care much about yourself."

"No one else has complained."

She snorted, deciding to leave him to his fate. If he hit the floor, there are enough men around who could lift him back to the bed. "No one else around here is going to complain to your face, Mr. High and Mighty. And you know that."

He made two smaller, wobbling steps, stopping and resting his hands on the dresser edge, sweat breaking out all over now. "You need not worry your pretty little head. Nothing will happen to Heritage or anyone here. Regardless what happens to me, the future of this place, and all the inhabitants, are assured." He paused, sucking in shallow breaths. "Now, is there anything else?"

"Yes, forget all this nonsense and come back to bed. I can't begin to tell you how terrible you look."

"I can only imagine."

She pressed closer to his side, feeling his pain. It was hard not to feel the assorted aches and pains prodding him. Sympathy warred with anger. "I don't understand you," she said softly, touching his shoulder, then jerking away as he recoiled from her touch.

She got a flash of him falling, landing in the dirt, the hard, breathless impact to one side. He felt like a smoking volcano swaying beside her, promising to blow—when was the question. She doubted he had enough steam left in him right now to manage much of an explosion.

"You're lucky. You could have done much worse," she said, touching his other arm. "You could have easily done worse than dislocating your shoulder."

He drew back, eyes startled at first. "How did you know?" he asked, pausing and wagging his head. "Never mind," he muttered, his eyes flattening into dark pools of determination, his jaw set in stubbornness as he wobbled once more toward the doorway. "I have things to do. Unless I'm mistaken, so do you. Now go get busy."

"I am busy," she persisted. "Busy trying to keep you from killing yourself. Trying to get you to stop this madness. My word, Ty, you can barely stand!" Tears choked her as she pictured Scotty again in her mind. Or was it Ty crushed under the horse she saw instead?

"And why the blazes is this crusade so important to you?"

Desperation gripped her. All she could see was a man falling in the dirty ground, pounded to death by slashing hooves. Horror and grief swept her like cold, blowing winds. She couldn't stand by and watch another man be hurt at the mercy of an angry horse.

"Maybe it's because I care about you!" she exclaimed, feeling her face flush under his sudden stare.

He blinked twice, clearly startled at her announcement. "That was your second mistake," he murmured gruffly, limping heavily across the hall into the bathroom.

Second mistake? What did he mean by that? What was her first mistake? Staring at the closed door, she knew it would be a while before he came back out. Drifting downstairs, his final words echoing around her mind, she limply dropped to a bar stool and looked over at Moose as he dried dishes.

"What is wrong with him?" she asked numbly.

"He's just upset at being done in by a horse. His pride is more hurt than his body right now. He's been in a bad mood since you left and it got worse. He was a devil for us to bring inside and tend to. But then again, he's always in a foul mood when you leave for the races. Now that you're back, maybe I can convince him to take some pain medication," he finished, picking up and rattling an industrial sized bottle of pills.

"Really? Why? Does he worry about his horses that much?" She felt foolish to ask such a question, knowing it had nothing to really do with the horses, but rebelling at the truth in her heart.

Filling a glass with cold water, he paused, studying her. "He loves you. And it scares him to death. It scares him far worse than thinking about anything those fool horses could do to him."

She sat there, knowing it was true. Just hearing Moose verbalize the truths made them so much more real. Where she had to accept them, putting them where she could no longer ignore their persistent nudging at her. The final heart string that she had thought was permanently knotted slowly came untied within her chest.

"Are you going after him?" Moose asked, hearing a couple thumps upstairs. "He won't travel far." He placed the tray with water glass and pill bottle on the counter.

"No," Season said slowly, still digesting Moose's words, still picturing the image of an exploding volcano. "I think I'll wait till after the smoke clears before I talk to him again."

Moose grinned, moving out from the counter. "If you ask me, it seems things are just starting to heat up," Chuckling, he headed for the stairs balancing the tray.

❦ 10 ❦

Season arose early the next morning, showered and headed downstairs for some coffee. Not even Moose was up yet so she measured the beans, poured the water, and turned the machine on.

She sat in the semi darkness, and listened to the percolating noises of the machine as it brewed, savoring the rich smell of freshly brewed coffee. When it finished, she poured two mugs and headed back upstairs. Topping the steps, she heard a telltale thump coming from Ty's room. Knocking once, she toed the door open, already knowing what she would find.

"Where are you going, Mister?" she asked, stepping into the room. He was half on the bed, with his knees on the floor, clearly having tried to stand up, slid down, and missed the bed.

He eyed her standing there with the mugs. The fresh coffee mixed with the manly, musky scent of his room both combined to fill her brain with cotton. She drew in a big breath, finding her focus.

"I have things to do," he argued. "It is only a bruised shoulder. I have spent way too much time lying about."

"Well, I disagree," Season said, setting the mugs down on his dresser. "You can't even stand. Besides, it's more than a bruise on your shoulder. And what about those ribs? Your body needs more time than a day in which to recover from all the stress and trauma it experienced."

"So you're a doctor now?"

"Don't have to be, though I wish you would consider seeing one. But I know you won't." She took a sip of her coffee, noticing how he eyed the mugs. "So what exactly are your plans for the day, if I may ask? Go muck stalls or take a brisk trot?"

Pulling himself up by one arm, he finally managed to make it to a sitting position once more, breathing from the effort. "Breakfast or a shower. I was trying to decide which one was more pressing."

"Um. Well I could offer you a better option," she suggested mildly.

He cast her a wary look. "What do you have in mind?"

"Relax. Nothing bad. I was thinking of bringing you breakfast in bed and then a sponge bath."

He grinned, eyes crinkling in humor for the first time. "Ah, sweet Season, you do know how to tempt a man. Tell me though, why not just do that fae touch on me instead? In ten minutes I would be all healed and ready to roll again."

"Ready to fall again, you mean." She shook her head. "Even if I wanted to, it's not fair to rob your body of this recovery and rest time it needs. Using any powers like that would be more of a way to cheat or short change your body."

He eyed her. "Um, yet you wouldn't mind using those same powers to keep me quiet here against my will. And that wouldn't be cheating or short changing me? It could almost be called kidnapping."

She scowled. "A little over dramatic, don't you think, Ty? Yes, I did consider it last night when you were being so pig headed and foolish. But today you are much more sensible, right?'

He didn't answer.

"Do you have any other explanations for what you call your behavior? Any I would understand?" She thought they might go another round. He glared at her, his thoughts closed, guarded, a suspicious, and weary look in his eyes. She wondered which one would win out in the end.

"So what are my options?" he finally asked, followed by a heavy sigh.

"Plenty," she said happily, seeing weariness was winning him over. "But I suggest you getting back in bed. Here's your coffee. I'll get you some breakfast next and then make sure you get a nice sponge bath. That's a good place to start. No need for crazy notions or kidnapping if we all behave logically. Right?"

He heaved another sigh, holding out his hand for the coffee. "I believe you are enjoying this a little too much, Season."

She grinned broadly, turning for the door. "Not at all. It's the sponge bath I'm looking forward to."

❧

"So how's the patient?" Moose asked as Season collapsed onto a bar stool, dropping her head on her arms and heaving a sigh.

"He is as bratty as that racehorse of his," she said, her voice muffled against the counter. "Do you have any strong chocolate?"

"I have some chocolate liqueur. Do you think that would cure him?"

"It's not for Ty. It's for me. Yes, that poured into a cup of strong coffee would help me a lot."

Moose chuckled. "I'll see what I can mix up for you, Missy."

Once he submitted to her orders, he made it clear it was only within the limits he still set. He was exhausting her with his demands and just the constant close proximity was wearing on her. The running up and down the stairs with trays of food three times a day was fine. Except he complained about the food Moose had prepared. More to irk her she suspected than an actual complaint at Moose's cooking. The worse part was the sponge baths.

She'd been flippant when she told him she was looking forward to them, now she wished Moose or the other men would take over. She tried her best to maintain a professional distance and wondered how nurses did it every day with patients. The water, filled with scented oils, gliding over his tanned skin had her biting her lip enough to draw blood. She swallowed back a few moans of excitement. The proximity to his skin, his muscles, his eyes, his perfect physique, was more than rattling her. And he knew it! From the smug look on his face, she saw he gloried in being able to cause it.

Today, after another bath, she felt as rung out as at the cloth she was using to wash him. Finished, she dumped the water down the drain and fled downstairs, in need of her own medication.

"Here you go, Missy," Moose set the mug before her, steam rising. Cocoa and coffee filtered through the air. "When was the last time you stuck your head outside?" he asked, resting his elbows on the counter beside her.

"I don't know," she answered, raking a hand through her hair. Had she even washed it today? She couldn't remember. "How many days since I got back?" she asked, taking a sip from the mug. The strong taste of liqueur felt good in her mouth. Chocolate cured a lot of wounds.

"Three."

"That's it? Three days? It sure feels like weeks with him."

Moose chuckled again. "I'm sure the Master will survive an hour without you. Why don't you go outside? Take a walk. Check the horses. Take a ride. Anything. Just get away for a little while. You need a break from him."

"That is a great idea, Moose. He's sleeping now anyway." She slugged the last of her drink down and handed the mug over. "Thanks. You're a real pal. Sometimes I don't know what I would do without you."

His chuckle followed her down the hall and to the front door. She grabbed her jacket from the peg and soon realized she didn't need it. When had spring arrived? She felt warm breezes blowing around and warm sunshine and noticed puddles of mud where the snow had melted. When did this happen? Standing there, a few feet from the door, she stared around her. All this happened in just a few days?

Flowers poked their colorful heads up, winking at the bright sunshine. To the left, away from the barns was freshly broken ground. A garden started. No doubt Moose's?

Looking beyond the farm, the towering mountains were shedding their snowy caps. Neighing horses drew her to the corral holding the rented training buckers. An involuntary shudder crawled over Season as she wondered which one of the brutes had given Ty that jarring throw. In retrospect, she knew she couldn't really blame the horses. They were not the killers Widow Maker was. And no one made Ty get on them except his own fierce pride. Blaming the horses accomplished nothing good.

Following the colorful little flowers, she made her way to the stallion barn. Maybe she could get a little work done upstairs. Walking the aisle, looking at the horses left inside, she knew she'd get no work done upstairs. She wasn't in the mood. Sky Hunter was out in the near paddock, cantering around with his buddy, Doodlebug. Richmond was grazing in another paddock. Bold Raven and a couple other stallions were in their paddocks, grazing or napping in the spring sunshine.

Black Warrior was alone at the far end, as he seldom went out at daytime without Ty. Stopping at the old stallion's stall, she wondered if he'd been out at all since Ty's injury. Few others could handle taking him in and out.

As if reading her thoughts, the old stallion shook his head, pawed and snorted, sounding as impatient as his princely son.

"I bet you miss him, don't you boy?" she said to the horse, careful to keep a safe distance between them. "And you're probably bored sick of being stuck in here too, aren't you?"

The stallion shook and pawed, throwing his long mane, covering his eyes.

"Wanna go for a ride, old horse?"

Again, Black Warrior snorted, bobbing his head.

She paused, a thought blooming. "Do you promise to behave yourself? No shenanigans?"

Knowing she was foolish for talking to him like that and crazier still for even thinking of what she was thinking, she knew there was no turning back. She rested her hand on the brass latch, and slowly slid the bolt over, her eyes never leaving the stallion's. Her every sense attuned to him. This could blow up into a horrible disaster.

If he bolted and she was unable to catch him, or if he remained loose in the barn when the other stallions were brought in later, he could cause a horrible commotion. Or worse, if someone walked in, not knowing he was running free, he could react violently. And don't forget how enraged Ty would be if his personal stallion killed or maimed an employee or other stallion. What if Black Warrior injured Sky Hunter? A shiver crept over her at the thought.

Yep, she was crazy to even think this, but she wasn't about to stop now. The horse's impatient whinny moved her forward.

Never breaking eye contact, her fingers picked up his leather bridle and she took one step into his stall, every muscle ready to spring back if he darted.

Docile, he stood, though clearly eager to get going. He wobbled his small ears as she lifted the bridle to his head and fastened the buckles.

"Okay, boy, so far so good," Letting out a slow breath, she gave the door a push and led him out into the corridor, to the cross ties and snapped him in place. Other than a restless pawing of his front feet, he waited like a well-schooled horse while she tacked him up. Gathering the reins, she swung aboard. Immediately, she could feel the enormous energy inside the stallion, the kind of power that had made him famous on the racetracks. Eyeing the track in the distance, she again spoke low and soft to the stallion quivering beneath her.

"How long has it been since you've felt a track beneath your feet? Fifteen years or so? Let's see if you remember what to do on one." Nudging him, she allowed him to pick his most comfortable pace. He may be a vicious monster, but he was still quite aged and it would be unfair to run him like a young colt. Warming up both their muscles, she simply held on as he made three easy laps around the track at a brisk canter. Still seeing he was ready to go further, she eyed the mountains in the distance.

"Why not, old boy? Let's go." Guiding him off the track, she pointed him in the direction of her favorite retreat and urged him forward, again letting him pick a comfortable gallop he liked.

If riding Sky Hunter was like riding the wind, this was like riding the fiercest storm. While he did not fight her, because she was letting him run as he liked, he still had so much unbelievable power and energy coursing inside him. Trying to rein him in against his will would be like trying to wrestle a tornado with one hand and rope a hurricane with the other. Just plain impossible.

She had to marvel at the sheer raw power the horse was made of. Like the toughest iron and steel and metal all combined into one creature and shaped like a horse.

And it felt so good to just go along for the ride. Black Warrior clearly was having a delightful time, tossing his head at the wind, glorying in stretching his legs longer and longer, his breathing coming faster as he pushed himself, nostrils expanding as he scooped in more air.

Was he reliving his days on the tracks? Was he just happy to be free of the confinements of the stall and barn? Was he simply delighting in the sheer freedom of the moment? Moving a hand to rest on his pulsing neck, she caught only the passion of the run, the dizzying drunkenness of the speed, the reckless abandon of being free with nature, and the simple pleasure of spring grass beneath his hooves.

As they neared the edge of the mountain woods, she felt him begin to slow down. Again, she neither encouraged nor pulled his reins, allowing him to pick his pace. He came to a walk and made his way through the trees, coming to a stop at a small brook, now swollen with fresh, cold melted mountain snow. Sliding off, Season allowed him to drink, moving upstream and kneeling down for a drink herself. Admittedly, her knees were shaking a little. She was actually riding the legendary Black Warrior!

"That was quite a ride there, Warrior old boy," she praised, patting the horse's neck as he drank deeply. Finished, he raised his head, water dripping off his muzzle. Season tentatively reached out to stroke his muzzle, finding it soft and velvety. He stood, watching her, making no moves to attack.

"You're not a monster like everyone thinks," she said softly, still stroking the velvet muzzle.

"You are not a devil horse," she declared, his dark eyes never leaving her face. "You are a sadly mistaken horse. A mere horse that people just don't understand." Ruffling the long hair covering his eyes, she planted an impetuous kiss on his black forehead.

In that one touch, she knew he was no danger. She connected with him, reading his heart and spirit, seeing what made him the creature he was. And she loved him.

"Okay, Black Warrior, are you ready to go back? Just an easy stroll back home? I probably should see how your daddy is doing." Swinging up in the saddle, she gently turned him around and let him move into an easy gallop.

Coming back into the yard half an hour later, she spotted Ernie, the delivery boy, getting into his car. She waved at him, smiling. Seeing the horse she was mounted on, his jaw dropped. Standing upright, he offered her a sharp salute followed by a youthful grin and he slid back into his car. She dismounted and started hot walking him, noticing the startled looks from the men passing by. Smiling broadly, she took him back inside, groomed him and then stabled him, ending with giving him a peppermint from the supply she kept cached away in the tack room.

"Thanks, Black Warrior, I needed that as bad as you did," she said, patting him on his neck as he noisily crunched the peppermint.

"Where have you been?" Ty's voice caught her as she topped the stairs and approached his room. Stepping in, she saw he was once again in the position of someone trying to get out of bed and failed.

"I've been out riding. I took Black Warrior up to the mountains."

Incredulous, he paused, looking at her. "*My* Black Warrior?"

Laughing, she bent to help him back to bed. "Exactly how many Black Warrior's do you have?"

"Just the one, of course."

"Then I suppose that was the one I took riding." She stood there, studying him. "I ordered some supplies that Ernie might have brought today. They would be good for you now that I think about it."

Again, she was rewarded with that wary look. "And what might that be? Eye of newt? Bat wings?"

"Epsom salts and some things like chamomile and lavender oils. It would be beneficial for a jarred body," she said as she adjusted his pillow, ignoring his barb. "Yes, after lunch, I think a good soak in the bathtub would be just perfect for you."

He slid her a long grin. "Are you offering to wash my back?"

"No, I'm offering to help your bruised body to heal. Nothing more and nothing less. I'll be back with your lunch in a little bit."

His call stopped her at the door. "Season, why did you take Black Warrior out?"

She smiled back. "Because he said he wanted to go."

⚬⚬⚬

One hour later Ty eased a contented sigh, slowly sinking deeper into the tub. Season had been right, the salts and oils were working on his battered body, erasing the aches and pains. And they smelled so much like her, making him feel drunk on the scents enveloping him.

What a woman. What had made her even think of taking Black Warrior for a ride? He smiled, recalling her cheeky comeback. Surely the horse hadn't verbalized a desire to go for a ride to her? Had he? With that woman, it was hard to say.

While his conventional mind told him it was impossible to happen, he

144

also had seen enough since her arrival to know nothing was impossible. At least with her.

There was an old television show, decades ago, about a talking horse called Ed. His drunken mind easily pictured his black stallion and her conversing over the barn door, and the horse clearly saying he felt up to a bit of a ride.

"Utter nonsense," he chided himself. "Absurd. The woman is playing with your patience."

Yet the images played through his mind, refusing to go. Eyes closed, relaxed, cocooned in warm water that pulled the pains from his body and smelling of lavender fields, he felt himself involuntarily drifting off. He sailed away to some ethereal place where women fluttered about like faeries and horses were able to speak English like a man. Grass grew long, butterflies and bees merrily buzzed and trees were home to mists and mysteries. Whispers echoed off each other, riding the wind. And in the center of this odd little place frolicked a coal black stallion, fiery and fierce. And a wisp of a woman, shimmering in her gown of the palest gold and hair hanging in a long tangle of brown curls, and with the prettiest, bewitching green eyes.

Watching them, he ached to touch her, to hear that beautiful laughter, wanting it to be for him. To see those enchanting eyes look at him and sparkle like the countless twinkling lights surrounding them. To seize that captivating spirit and hold her, to see if she were real and not some imaginary figment. To perhaps love her, capturing her with a kiss. To keep her, learning her secrets. To join in courtship with her, loving her as woman like her ought to be loved—tenderly, slowly, and fully.

What a lucky man one would be to come out of that surreal place with the heart of the woman and the friendship of the stallion.

11

"You have done well, Missy. The Master has come back quicker than anyone expected," Moose praised over breakfast a few days later. "You must have a magic touch with him." He winked at her.

"Not quite the touch," she hedged between bites. It was more likely the fear of magic that kept him more or less submissive to her, she figured. "He's been a real handful, that's for sure."

Moose grunted in agreement, nodding his head once. "No one else would envy you the job of tending to him."

"Yes, funny, but I did notice a complete lack of willing volunteers lining up that day. Or any day since," she pointed out, smiling. Who could blame the poor guys? Certainly not her. But it hadn't been all bad, she had to remind herself. There had been a few moments that would forever stay etched in her mind. Moments when she was privileged to see the tender side to Ty.

Like last night for example. He had just started coming downstairs since his second soaking bath, promising to just sit and relax, stating he needed a change of scenery. Agreeing he probably did, she relented. Coming back inside last night, she went to check on him. What she found melted her heart. Following the dim lights to the library, she halted half way in the room, hand on her chest.

He was lying, stretched out on the sofa, open book splayed across his chest. One arm was flung up over his head, the other folded by his side. His bare feet hung over the edge of the sofa. About to call his name, she realized he was sound asleep, the lamp light making him appear so much more relaxed and ... tamer. Gently plucking the book from his chest, she listened to the light, regular breathing, watching the steady rise and fall of his chest. She giggled at his soft rumbling snore. Finally, pulling a light blanket from the ottoman, she spread it across him and reached over to extinguish the lamp above his head. She could have stayed and watched him sleep forever, but in the end, she forced herself to go upstairs alone, knowing she'd been privileged to see a rare side of Ty Masters.

***

The next day Ty stood at the window looking wistfully out at the bronc horses in the corral. Season came in, leaned against the threshold, her arms crossed. He turned to her, taken aback by the sad look in her eye.

"Is there something you needed?" he asked.

"Ty, I don't think you're getting this," she said. "Come on, let's take a trip."

Surprised, but pleased at the suggestion of going somewhere, he headed for the door. "Are you willing to have me drive us?"

"We're not going by car. Take my hand."

Ty's hand touched her warm, soft skin. Before he could enjoy the pleasure, they were gone, magically transported—elsewhere. He looked around at the dirt floored arena below them and heard the snorting horses and the yelling of the crowds around them.

"Season!" He hissed in amazement, eyes round, and his heart pounding. "What have you done?"

"Relax, they can't see or hear us."

He blinked, looking at the people seated next to them. "You mean to say we're ... invisible?"

She nodded, her eyes on the scenes below.

"Another of your skills?"

She nodded again, this time turning back to look at him. There was no mistaking the despondency in her eyes. Swallowing hard, he looked around the groups of people. A young woman seated by herself two rows away caught his eye. Sudden realization dawned on him, sending a shiver over him. It was Season, years younger, cheering on a young blond man on a horse in the arena below.

My word! She'd taken him back to the event she attended with her cousin. Was this the final one in which he met his death? If so, the younger Season had no clue of what was to come. Looking so lovely, she enthusiastically cheered on the plucky rider down below.

Were they really invisible? How could she manage such a feat? As if to confirm his doubt, Season waved her hand before the face of the person sitting next to her. The fan was oblivious, staring at the rider below. Ty swallowed around the knot in his throat.

In the past, he had sensed her, wondering if she were somehow near him and he wasn't able to see her. This, right now, confirmed she could. Accepting that fact as real, he watched her return her attention to the rider, her expression so sad compared to the one worn by her younger self just a couple of rows over. He shook his head. This was madness!

Just when Ty thought he was growing dizzy, the ride was over. Her cousin had defeated the horse and hopped down, arms raised in victory. Cheers erupted around the stands. Suddenly, without warning, the horse twisted around, plunging into the young man. He was instantly swallowed by the size of the brute, ground into the dirt floor.

The younger Season gasped, horrified, rushing forward as she screamed his name. Scotty. Even the Season beside him leaned forward, about to lunge, barely able to restrain herself, tears falling silently. Ty ached for her pain, so real today as it was that day long ago he was witnessing now.

He wordlessly took her into his arms, cradling her head into his shoulder, blocking her view below. Holding her, he watched the younger version of herself rush past the crowds and the horse to reach her dead cousin. She dropped next to him and cradled his body in her arms. She sobbed loudly, tears running unchecked down her face as she sat in the dirt and rocked his mangled, misshapen body. Her pain was so real, it stunned him, leaving him trembling at the raw sights and sounds.

Suddenly, they were back in his library. Shocked, it took a moment for him to readjust his mind. Watching her cool gaze, he suddenly felt horrible. Lowest of the low.

"I'm sorry you had to show me that," he said slowly. "But I still have to ride that horse."

Something flickered in her eyes. "Then you are a bigger fool than I realized, Ty Masters." Spinning on her heel, she left the room.

⌘

"I need a break before I go batty," Ty complained a few mornings later after breakfast. "I feel better, enough so to get up and walk around."

"You have been up and walking around," Season reminded him, as if consoling a pouting child.

He shot her a dark look. "I mean as in outside. To see something different."

He had a point. It had been just over a week and so far, he had only been as far as the library in the last day or so. And the trip back to the past, of which neither spoke of again. Perhaps a short walk outdoors would be good for him. It would certainly be good for her.

"Fine. Just a short walk outside, get some fresh air. No riding, no climbing, or anything else crazy," she warned, ignoring his scowl. "Come on then."

The sunshine was warm as it greeted them, only too soon disappearing behind some thick clouds.

"It's spring already," Ty said in awe, standing on the front steps.

"Yes, it surprised me a few days ago too. I swear it was still winter just a couple days ago."

"To the stallion barn," Ty commanded with a pointed finger. "I want to see the stallions."

Season slowly stepped off the step, taking his weight, staggering a little. Where were the men when she needed them? Hiding no doubt. If Ty noticed their absence, he did not mention it.

A clap of thunder drew her eyes upward. "Uh, Ty, are you sure about this? Maybe tomorrow might be better."

"By tomorrow I shall be mad as a hatter."

"So how will that be any different?"

"Funny, babe."

She cringed under the nickname, deciding if he wanted to continue, so be it. But she would bet a thunderstorm was coming.

They made slow, awkward progress across the yard to the stallion barn. He stopped frequently to marvel at the flowers and other sights, to check all was still well in his kingdom. Ten feet from the barn door, the thunder crashed overhead, the skies opened, and icy-cold rain poured out like overflowing buckets. Instantly, both were drenched with chilling water.

"I tried to warn you!" Season exclaimed at Ty's surprised yelp. Flinging the door open, she ushered him inside and slid it shut behind them, the rain driving hard and biting the wooden door.

"We need to get some of this soaked clothing off," Ty said, looking around. "Up there," he said, pointing to the hay loft.

Skeptical, she shot him a look. "Are you sure? Up the ladder?"

He nodded. "The view will make it worth the effort," he promised her.

It took some effort, but they made the climb. Straddling bales of hay, Season opened the loft door, amazed at the spectacular view of the storm's fury. Thunder cracked, lightening flashed, and rain fell in heavy sheets. Inside they were safe, watching the fury though the loft door. It was, she had to admit, worth the effort.

"Here, take your shirt off, let it dry," Season said. She took it as he handed it over and wrung it out. She took her over shirt off, wringing it out as well and leaving her camisole on, acutely aware of Ty's interested stare. Okay, she knew a wet lacy camisole left little to man's imagination, but there wasn't much she could do about it now. She draped both shirts over other bales of hay, hoping they would dry soon.

Drawing his eyes away, back to the storm outside, Ty heaved a sigh. "I have always enjoyed watching storms," he admitted. "When I first bought this place, I soon discovered this was the prime spot for storm watching. Perhaps because in England there are so many thunderstorms."

Season moved closer, eager to hear something personal. "Perhaps in some way it reminds you of England."

"Perhaps," he said, nodding, still not taking his eyes off the raging storm outside. "It's one of the reasons I so love it here." He ran a wet fingertip over her camisole strap, igniting a warm trail over her shoulder, but kept his attention on the storm.

She saw a wistfulness in his eyes, felt a heaviness in his heart. Was he homesick for his native land? Did the thunderstorm take him back somehow?

Unable to stop herself, she moved until she was sitting behind him, straddling the same bale of hay. Cupping her hands, she blew a gentle breath into them and vigorously rubbed them together. Reaching out, she gently touched Ty's shoulder, waiting for his recoil. There was none. There was an initial quick intake of breath, then he stilled, then he slowly relaxed against her touch.

Using first her fingertips, she explored the muscles beneath the skin, moving in sweeping circles, finding the sore spots. Closing her eyes, hearing only his shallow breathing and the fury of the storm outside as rain pelted the tin roof in rhythm, she massaged his shoulders, first one and then the other.

He relaxed, melting into her touch, his head bobbing to rest on his chest.

Next, she moved up to his neck, rubbing her fingers along from his jawline back and down to where it met between his shoulder blades and then rolled over around his throat to his collar bone.

From there, she moved over his chest, weaving her fingers through the curly hair. A low groan escaped him as her fingers traced around his nipples.

Reaching the ribs, she sought the cracked ones. Finding two, she gently worked to knit the bones beneath her touch, drawing him back against her chest.

"Oh, mercy, Season, you shall be the death of me," he murmured, eyes closed and voice thick.

She smiled, silently continuing her ministrations. The thunder outside complemented her touches, lighting flashes streaked across the sky, and rain drummed the roof, all echoing her trailing fingertips across his skin. The steady pelting of the raindrops beat the wooden walls like the steady pounding of their heartbeats. They all worked in unison, in harmony, building to a fevered pitch before releasing with another savage rumble.

Finally, Ty sucked in a deep breath and captured her hands, stilling her movements. He swiveled her around to face him, waiting till she straddled the same bale.

"Why did you not do that a week ago?"

She smiled. "Do you feel better?"

"Much." He paused, as if taking stock of himself. "What did you do to me just now?"

"Nothing special. Just a massage."

"Right," he replied, sounding far from convinced. "Odd, but the storm has abated as well. More of your handiwork?" He cocked an eyebrow outside.

"You give me entirely too much credit, Ty." She laughed. "Sudden, random spring thunderstorms are to be expected here. You should know that. It was already starting to build before we came outside. Remember?"

"What was that song you were singing?" he asked, ignoring her question.

"I wasn't aware I was. Sorry, I don't know. Must be some unconscious reflex I suppose."

He gave her a long look, unspoken questions in his eyes. Finally, he gave a wag of his head. "I just never know what to expect with you. If just a massage can make me feel better now, why not do it a week ago?"

"Because it wouldn't have had the same effect then."

He laughed, rich and quick. "Oh, I disagree. You have no idea the effect it had."

"I mean, the effect on your body," she clarified.

"So did I."

❧

The plane rose steadily higher, banking right and heading southeast. Seated beside Season, Ty slid her a long, guarded look. She and Ty had maintained a distance since the afternoon they rode out the thunderstorm in the hayloft a few days before. With effort, they both kept their relationship purely professional, staying focused on Sky Hunter's big week.

And now it was here. It was Season's first flight in which Ty traveled with, and was staying with, for the week. This was going to be the first race in which she did not have the evenings to look forward to his silky soft voice reaching out and caressing her through the phone lines, complaining about everything that had gone wrong, whether her fault or not.

Instead, she had the living, breathing man only a few feet away for a whole week. There was no escape. She could feel the tension from the guys, noticing how they tried, and failed, to act casual just because the Master was on board. There were no card games, no music, no jokes from Stan, no relaxed comradeship. She guided a strand of hair behind her ear. It was going to be a long week.

Finally, once the horses were settled, she leaned back in her seat, closing her eyes. She was going to need some peace of mind to stay focused this week. And it was definitely going to be a test of sorts for her based on how well Sky Hunter ran and behaved.

Touching down, the men eagerly set to work, as if glad to have something to do with the watchful eye of the Master upon them. Taking her customary place in the back of the trailer with the horses, she overheard Ty's surprised question to Eddie. "Why is she staying back there?"

"She always rides with the horses, Boss." She hustled in behind Sky Hunter, eager to escape his startled response.

At the barn, Season stayed glued to Sky Hunter. The festival atmosphere of the place was making the big colt more nervous than normal.

"Is he always like this?" Ty asked as he stood and watched him break into a light sweat and mill around his stall, nearly crushing Season half a dozen times.

"It's Derby Week," she pointed out, trying for patience for both the colt and the man. "There is a little more commotion right now than normal, so he is overreacting a little more than normal. Give him some time." And space.

Please, Hunter Boy, don't make me look so bad in front of the boss, please.

Dodging his hooves as he swirled around in yet another circle, she turned her back on Ty, capturing the colt's halter in both hands, forcing him to stand still. He bobbed his head, snorting at the touch. Placing both palms on either side of his cheeks, she laced them under the halter, moving her fingertips in slow circles over his face. Closing her eyes, she crowded out the sounds of laughter and the din of endless noises from all around them.

Whispering soft and low, she pleaded Sky Hunter to settle. Beside her, Doodlebug nosed first her and then Sky Hunter's shoulder, nickering.

Sky Hunter's small ears swiveled around, catching every pop and boom around the barns, gradually pricking them forward to catch Season's soft, lilting, whispering coo. The more he heard her whisper soft coo and felt her feathery strokes, the more he forgot about the monsters outside the stall. His dropped his massive head to her shoulder like a giant lapdog, eyes half closed and nickering softly.

"Good boy," she praised in another soft whisper. Patting the white blaze on his forehead, she gave him a gentle kiss. "Such a good boy."

Turning, she was startled to see Ty standing at the stall door, transfixed.

"You just hypnotized that horse."

"I did not," she said, still keeping her voice soft and low. "I just took his mind off the bigger worries outside and gave him some good thoughts to consider inside."

Holding the door open for her, he slid the bolt shut behind her. "I sort of feel I'm in your way," he admitted slowly, looking around. "All of you."

She smiled at that. "We are a good team. You have even said that. We all know what to do and just do it." She winked up at him. "Besides, we're a bit more on our toes because the boss is here this time."

"Ah, so it's my unusual appearance that makes for such efficiency?" he joked back. "Perhaps I must clear my calendar so I can travel to the races more often."

She gasped in mock horror, looking around to see if anyone overheard. "Don't you dare! It would forever ruin our fun and games. These trips would become nothing more than just plain and simple work. How positively dreadful!"

Their eyes met over the shared laughter, holding a few seconds longer than intended.

"Well, I need to see to Winter's Dawn," Season said, letting out a sudden breath. "Excuse me, Ty," She gave him a quick bow.

"Until later," he offered her a salute.

⁂

"So, Season, now that we have made it here, what are your plans for Sky Hunter?" Ty asked her later over dinner.

Swallowing a bite, she gave him a puzzled look. "Well, I rather thought we would race him," she said, earning low chuckles from her coworkers.

"I believe you were the one so confident he is Triple Crown material. So here we are, on the first leg so to speak," he clarified. "What do you plan to do differently to make sure he wins?"

"Depends on how soon he settles down from the festival atmosphere that has him so nervous. Other than that, just let him run his own race."

"And Winter's Dawn? Will she earn her Triple Tiara as well?"

Season shook her head. "Not this year. She's too social still. She might place well in the races, but she won't win the Tiara. She just doesn't have it in her right now."

Ty set his wine glass down. "That is a shame. It would have been nice to attend the post balls with both a Triple Crown winner and a Triple Tiara winner at hand."

"Well, I suppose so, but I won't be attending any balls while in town."

He raised an eyebrow. "Why not? For someone so sure your horse is going to win, you don't plan on attending the Julep Ball?"

Heat flushed her cheeks and she moved food around her plate. "I ... I didn't bring a gown," she muttered to her plate. How could she admit she did not own any fancy ball gowns?

Cocking his head to one side, he studied her carefully. "No matter. We can certainly find you a suitable gown in one of the shops in town. You would look stunning in something blue," he paused, a distant look in his eye. "Or perhaps pale gold."

More heat filled her face, from his lingering, faraway stare. "Maybe. We'll see," she commented, hoping it was the wine making him look at her that way with talk of balls and gowns and wearing that dreamy look. It was upsetting. And the stares from her coworkers weren't helping.

⚛

"Season, I have to ask you this, please don't get mad, okay?" Eddie said, getting her attention the next morning. They were saddling up Sky Hunter in the pre-dawn darkness. They were alone for a few minutes while everyone else went to do other tasks.

"I never get mad at you, Eddie. What's up?"

"The guys and I were talking last night, after dinner you know. And we were wondering about you and the Master." Eddie hesitated, looking around them before plunging ahead. "Are you two dating or something?"

"Ty and me dating?" Her hands stilled on the bridle. "What makes you ask that?"

"Because you two sure act like it sometimes, especially last night. When you're not arguing with each other. And because you call him Ty. No one ever calls him by that name, except you. Not even the other trainers called him that."

Goodness, did they really act like they were dating? Mercy!

"Eddie, no, we aren't dating. Ty and I just have a close working relationship. That's all."

His face squished up as he considered her explanation. "Well, it sure looks like it's a real close relationship."

"I guess I never noticed that. But to be honest, most days he drives me crazy," she assured, giving him a smile. "Tell the guys it's just business. Now, as for our star here..." She smiled, patting the horse's neck. "No one else is out there now, so let him warm up and run his own pace. Don't make him think he has to fight you. We don't want him tiring out before his big day."

"Right," Eddie sounded doubtful. "This guy? Tired out? I'd love to see it happen."

Taking a moment to survey the grandstand, now void of people and shrouded in overhead lights piercing the darkness, she had to wonder if this was the track in which she had seen Sky Hunter winning in one of her first visions with him. *Perhaps.*

Selecting a seat, she sat down, watching Eddie and the black horse down below. He was frisking, enjoying it now that there was no extra noises and commotion. That would change within the next couple of hours. Her fear was he remained so worked up over the festival noises, he would have nothing to draw from when pressed for the big race on Saturday. All kidding aside about his abilities, he was still just a horse and everyone had their limit. The Derby would test his like nothing had yet so far.

"My money is on the black colt," Ty said softly, easing into the seat next to her.

She smiled at his joke. "I should hope it is. His owner assures me he is an expensive horse."

"Funny, babe," he said, chuckling at her comeback. "So what are your plans with him?"

"You keep asking me that." She turned to him for a second. "And my answer is still the same. Do you have other plans in mind?"

"Actually yes. Since you failed to pack properly for this trip, I plan on the necessity of taking you shopping for a proper gown tonight and then I plan on taking you to the Julep Ball after the Oaks race. We might even make a few more balls before we leave town."

"What about the men?"

He looked puzzled. "They would look rather odd in a gown, I should think."

She laughed. "No, are they going to the balls too?"

"If they packed properly and brought their dress clothes along."

They lapsed into silence, watching Eddie and Sky Hunter circle the track again, lost in their own thoughts.

"He is something to see on a track. Even better in real life than on television," Ty said finally, his voice heavy with satisfaction.

"Wait till you see him Saturday. He's like an explosion of dynamite coming out of the gate. You can actually feel the propulsion when he starts out."

He slid her a look. "You may feel it perhaps. The rest of us mere mortals aren't so lucky."

"Ty," she warned, checking the colt's time as he swept past them. "You forget I'm just like the rest of you mere mortals."

"Oh, babe, you are so wrong there. You have no idea how unlike us you really are."

Going down to the track to help, Ty's words of awe continued to ring in her mind.

❧ 12 ❧

Winter's Dawn entered the starting gate like the Belle of the Ball that she was. So far, she'd been enjoying her Derby Week experience as much as her half-brother was disliking his. Every workout on the track was a social event to her and so they used it to their advantage. They exercised Sky Hunter early in the morning and late at night, always under the cover of darkness. Winter's Dawn was taken out to exercise during daylight hours, when the track was busy, when the stands were occupied, and when noise and activity kept her ears swiveling merrily in every direction.

Now, at last, they were ready for her big debut. The Kentucky Oaks, the derby for the fillies.

"You'll be fine, Dawnie girl," Season cooed in the filly's ear. "Just pay attention out there." Season couldn't put a finger on it, but there was something different about Winter's Dawn this morning, how she carried herself, how she acted. But she couldn't pinpoint it. "What do you think, Eddie?" she asked, "Does she feel different to you?"

"Maybe a little." He frowned, turning her in a tight circle. "Maybe it's just the excitement?"

"That could be it," Season agreed thoughtfully, tapping her chin. Not able to think of a reason not to race her, she turned the reins over to Tommy who ushered the filly into the gate. Season opted to stay in the paddock area to watch, to be closer, rather than join Ty up in one of the lounges. Between shopping for a gown, attending the Parade on Thursday with him, and having him constantly underfoot at the stables, she was just at the point she needed a little time away from him.

Her mind drifted momentarily away, back to the afternoon before. It was during the lull between practices and dinner when Ty summoned her, saying to be ready for a short road trip. She met him at the rental van at the appointed time, wondering what he had in mind. All serious, he simply said he was fulfilling his obligation to society. Rather cryptic, until they stopped at a row of clothing shops. He took her arm, and without another word, and a silly little smile on his face, he escorted her into the third shop down the walk.

Their visit had been arranged beforehand. Within seconds of their arrival, she was whisked away to a separate room and shown racks of gowns. With her protests ignored, she tried on several of the shimmery, beautiful dresses, half afraid to know their cost. More than she was able to afford.

"That one," one of the two attendants told her finally. "That is the one."

Stepping back, Season looked at her image in the full-length mirror. She did look rather good. The gown was the palest shade of lemony gold. Strapless, the bodice wrapped her body like a silken glove and billowed into waves of shimmering silk that rustled around her legs. What would Ty think of this gown?

Reluctantly, she shrugged it off. She was assured that Mr. Masters had authorized her a fine gown, gloves and shoes, no questions asked. Mighty generous of him once again.

Dressed in her regular clothes, she returned to where he waited while the attendants carefully packed everything up for her. Ty already had a small box wrapped up next to him. Taking the packages, again without words but smiling happily, he escorted her back to the van and to the hotel. She smiled at how pleased he was with himself.

"I shall see you at the track in a short while," he said, taking his small package and leaving her at the door to her room.

Now it was post time for the Kentucky Oaks, Winter's Dawn big performance and she needed to bring herself back from that surreal shopping trip with Ty.

Winter's Dawn broke fourth from the gate, tied with another filly.

Pounding around the half turn, they looked good. Winter's Dawn was up nose to nose with the third-place horse. She might actually win, and if all went well, she would certainly place in the money. She lengthened her stride going into the final turn, trying to catch the number two filly.

Something suddenly froze inside of Season, making her heart skip several beats. Eyes still glued to the filly, she felt the horrible picture unfold before she saw it. A popping sound echoed louder than the pounding hooves, Winter's Dawn lurched to her left like a ship listing at sea. Eddie reared back in the saddle to avoid flying over her neck as she toppled toward the railing.

The rest of the field thundered past her as Season rushed out onto the track. By the time she breathlessly reached them, Eddie had dismounted and Winter's Dawn was waving her left front leg uselessly off the ground, holding it as she whinnied plaintively.

"Dawnie, oh, Dawnie, what happened, girl?" Season cried as the filly gave her a painful whinny. Laying her hands on the filly, she could feel the shocked pain beneath the trembling body. "Oh, baby."

Eddie stroked the filly, breathless himself. "She was doing just great. It just happened."

An outrider reached them. "Do you need an ambulance for her?" he asked.

"Yes, please. If we can get her back to the stable," The roar of the crowd told her the Kentucky Oaks had finished and another filly had taken first place.

By the time they had Winter's Dawn safely in the stables, Ty was waiting for them in her stall. Fierce lines etched his face as he stood, arms folded across his chest, waiting for the track veterinarian and Season to finish their examination. The vet was taking films with his portable x-ray machine. Season's heart felt crushed as she realized the filly's injury and saw it confirmed with the veterinarian's sad shake of his head.

Turning, she looked up into Ty's face, knowing how this was going to impact him. His high hopes for Winter's Dawn ... and now this. Her heart just crumbled.

"Bowed tendon," the vet said gently, shaking his head again. "I'm sorry, Mr. Masters." He hesitated a moment before adding, "Who do you know would want to intentionally cause this kind of harm to your horse?"

"Intentionally?" Ty blinked, looking from the vet to Season. "You mean someone purposely did this to Winter's Dawn? Deliberately?"

"Yes, Mr. Masters, that is exactly what I'm saying," the vet confirmed, closing his medical bag. "Bowed tendons happen in horses, it's a fact of anatomy. But someone well-schooled in the composition of a horse's leg can also know how to make a tendon bow. Come look at this."

Season moved aside as the vet motioned for Ty to kneel in the straw in front of the filly. She only half heard the kindly old vet's descriptions and explanation as he pointed things out to Ty. She did hear Ty's surprise and disbelief. Not only did his prized filly just suffer a potentially devastating and career defining injury, to make it even worse, someone purposely caused it to happen.

"Thank you, Doctor, I do appreciate the education and your frank candor," Ty said finally. He stood up and gave Winter's Dawn a sad pat. "Of course we want the best for this girl. I value your opinions as well." He cast a look over at Season before ending, "I shall require a word or two with my trainer." He shook the kindly old man's hand and escorted him to the outer corridor.

Coming back inside the stall, he stood there, watching Season as she caressed Dawnie's velvet nose. Turning to face him, her heart bled for the mixed emotions she saw there. Anguish, disbelief, worry, dread, and so much more. She considered going to him, to feel his strong arms around her. Instead, she stayed at the filly's head.

"It was a great race," she said lamely. "Dawnie was really looking good."

Ty nodded. "Right up to the point where she pulled up lame."

"I suppose you have a list of suspects."

"Ironically, no. My mind is a total blank as to anyone who would harm a horse to get at me," he said. He stepped inside the stall, shrinking the small space. "How about you, Season? Do you have any ideas?"

"No, none at all. Like you, I can't think of anyone who would stoop to hurting an animal just for revenge. And Dawnie is such a sweetheart."

They lapsed into silence, the only sounds the soft nickering of the filly.

"Can you fix her, Season?"

His quiet question took her by surprise. Turning from the filly back to him, she considered it.

"Not a hard question. Can you do your stuff and make her right again?"

Had she not been asking herself that same question for a little while now? "I don't know, Ty. A bowed tendon is a tricky thing. I can probably at least relieve her pain and discomfort while she heals. But can I shortcut months of proper healing? Can I make her one hundred percent again?" She gave him a disappointing shake of her head. "No, I can't."

He sighed deeply, raking a hand through his hair. "Do what you can for her. In the meantime, the good doctor won't say this was deliberate and we'll continue on just like it was an accident. We still have races and plans for our time here. And security will covertly be tightened around our horses. No one outside of yourself, me, and the good doctor will know of today's conversation."

"Sounds like you have a battle plan," Season said quietly. "Here, I think she is cooled enough for me to try touching her. Take her head please."

⚜

Ty cradled the filly's head in his arms, standing above Season as she knelt in the straw beside Winter's Dawn.

Bringing her hands together in a loud clap, she rubbed them vigorously, until Ty thought he could almost see vapors of steam rising from them. He could feel the heat coming from them and remembered a time not too long ago that she done something similar to him. That delightful day they were caught in the rain, and she had nothing but that see-through scrap of lace and equally lacy underwear. He thought he might die of pleasure up in the hay loft that day. It was a great disappointment when their clothing dried and the storm subsided. And she insisted he return inside to rest. Rubbish. He wanted to push her into the hay and claim her so badly.

"Easy, Dawnie girl," she crooned, laying her palms against the filly's left front leg. Her soft words brought him back to the issue at hand. Winter's Dawn shivered once, snorting in surprise. Ty murmured a low word of consolation to her, knowing how it felt. Dislocated shoulder or bowed tendon, he knew firsthand that Season had the touch to ease the pain.

Her gentle chanting filled the stall and he was glad he had the foresight to chase all others away for now. Magic hung in the room. He felt the filly relax in degrees beneath his arms and he struggled to hold her head, finally just letting it hang as she wanted. Moving his hands up to weave into her silky mane, he felt as hypnotized by the chanting and magic as the filly, his own eyes dropping and his body relaxed and heavy. Shifting slightly, he braced his legs, letting his eyes finally close.

The next thing Ty knew Season was at his side, an amused grin on her face. The filly was half asleep, head hanging low, her nose grazing the straw.

"Ty, I think she is feeling better," Season whispered. So was he. He did not recall any dreams, but he sure felt like he was just waking up from a good one. The woman was bewitching them both.

Clearing his throat, Ty knew there was color in his cheeks. Taking her elbow, he guided her out of the filly's stall.

"I believe she will be fine for now. It's time we return to our hotel. We still have a ball to attend tonight."

"Do you still plan on going tonight? Even with Dawnie?"

He arched his brows. "Why wouldn't we go? Winter's Dawn is fine for the moment. Come now, Season Moriarty, I want at least one dance with the loveliest woman at the ball." Still holding her elbow, he led her down the corridor toward where the rest of their group was waiting. "Just leave any discussions concerning the filly to me at the moment," Ty cautioned, his breath hot on her neck, her shampoo sharp and sweet in his nose.

She nodded wordlessly. He would say very little to direct questions and ignore the unspoken ones. And he had called her lovely.

⊗⊗⊗

One hour later, after a relaxing soak in the tub, Season stood by the closet, fingering the silky material of the gown, sliding her fingertips over the long skirts. She felt like a princess just by looking at it hanging in her room, she could hardly wait to put it on. Soon.

The peal of the phone startled her. Picking it up, Ty's honey smooth voice rumbled over the line.

"Can you come over to my room?" he asked, the request sounding more like an order.

"Right now? Before the ball?"

"Right now. Come as you are. This shouldn't take long," he added before hanging up.

That did not sound good. Pulling on a pair of jeans, a tee shirt, and sneakers, she grabbed her room key card and headed for his room around the corner.

He swung the door open at her first rap and stepped aside, letting her in. He was partially dressed for the dinner and dance, wearing black tuxedo pants, and a crisp white shirt with the sleeves rolled up. He had freshly showered and shaved. He smelled so clean and masculine. To get her mind back to the seriousness she'd heard in his voice, she dragged her eyes around the room.

Somehow, she'd expected him to have a huge suite like a penthouse, but his room was a lot like hers. The only difference she could spot was while she tended to use either the soaking bathtub more or channel surf afterward while falling asleep, he appeared to have set up a portable command central of Heritage at the corner writing space. A laptop computer and several discs fanned out over the desk.

"Have a seat," he said, ushering her to the chairs. "I have something to show you."

Wordlessly, hands on her knees, she watched him slide a CD into the laptop and turn the screen to her. Based on his vibes, and deadpan expression, she knew this was going to be bad. She squeezed her right knee to keep it from jumping.

"This is a copy of footage I obtained from Churchill security," he explained. "This is the view of the corridor outside our horses' stalls."

Together they watched the clock move forward as people came and went along the corridor, none taking any special interest in the Heritage horses section. Until ... Season felt Ty hold his breath, as Eddie came into view, escorting a woman into Winter's Dawn's stall. She leaned closer to watch.

The unknown woman carried a clip board, the heavy, metal kind that could be used to store small equipment inside and clip documents on the outside. She wore a light jacket of green with khaki pants and high black boots. Her brown hair was pulled into a ponytail, jutting through a dark yellow ball cap. Only her face remained obscured from the camera's lens. Season noted the time, it was a half hour before the filly's race.

She watched the stall door, both hands gripping her knees, as the camera rolled, ticking off the minutes while Eddie and the woman were inside with the filly. Fifteen minutes later, they emerged, shook hands, and separated paths. Again, the woman's face remained facing away from the camera. She could be just about anybody but Season suspected she was the reason Winter's Dawn bowed her tendon. She glanced at Ty.

Grim faced, he turned off the computer. Tension rolled off him like smoke.

"Eddie?" she finally whispered, her voice sounding as hollow as she felt.

"Who is the woman, Season? Is it you?"

The quiet accusation stunned her. Shocked, she could only stare for a moment. "It's not me! I can't believe you can even consider that."

"She looks like you," he returned quietly, staring at the now blank screen, his hands on the tabletop. "Right down to the pony tail."

"She may look like me but she isn't me." Hurt and anger recoiled within Season. "How could you even think that?" she asked again, this time demanding an answer. *How could he?* "I would have nothing to gain by hurting a horse. Damn you, Ty Masters! If I wanted to get you, I have only to snap my fingers or—"

He held up a hand, stopping her angry tirade. "Yes, I know, you can turn me to a toad with a word or douse me with water or any number of witchy things in your bag of tricks. Right now, I want to know who that woman is who visited my filly without my knowledge or consent."

Witchy? Bag of tricks? "Seriously, I would be more careful of the phrases and terms you use, if I were you," she retorted, arms crossed over her chest. "What made you think I would stoop so inconceivably low?"

"I don't know what to think right now."

The softly whispered admission, and the downcast eyes, paused Season's anger. He looked so vulnerable, she wanted to reach out to him, touch him. But the bitter sting of his accusation stilled her, warring with the desire to comfort and be comforted.

Casting her eyes around the room, she searched frantically for some explanation. Something to make sense of this unbelievable mess. Nothing came to mind. The woman did not look the least bit familiar. Eddie had said nothing to her about a visitor. And, like her, he had nothing to gain by hurting the horse, and everything to lose. It just didn't make sense. She clenched her fists, and unclenched them, as she tumbled the questions through her mind.

"We can talk to Eddie tonight. Ask him about it," she finally suggested.

"There might be a good explanation for that," she gestured to the laptop screen.

"If so, then who else would have hurt the filly?"

Again, the quiet pain in his voice tore at her heart, she wished she knew how to help ease the pain away. She wished he'd never accused her. The bitter taste of words he could never take back sat between them.

"I don't know. But why would Eddie deliberately hurt one of the horses? Why would he stand by and watch someone hurt Winter's Dawn?"

A long silence filled the room, hanging heavy with tense and sorrowful emotions.

Ty looked over across the table at her. "Season, can you use your abilities to see ... you know ... to see what happened? Inside there?" he gestured to the screen.

"No. It doesn't work that way." She gave a sad shake of her head. "I tried to read Dawn today, during the massage. There was nothing there. Whatever happened did not traumatize her beforehand."

"There is a small consolation I suppose," Ty muttered, lapsing into silence again. Finally, he spoke another question. "You can see into the future. What about Sky Hunter? Is he in danger?"

"I think it's safe to assume both horses are in danger." She met his stony glare. "Ty, that wasn't me in that footage, okay. So some woman entered that stall with Eddie. Now, whether she had anything to do with Dawn's injury or not, I don't know, but someone sure did. So, yes, Sky Hunter is in some danger."

"Would he tell you if someone hurt him?" He cracked a ghost of a smile, fleeting and vanishing like a phantom. "Like his sire told you he wanted to go for a ride."

"Ty, he would only tell me the same way he would tell you, by acting crazier than he normally does. By acting like he was hurting. By being different than what we expect from him. And you can hear any of that from his mouth without any special abilities."

Another fleeting smile crossed his lips, vanishing as quickly as it came. Heaving a deep, heavy sigh, Ty pulled the CD from the laptop and dropped it into a protective case.

"This conversation stays between you and me. Right now, we have a dinner and dance to prepare for. We shall attend, wine and dine, acting for all the world as if nothing is wrong." He paused, looking so sad it ripped at Season's heartstrings. "Later we shall address this," he said as he held up the CD case. "And tomorrow, Sky Hunter will have his run for the roses. In the meantime, additional security has been added to our corridor. No one will be able to sneeze near those horses without me knowing about it."

Standing up, he waited for Season to follow him. Reaching the door, he checked his watch. "We have twenty minutes to prepare. The men are taking the van for their events so I hired a limo for us. I shall call on you in twenty minutes, Miss Moriarty." His voice dropped a pitch, his eyelids heavy. "I cannot wait to see you again."

Butterflies took flight in her stomach, leaving her reeling as she stepped out into the hallway.

Suggestions of a different nature rolled off him, this time whispering of yearnings and desires not spoken. Subtle hints of heated thoughts barely concealed. Despite the burn of his accusation, her body responded with heated desires of her own.

Twenty minutes! She would barely make it! And he hired a limo too!

Flying around the corner, she slapped the key card into the slot, waiting impatiently for the three seconds it took the card to read, turn green, click, and unlock the door. Inside, she kicked out of her sneakers, yanked off her tee shirt and peeled the jeans off, tossing all of them into the corner. Sweeping her hair into a bun, she secured it and then walked to the gown.

Breathlessly, almost afraid, she inched it off the satin hanger and allowed the cool fabric to flow over her. Smoothing the folds and ruffles into place, she stepped back and looked in the mirror, seeing a pink cheeked princess looking back at her. The pale lemony color accented her complexion well and she would barely need any makeup. Taking her socks off, she slipped the studded ballet flats on.

Swirling once around the room, delighting in the rustling sound of the long skirts, she laughed, a happy giggle. Butterflies and giggles bubbled up inside her, spinning around her and making her dizzy. She and Ty were going to a ball, riding in a limo, and she looked like a fairy princess. And someone was seen going into Dawn's stall hours before the filly pulled up lame in her big race. Butterflies and giggles.

How inappropriate it seemed now, but how good it felt.

✵ 13 ✵

It had to be the wine, Ty decided a short time later. He was completely enchanted, caught under one of Season's spells and he was perfectly content to stay this way for the rest of his life. It was entirely wrong and illogical so, therefore, it must be the magic and the wine working together to bewitch his tangled mind.

She was enchanting. The moment he called around to collect her to take her to the waiting limo, he was spellbound. She radiated in her dress, stabbing little darting memories through him of the woman in his dream. The pixie faced fairy in glittering gold who frolicked with the black stallion in the mystical pastureland of his fantasies.

Standing there, he felt his tongue turn to rubber. It took all he had to coherently say a few words as he beheld her. She was a surreal vision, alluring, coaxing him closer with a tantalizing smile.

"Very nice," he had said, meaning every syllable. "But it needs something." He withdrew the wrapped package he'd obtained from the dress shop and watched, fascinated, and a little breathless, as she unwrapped it. Her startled intake of breath undid him like ribbon falling off a spool.

"They are just beautiful, Ty. How lovely," she whispered, gently fingering the sparking diamond choker and earrings. She held the blue velvet box to the light, but their sparkles couldn't compete with the ones in her eyes.

"Yours for the night," he apologized, wishing now he'd bought them instead of just renting.

Making a mental note to remedy that later, he forced his hands not to shake as he fastened the choker around her delicate, soft neck, his fingers itching to turn her around and take her lips in a long, deep kiss.

Now, listening to her laughter, merry and light, seeing the jewelry compete to outshine her eyes, and smelling the intoxicating blend of oils that will forever be her scent, he knew he was enchanted. Utterly spellbound. And he loved it. He could hardly wait for dinner to be done so he could lead her out onto that dance floor, just to hold her in his arms. Hold her close and lose himself in her bewitching charms.

Right now, watching her bright red lips, wet with the wine, he could only imagine what she tasted like. His mouth pooled with desire to taste the wine on her lips. Finally, after his tormented imagination could take it no longer, the band assembled, warming up their instruments.

"My lady," he asked, eagerly pushing the chair back and reaching for her hand. He had to stamp a claim on this fairy before she was whisked away by someone else or she disappeared into the night. Taking her hand, he noticed the stares from the other men, heard the whispers from the women. He felt like king of the world, holding Miss Season Moriarty beside him.

She melted into his arms, her sweet scent pouring over him like warm water, her smile radiant as she turned those lovely, emerald green eyes up to him. Lights strung overhead twinkled off her coiled hair. She dazzled as he turned her around the floor. He felt as tall as a mountain. The song was soft and slow.

Halfway through the song, she rested her head against his shoulder, moving even closer to him, her hands in his, her bare shoulders burning through his tuxedo, lighting him up. Rapture exploded within him.

Time stopped. It simply ceased to exist, to progress forward. Only the music continued. Coming from some invisible source he could only hear and not see.

He no longer noticed the other dancers. They were alone on the floor, gently sweeping across the wood, alone in each other's loving embrace. It felt like their feet never touched the floor. The strands of sounds were hauntingly beautiful and tender, poignant, lulling.

Hearing her soft sigh against his heart, Ty knew he was forever lost.

The song came to an end. She lifted her head, tilting her face up to his. Impulsively, he dropped his lips down upon hers, closing his eyes, and tasting wine. Drunk with the taste, he pulled a hand up to her slender neck, bringing her against his chest. Suddenly he couldn't breathe. Every sense was filled with her, engulfing him. Like a drowning man, he reached for more, praying it never ended. If he stood where he was for the rest of his life, holding her in his arms, he would be the happiest man alive. He felt so alive holding her. So fulfilled. So complete.

Suddenly, as if rousing from a dream, Ty stilled. Inhaling a deep, shuddering breath, he became aware of other dancers and a new song, he waited until Season lifted her head to blink at him.

"What have you done to me?" he asked, not unkindly, his voice thick. "I'm under your spell."

She laughed, lilting and sweet. "I have done nothing to you."

"Indeed, you have." Taking her by the elbow, he guided her back to their table, his hand gentle at her back. "You have made me fall for you," he whispered at her ear, bringing her chair for her.

"Ty Masters, I doubt seriously anyone could make you do anything you don't wish to do."

"Only you." Raising his wine glass, he offered a toast, wishing the dream did not have to end.

Upon returning to her hotel room, Season sank into the tub of bubbles, still giddy and exhilarated. The night with Ty was beyond her wildest dreams and she was sorry it had to end. No, she hadn't cast any spells on him, though she knew he believed otherwise. She was just as captivated and enchanted as he was. It was magical to her as well. It was unbelievable, deliciously good. She could hardly wait to see what tomorrow would bring.

⚜

Season joined the men downstairs at the hotel's restaurant. Eyeing the men assembled around the table, she noticed Ty was absent and all the men had a 'been-out-too-late' look about them. She hoped she didn't look as beat as they did.

"Hey, it's Derby time," she cheered. "Sky Hunter's big chance for the glory. Come on, guys, shake it off and wake up." She handed the coffee carafe around.

"I believe some of us have over indulged last night, Season, and will be a bit before they manage to shake it off," Ty murmured dryly, approaching the table and pulling out a chair. Accepting the carafe, he poured himself a mug, and breathed in the heady aroma. Without taking a drink, he set the cup aside untouched and opened up the newspaper he was carrying. Clearing his throat, he continued. "It seems all the members of Heritage Farms have made it into the society pages today. It appears we have collectively attended some rather interesting sounding events." Cocking an eyebrow around the circle, he read paragraphs naming Eddie and the others of the team at their chosen events.

"Let me see please." Season reached for the paper as he concluded. Glancing at the article, another one caught her eye, making her gasp. A photo of her and Ty was pasted in the middle of the page, at the ball last night, caught in what could only be called a lover's embrace, light sparkling around them and the headline boldly reading *'Ty Masters and female trainer at Jubilee Ball, dancing on moonbeams'*.

Yes, it did rather look like some moon dust had been sprinkled about, but she swore she had nothing to do with it. Reading the article, there would be no convincing anyone she and Ty were not romantically involved. Both their expressions were heavy with unspoken desires and promises of later. Had they really looked that way last night? But after they left the ball, they went to their separate rooms. However, no one looking at that photo would believe that. The article ended with a recap of Winter's Dawns' tragic injury and the high hopes Heritage held for Sky Hunter at the Derby today.

"Oh my," she whispered.

"Indeed."

Returning the paper, she brushed fingers with Ty, knowing he was keeping his thoughts guarded from her today. The briefest touch of their fingertips let her peek inside. Just enough to see quick flashes of thought.

He wasn't disappointed or upset, as she first had thought when he approached the table. Peering carefully at him, she felt he was still deeply awed from their evening together and seemed unsure how to proceed next, especially in light of the highly suggestive photo and article. Worries crowded his mind about Winter's Dawn, Sky Hunter, security and safety, and something about the jewelry. A new emotion filled him too, one she wasn't quick enough to identify before it darted away. To keep his control intact, he pulled up the guards that always protected him and kept people at bay. Knowing she was reading him again, he resisted it, giving her a smoky look.

Releasing the paper, her eyes held his for a lingering second. "Keep the picture," she suggested, then saw he'd already intended to do just that. Good, she intended to buy a copy of the paper herself and clip the entire society pages section for a keepsake.

⚜

The day finally dawned bright with clear blue skies overhead by the time activities were in full swing at the barns. The steady noises of the various activities throughout all the barns reminded Season of droning bees. Buzzing, busy, everyone was bustling in their duties. Much to do. Time was short.

And Camp Heritage was no different. Ty hovered like a protective papa as Sky Hunter was prepped, prepared, and generally fussed over. Still under the cover of darkness he'd loped around the track during his early run, as the sun's rays pierced the darkness, chasing it away.

Now, closer to race time, it took all of Season's concentration to keep the nervous colt from exploding from all the media, noise, excitement, and constant buzzing going on.

"Can't you do something to calm him down?" Ty demanded as Sky Hunter kicked out at his stall wall. Even placid Doodlebug was unable to calm his ruffled nerves this time. Ty's patience was wearing thin as he watched the colt spin in circles and throw his head around, snorting.

"What exactly do you suggest?" she snapped back, then immediately regretted it as Sky Hunter grew even worse. She drew an exasperated breath. "Ty, if you aren't going to help us, please go away," she politely requested, her teeth clenched as she held Sky Hunter's halter.

She didn't need eyes to know her comment was overheard by her coworkers and they had stopped working and waited, breaths held. No one ever dared order Ty Masters around. Except she just had.

"I shall be over at Winter's Dawn's stall," he muttered, stomping away, his expression dark.

Blowing out a deep breath, Season turned back to the lathered colt. "Back to work everyone. We still have a lot to do before post time." She would deal with his temper later.

The band was playing '*My Old Kentucky Home*' as Sky Hunter entered the gate. From her position at track side, Season knew there was little left to do now except let the horse run his race. Eddie would ride the best he could. Her palms were sweating as she waited.

The colt shot out of the gate like a black bullet, taking an early lead. A sorrel horse galloped close behind and a pretty bay horse brought up third position. It was going to be a close, challenging race. It would be a great test for her colt. She remembered the showy bay now. He was Sun Waltzer, a challenging threat to Sky Hunter during some of the earlier prep races and workouts.

Dirt flew under their hooves as they pounded down the track like runaway locomotives.

Fists clenched at her sides, Season swore she felt the earth shake as Sky Hunter thundered past her. Sun Waltzer pressed close by, not giving up so easily to the black horse. Racing side by side, the sorrel stayed at their haunches, trying to wear them down.

With a burst of new speed, Sky Hunter snaked out his head and dug in hard, enough to push further ahead of the irritating challengers, sweeping first under the wire.

Sky Hunter had just won the Kentucky Derby, the first jewel in a hopeful Triple Crown.

From out of nowhere, Ty appeared, taking her elbow. Wordlessly, he guided her to the Winner's Circle where already a wreath of roses was being placed over Sky Hunter's mane and Eddie waved breathlessly at the crowds.

Accepting their congratulations, Ty pressed next to her side. Season could feel his warm breath on her neck and smell his clean scent. His hand protectively resting on her shoulder, she felt like the Belle of the Ball. Catching his eye in a fleeting moment, heat crept up her neck, reaching her cheeks.

Only later, after the photographers and reporters finished with their endless snapshots and questions did she notice it. Leading Sky Hunter back to his stall, shoulder to shoulder with him, did she feel the slight limp on his left front leg. It was very slight, but she still felt it nonetheless.

Cold shivers of dread washed over her. Not again. It can't be happening again.

Reaching the stall, she touched Ty's arm, leaning close. "Can I have a minute with you alone? In here?"

Something in her voice or eyes, or maybe both, stopped him. Ushering the others out, he stepped in front of the colt, arms crossed, looking to where she was kneeling at his left leg. When she looked up at him, her world crumbled. His expression said it all.

"Not again?" The words came out sounding like gravel.

His disbelieving, hollow question ripped at her heart, echoing her own worse fears.

"He finished the race," she pointed out cheerfully. "He's not in pain. It's very minor."

"Is the tendon bowed, Season?" Only his face betrayed how close he was to coming unraveled.

"I'm not sure. It's a ... well, it's something. We probably ought to get the vet to be sure."

"Can't he just tell you what happened?" Ty moved one arm to the colt.

"No. I already tried that," she said, blowing out a breath. But she tried it again, resting her palms against the colt. Nothing specific, just lots of fragmented, disjointed pieces of pictures and images. "I think this horse has ADD," she said with a ghost of a smile. "It would certainly explain a lot about him."

Not appreciating her attempt at humor, Ty moved to the stall door. "I shall fetch the vet. Stay here with him until we return."

Heart sinking, Season sank down in the stall next to Sky Hunter, rubbing his nose as the colt lowered his head and butted her shoulder. All she could do was wait.

※

"Well, it's not quite bowed, not like the filly's is," the vet declared, standing up and giving Sky Hunter an affectionate pat. "But someone tried mighty hard to make it so." He leveled his gaze at Ty. "Someone out here does not like you very much, Mr. Masters."

Season glanced over at Ty, saw him flinch, and looked back at the vet's x-ray pictures.

"Is it the same pattern or method used as for Winter's Dawn?" she asked, knowing Ty had to be wondering the same thing.

The kindly vet, sworn to secrecy, tilted his head as he considered the question. "Yes," he finally nodded. "I would have to say it was the exact same method used on both horses. Except it worked on the filly and almost worked on this big fella." Again, he patted the colt's neck.

"He ran a great race today. And a lot of horses would have crumbled under the stress and pressure of that kind of race. You both should be proud of the heart this animal has."

"Thank you, doctor. Very kind words," Ty said, finally breaking his silence.

"Would you conclude the failed attempt at Sky Hunter could be due to the individual being interrupted?"

"Yes," the vet nodded again. "That would be a good, logical assumption. Look here," Again, he drew them to Sky Hunter's leg. "It's close, but not quite. Maybe another minute or two might have made a completely different story for this fella here and for his racing career altogether."

Grimly, Ty nodded. "Thank you. Again, I appreciate your candid honesty and security. Season, I shall see you in my quarters in one hour." Turning, he led the vet from the stall.

One hour later, heart thumping, Season knocked at Ty's hotel room door. Wordlessly, he swung the door open, gave her a slight smile, escorted her to the command central sofa and slid a CD into the computer, making sure his thoughts were carefully guarded from her.

"The footage from the last twenty-four hours outside Sky Hunter's corridor," he explained, leaning back to let her view the film.

Seated next to him, thighs almost touching, feeling his barely concealed vibrations, she found it hard to concentrate on the people coming and going along the corridor. She spotted herself and Ty, Eddie, and his valet, and the groom all going and coming from view. Listening to Ty's breathing, she was lulled into a relaxed state as the familiar faces paraded past her eyes. Some were acquaintances of Ty's come to visit him at the stall area.

"Wait! There!" Sitting bolt upright, she pointed to the screen. "There she is again. It's her."

Not looking surprised, Ty stopped the footage, rewound it briefly and started it forward again at a slower speed.

Eddie and the same woman with the big metal clipboard came walking along the corridor. This time she wore a wide brimmed hat. The way she was bobbing her head, she must have been listening to Eddie doing most of the talking. Pausing a moment, they both slipped inside Sky Hunter's stall.

Season checked the time. It was mid-morning, just as they started breaking up for quick lunches before post parade. Not even a full two minutes later Tommy, his valet, came along leading Doodlebug, entering the stall. Like a flash, the woman slipped out and vanished from view like a wisp of smoke. The footage continued on, showing Eddie and Tommy coming out of the stall a few moments later, securing the door, and walking up the hall.

Turning off the CD, Ty waited, his expression neutral.

"Is that the only time she shows up in there?" Season asked, pointing to the blank computer screen.

He nodded stiffly.

"Where is Eddie?" he asked, his voice coming out like rough sandpaper.

"He went to that jockey charity ball. He won't be back until late I suspect."

"He needs to be questioned about this ... woman. As does Tommy."

Season nodded. Clearly, whatever was going on with the horses, Eddie seemed to be at the scene both times. "You know, I never thought to check with Doodlebug about what he saw. He wasn't in the stall with Winter's Dawn or with Sky Hunter until the last moment, but it still might be useful just to check."

"Pick his brains?" Ty commented dryly, shrugging indifferently, removing the CD and placing it in a clear case.

"Something like that. Yes."

He shrugged again, his thoughts and expression well-guarded.

"Let me question Eddie and Tommy tomorrow," Season requested impulsively.

Ty lifted one eyebrow in surprise.

"Eddie wouldn't lie to me. I believe that. I also think there has to be some logical, explainable reason for this. Besides, everyone else is scared to death of you. That might color what they say during an inquisition from you."

That earned her a truly amused smile. Leaning back again, he slid his eyes over her. "So why are you not scared to death of me as all the others?"

"Because I can turn you into a toad if I need to."

"Good point," he agreed. "Question them tomorrow. I shall expect a full, truthful report from you before lunch. And then we shall return home. We have two injured horses who need attention."

"Fine." She started to get up, then hesitated. "What about tonight?"

Leaning forward, his smile almost wicked in the dim lighting of the hotel room, he brought her to him.

"Tonight, I plan on risking becoming a toad."

Capturing her lips, he branded her with a hard, searing kiss, feeling the surge of energy that transferred between them. She felt the unspoken whisper of their combined needs as she lifted a hand to work loose the buttons on his shirt. He grinned and tugged her tee shirt off, tossing it carelessly into the corner.

Within moments his shirt and both their pants lay scattered on the floor. Season lay back on the sofa, arching toward Ty as he lowered himself to her, his lips nibbling at her earlobe.

A giggle escaped her.

❧ 14 ❧

She was a picture of grace and beauty, a lovely, ethereal apparition in pink. A long gown cascaded to her pink painted toes, and swept the floor behind her. Red rosettes draped over her like a garland of fragrant roses. Music filtered into the room, filling it with horns and flutes and sweet melodies as she glided over the bare wooden floor. A slow waltz began, hinting at romance. He drooled in anticipation.

Eagerly he sought her eye, trying to catch her attention. So many others crowded near, almost pushing him out of the way, blocking his view of the vision of beauty in pink pastels and red rosettes. Feeling the need to hold her for a dance was a physical thing. He had to get to her. He would climb a mountain of people if need be.

Forcing his way through the growing crowd, feeling the air grow thick with too many bodies in one place, he tried to shout her name only to discover, horrified, he couldn't speak. Only a dry croak came out.

What the bloody hell? he thought in bewildered amazement. Was he losing his mind?

Finally, slowly, like a fine porcelain doll, she turned his direction, wearing a pretty, pouting smile. The kind that begged men to kiss those pink rose bud lips. For one fantastic second, their eyes connected, locking. With all the elegance and serene femininity of a grand queen, she stepped across the floor, through the parting crowd, to reach him. Her hibiscus scent reached him first and he breathed deep, taking it in.

Stopping one foot away, she reached out to take his sweating, trembling hands into her white gloves. All he could do was breathe in every exotic, sweet, and spicy scent that mixed with the hibiscus. It wafted around him like wispy curls of deliciously mixed aromas.

The music intensified, matching the crazed beating of his own heart. Suddenly they were the only two people on earth, the crowds melted away, leaving just her in his arms. As it should be. He could swear they never touched the floor, but danced above it. Just as he thought he could die happy, the floor tilted.

Thinking initially an earthquake was rumbling through, he looked at her, instantly horrified to see her pink gowned beauty was gone. As if by the cruelest magic spell, she'd changed into Winter's Dawn, now waving her foreleg accusingly at him and moaning pitifully. Mouth agape, utterly stunned, he looked down and saw he was an amphibian.

Yelling, gasping, flailing his arms, Ty sat bolt upright in the dark, his heart pounding crazily.

Good mercy! Bloody hell!

Raking a shaking hand through his hair, he turned for the bedside lamp, flooding his bedchamber with light. Had his little witch cast a spell on him somehow? He sucked in a ragged breath.

Swinging his feet to the carpeted floor, he stumbled to the bathroom, flipping that bright light on as well. Light, oh how he wanted light. Lots of light.

Gulping down two glasses of cold water, he struggled to bring his labored breathing under control. Splashing cold water over his face, he looked back into the mirror. Squinting, he saw he was indeed the same old Ty Masters he'd always been. Human. Male. Two eyes, one nose, a mouth, tousled hair, trimmed mustache. Everything seemed to be as it should be.

Good.

He proceeded to inspect further down. Two arms, ten fingers, yes, everything all appeared accounted for as he worked his way down.

So the vixen hadn't bewitched him.

It was a dream, a horrible nightmare. Still haunted by the pained, accusing look in Winter's Dawn's eyes, he found no humor in the term night mare. Moving to the bureau, he gripped the society page article, carrying it back to the bed. Seated on the edge, he stared at the photo snapped of he and Season, dancing, holding each other in a lover's embrace, like they owned the moon.

Yes, they had made love last night, just as the photograph implied they would surely do. He'd been kidding, more or less, about risking becoming a toad. Just enough to stay lingering in his memory apparently. Just like the night she had led him up into the woods, they had come so very close to crossing that line and this time they did, breathless and excited. Last night Season took him to the brink of control, then she took his hand and led him over the edge, into a realm he'd never dreamed existed. Making love to her was unlike any woman he'd ever known before.

And it sure buggered things up.

Their relationship was complicated—predominately business by design and lately romantic by passion. After last night, there was no turning back, for either of them.

Now, in the aftermath of that dream, he clutched the snapshot of them. This was proof positive he had at one time danced with her, held her close, smelled her, touched her, felt her curves fitting into his, and tasted her sweetness on his lips. It was all there in the photograph. It was magical and bewitching. Just like her.

The real and true memories of that ball would chase away the implied memories of his dream.

⚜

S eason greeted the dawn with a big yawn and a long stretch. She hadn't slept well last night, despite the very comfortable bed and ultra-soft pillows.

Upon leaving Ty's suite, she left phone messages with Eddie and Tommy that she wished to meet with them before breakfast privately and now she was rushing to shower and prepare for her questioning.

Though she was positive they were innocent and would tell her the truth of what was going on, she still was pretty much clueless about how to handle this. She almost regretted asking Ty for the task. He was no doubt better suited for this kind of interrogation, but she doubted his bulldozing tactics would achieve much with them.

Dropping her shirt to the bathroom floor, she stepped into the shower, welcoming the warm spray, hoping for a burst of inspiration.

❦

"It was pretty much like the tapes showed it and how we suspected it," Season began, taking a seat at command central after Ty escorted her into his quarters. Shaking her head at his offered glass of orange juice she tugged at her braid, trying not to notice his own hair was still damp and slightly curly from the shower. He smelled shower fresh too, dragging Season's mind off from her appointed task.

Taking a sip of orange juice from the glass, Ty leaned back into the sofa, waiting, his eyes cool and calm, his thoughts guarded again.

"So you completed your questioning already? That was fast. And what did you discover?"

Glad for the bit of praise, Season plunged in. "In regards to Winter's Dawn, the woman approached Eddie down in the corridors. She said she was the track vet and scheduled to examine Dawnie before her race. Eddie thought that was sort of odd, but she said something about being a new track regulation, just implemented this year. She added that you knew about it too. She mentioned you by name as being in the know."

Season paused and Ty nodded grimly.

"So he just escorted her to Winter's Dawn stall and hung in the background, figuring vets know what they are doing. He was pretty sure she was in and out in only a few minutes."

"The tape showed a bit more than 'a few minutes'," Ty pointed out, taking another sip of juice and setting the glass down. "Did Eddie happen to notice any tools or equipment she might have used? Did she give a name?"

"No, he said she opened her clipboard, but he wasn't paying any attention. If she gave her name, he forgot it."

Ty frowned, not impressed. Eddie would surely hear a few words regarding his lack of attention to details later on.

"All right. Next," Ty prompted.

"It was pretty much the same with Sky Hunter. Eddie admitted to being kind of surprised to see her again, as she found him as he was coming to Hunter's stall. Still believing her story about being a track vet, he took her in, but noticed Sky Hunter was a bit more flighty than normal. To his credit, it's hard to sometimes tell what is making that crazy horse act more flighty than his normal flighty moods." Knowing she was taking a risk to point out how Sky Hunter's behavior did not help the situation, she still had to point it out.

Ignoring her barb, Ty pushed her on. "And Tommy? Was he any more observant?"

"A little. Tommy only saw her a moment, as he came in with Doodlebug. The woman sprang up from her knees in front of Sky Hunter. Eddie was holding the colt's halter to make him stand still for the exam. She pushed something small into her clipboard, slammed it shut, murmured a few words and was gone. Even Doodlebug was acting weird."

"Odd for him."

Season nodded in agreement. "That is why I took a taxi down to the stables this morning."

Ty's head snapped up, blinking. "You interrogated the horses as well?"

"They seemed like credible witnesses," she said in defense.

Ty opened his mouth to speak, changed his mind and sat, waiting instead, giving her a hand wave to proceed.

"Winter's Dawn showed lots of pain and fear. She felt a badness from the woman at first. No pain, just distrust."

"Badness?"

"Yes. Horses sometimes lack the words to describe things like we would. It's more pictures and feelings."

"Um," Ty nodded, his lips thinning.

"It was only later Dawnie felt the sharp stabbing pain in her leg during the race. Sudden slices of tiny razor blades biting through her leg."

"She told you this?"

"Not in those exact words." Season hesitated. "Let's just say you don't really want to know how I know those were her exact feelings."

"No, I don't. So what about the other two? So far we can't connect the woman's visit to Dawn's feelings."

"Sky Hunter also sensed a badness, something not to trust. No pain, just mistrust. Not a lot coming from him I know. But Doodlebug had the best information though. He saw a person who wanted to cause evil, who had black in her heart, who smelled of wickedness and wasn't to be trusted at all. A predator. A hunter. He also saw a small instrument with a handle, maybe a knife or pen or a razor."

Ty sat up straight, stunned. "Doodlebug told you all that?"

"In pictures. Yes," Season nodded.

He fell silent for a moment, fingers steepled under his chin. His lips twitched ever so slightly. "So you are telling me the best witness we have is that pony?"

"I guess so."

"I hope Eddie and Tommy will be properly chagrined when they find this out."

"Ty," Season touched his arm. "Don't be too hard on them. They only did what they were led to believe were part of the track rules. Refusing would have gotten Eddie suspended or you fined or both if this had been a legitimate regulation. Remember that when you talk to them, okay?"

Ty slowly favored her with a smile. "Sweet little Season, defender of everyone." His voice was soft and sweet as a silky caress. "What a shame I can't pursue that further. Right now, we have work to do before we fly home with our injured horses and a wreath of red roses." He gave a deep sigh. "I can say I have never experienced a Derby such as this." Running a hand through his drying hair, his gaze turned smoky. "Season Moriarty, whatever shall I do with you?"

"I'll leave you to decide that on your own, Ty Masters. Thank you for the dance. And the gown," she added sincerely, climbing to her feet. Giving him a smile and a salute, she led herself out, heart hammering in her chest by the unspoken desires mirrored in his eyes.

Three hours later they were flying through the sky. Even with a Derby win under their belts, the mood was decidedly subdued and concerned about the next race.

Ty's preferred veterinarian team met them as soon as they landed at home. After a careful and thorough inspection of all three horses, they outlined a treatment plan for Winter's Dawn and met with Season for an exercise program for Sky Hunter until he left for the next race, Pimlico. Their expectations for a complete recovery for the filly were guarded. Season planned to boost her odds using all methods available to her and silently vowed to see the filly race again next year.

Once the horses were stabled and all plans hammered out and the vet team gone, Season escaped to a relaxing bath upstairs. Pouring scented oils of mint and chamomile into the warm water, she lit a few candles, put in a favorite CD, dimmed the lights and slid into the inviting tub. Sheer bliss welcomed her and she let the worries of the last few days roll off her skin. It was late and tomorrow was another day to start anew. Right now was her time.

Exiting the bathroom later, wrapped in her fuzzy bathrobe, she unexpectedly slammed bodily into Ty, standing in the dim hallway.

"Oh!" Startled, and surprised her senses hadn't detected him, she fought to keep her balance.

Chuckling in the semi darkness, Ty reached out and easily caught her, held her, breathed her in. "It isn't often I get to take you by surprise," he said, exceedingly pleased with himself. "It seems you always are the one who takes my breath away, not the other way around."

Gathering herself and her wits, Season challenged him, seeing his broad smile in the darkened hall. "I seriously doubt I take your breath away all that much."

"If only you knew, sweet Season," Ty said heavily, releasing his hold on her. She stepped away and he stepped into the warm mists and lingering scents in the bathroom.

Three days after returning home, Season came into the kitchen in search of coffee after running Sky Hunter. The second week of May was bright and warm and she loved being outside, relishing in it. Entering the kitchen, she scooped up both a mug and a cluster of grapes from the bowl Moose always kept filled on the counter. Sitting at the small table, she took a break, popping grapes into her mouth and chewing with satisfaction.

"There you are, Missy," Moose announced, coming into the room. His beefy hands were black with dirt and Season knew he'd been out working his garden, a true delight he looked forward to each spring. As much as he enjoyed putting up the preserves and fruits of his labor in the fall, all the members of Heritage enjoyed sampling those labors through the winter months.

"Were you looking for me? Sorry, I was out with Eddie and Hunter at the track."

Moose shook his head. "Not so important as to track you down, but a package came for you today. Special delivery." Scrubbing his hands in the big sink, he dried them off and walked over to the storage area. Coming back, he carried a suitcase sized parcel, wrapped in plain brown paper and tied with blue silken cords. Surprise stole over Season as Moose lay the package on the counter.

"It looks expensive," she said, running her hands over the paper, listening to it crackle under her fingertips. If this wasn't a dress, she would eat a horse shoe. "No name of sender. No return address," she pointed out. Just her name and Heritage's address. "Ty?" she asked, lifting her eyes to meet Moose's.

He shrugged. "My guess is yes, but you'll never get him to admit to it. He was here when it came and as far as I know, he has not left the place since your return from Kentucky."

"He can use the phone and computer. He has access to the outside world."

"He'll never admit to it. Now, go try it on and let me see how beautiful you are." His warm praise made her glow.

"Let me shower first, okay. I don't want horse smell to get on it."

"I'll be down here waiting on you," he promised, picking up a wash cloth.

Alone in her room, barely dry from her hasty shower, she opened the wrapper on the bed. Pale cornflower blue silk unfolded, a small card dropped to the floor.

"For the dance at Pimlico."

Typed, it bore no name. Gently fingering where Ty would have signed it, she set it carefully aside and pulled the dress on. The silk felt cool against her warmed skin. Falling to the floor in silk pleats, one shoulder was bare and a row of blue rosettes ran down the other shoulder to her bust line. Around her waist was a satin sash that tied in the back with a pretty bow and ribbons of rosettes. In a word, it was ethereal. It was perfect. It was unexpected. She already had the pale lemon gown from the Derby, she hadn't expected a second one. This time, she would pack properly for the dance before the big race. Further inside the box sat a pair of sky blue flats, wrapped in a protective cloth bag. Gingerly she took them out and slipped them on.

Eagerly now, aware of the blush to her checks, she rushed downstairs to show Moose.

"Oh Missy, no wonder the man is in love with you," he said softly as she swept into the room, holding her hair up haphazardly in a bun. "You'll turn plenty of heads in Maryland next week wearing that. The Master will be fighting the boys off for sure."

"He doesn't have to fight them off. The boys I mean. He has never actually said he loves me." Season let her hair fall down, hands curling into the silky pleats.

Moose favored her with a long look, his hands stilled on the counter. "The Master has been a mighty man. You are making him into a better man. Give him just a little more time and he'll say the words your heart wants to hear."

"Moose," she cried brokenly, wanting to rush into his arms like she would with her dad.

"Now, now, Missy..." Moose reached around the counter and touched her bare shoulder, connecting with her. "It will all work out. Now, go change and save that for later on. We can't have it get smeared with garden dirt or horse smell." Giving her a wink and a smile, he spun her around and gently pushed her for the stairs. "Don't want the Master to catch a glimpse of you in that before it's time either."

Ty! She'd forgotten he could walk into the house at any time as well. And see her in the blue gown. Looking over her shoulder, she winked back at Moose, gathered the long skirts and dashed upstairs, to change back into real clothes and carefully fold the lovely present away for safekeeping.

Next week she would unveil it for Ty's benefit. Next week Sky Hunter would run for his second jewel of the Triple Crown she knew he could win. Ty would be happy if he just ran and placed safely. She wanted the win with a new record. She wanted Ty to see her in this gown and melt.

❧ 15 ❧

Through the clouds, the plane descended into Maryland, home of Pimlico race track and the Preakness Stakes. Landing, Ty went off, stating he planned to have some words with the track security officials. Nodding, she returned to the task of settling the two horses, Sky Hunter and his trusty, unflappable stablemate.

"Weather forecast is supposed to be like this all week long," Season lamented later at dinner. "Sloppy track, gray skies, periods of rain and thunderstorms. Eddie, you might want to carry an umbrella out onto the track," she ended with a grim smile.

"Not that it would matter much on board that locomotive," Eddie said. "I might just fly away in the wind current."

"Wouldn't that be a sight," Ty said, his smile not fully reaching his eyes. "We shall contend with the weather and the track. Fortunately for us, the horse doesn't mind rain or sloppy tracks."

Was that more than just a passing remark about the fact that Winter's Dawn hated rain and sloppy tracks and her future rested heavily on Ty's mind? Season had to admit she felt the same way. She had noticed Ty seemed a little more stressed since they landed and he went off to meet with the security officials.

He had to be wondering if that woman would show up and try something here. She had been wondering the same thing. Plus Moose had confided just before they left that Ty still planned to attend the rodeo festival when they returned next week.

Whether he planned to still ride that crazy bronc, she did not know or dare ask. To be honest with herself, she was more concerned about how she was going to feel if he did carry through with his original plan. So far, he was keeping those thoughts well hidden from her. He may do insane things from time to time, but he was no one's fool and knew how to guard himself from her attempts to read him when he chose to. Clearly, he had taken the time to learn and understand a few things about her gifts.

⌘

In keeping with their Derby pattern, Season and Eddie worked Sky Hunter under the cover of darkness early the next morning, before the rest of Pimlico woke up. By the time everyone else was stirring, their colt was cooled off and back in his stall.

Ty caught up with Season as she rounded the shed row. Catching her arm, he slowed his long stride to fall into step with her.

"Tonight, I'll call for you at six o' clock." He pulled her to a stop, capturing her chin in his fingers. Lights dancing in his eyes, he asked, "Did you manage to pack properly this time?"

"Why, yes, I did," she replied, biting her lip to keep the smile away, liking this little game they were playing. "Whatever do you plan to do with me at six o' clock, sir?"

"More than even you can imagine," he replied huskily. A wicked grin split his face. "But for now, it shall have to just start with the dance. After that, sweet Season, we shall have to wait and see."

⌘

At five fifty-five promptly, Ty knocked at the door of Season's hotel room. His palms were sweaty.

Taking a moment to pinch himself, he was assured this wasn't a dream this time. Lately, it was hard to tell. Nervously, he took turns rubbing them down his tuxedo pant leg, holding the small box carefully with the other.

Beyond the door he heard rustling sounds, each one making his heart pound just a little faster. Was she wearing the blue gown? He couldn't wait to see her in it. That single thought had just about consumed his mind all day long.

The rustling noises stopped and the door swung open, letting sweet smells escape. They swirled around him, then evaporated, taking his breath away with them.

"Aren't you going to say something?" Season asked, holding the door, a smile on her lips.

He couldn't speak. Perhaps this was a dream after all. Stunned, he stood there, quite sure his mouth was hanging ajar. Oh, he'd known she would be beautiful in that blue gown but he was totally unprepared for this vision of mythological elegance. Fairies and goddesses were not half as lovely as this woman was.

Could this be the same woman who tempted him with her exploits? Who rode unruly horses with impunity? Who could go invisible and bend time? Who challenged his every course of action and thought? Who drove him half out of his mind nearly every single day? Who tormented his dreams at night and threatened him with the quiet strength in her eyes?

"Ty?" Her smile faltered. "Thank you for the dress." She took a step back. "Don't you like it?"

Like it? The question burned his mind. He absolutely loved it on her. So much so he never wanted her to take it off. The only thing better would be the sight of her with nothing on at all.

Reining those thoughts in to a hasty stop, he thrust the box out to her, clearing his throat.

"It looks just fine," he said, once he found his tongue. "I believe, though, that these will go along nicely."

Opening the box, she gasped. "This is the same jewelry I wore in Kentucky."

He nodded. "I purchased them after I saw how lovely you made them look that night."

Blushing, she lifted them up to the light. Blinking and sparkling like old friends, she slipped the earrings into place. Holding the necklace out to Ty, she waited for him to fasten the clasp.

How could she disarm him so effortlessly, he wondered as his trembling fingers touched her silken skin. Before she closed the door, she picked up a small clutch bag and threw a light shawl over her bare shoulders. Favoring him with a bright smile, she offered him her arm.

"Ready for an unforgettable evening?" she asked, just a hint of amusement in her voice.

"Season, everything I do with you is unforgettable."

⚜

F rom the very beginning it was unforgettable. The limo ride was entirely too short. Season chatted and laughed merrily, making him feel like a king hiding a special treasure. He savored the moments alone in the car with her, knowing all too soon they would arrive and he would have to share his treasure with the public and he was reluctant. He wanted to keep her all to himself. Especially tonight, when she looked so invitingly good. So temptingly delicious.

Dinner was a grand feast, fit for a king and queen. Ty rushed through the piles of food, his eyes staying on Season as she slowly savored every bite. When hot melted butter escaped the lobster fork, trickling down her chin, he ached to catch it with his tongue, tasting the buttery goodness of her lips. Then she brushed it away with a dainty dab of her napkin, looking embarrassed by her messiness.

Ty felt no shame for his thoughts. He impatiently fretted for dinner to be over, so he could take her out onto the dance floor, away from the people at their table foolishly bent on conversing on boring topics. Once they escaped to the dance floor, he could hold her there the rest of the evening.

Tonight, she belonged solely to him and damned the social photographers who implied anything. Tonight, he wanted to dance in the air with Season and know he held the most wonderful woman in the room.

At long last dinner was finished, the conversation died down and the music began. Ty was ready to whoop with unbridled joy. All but jumping from his chair, Ty leaned in for Season. "A dance, my lady?"

One more delicate dab with her napkin, a smile around the ring of people at their table, a final sip of wine, and then she allowed him to guide her out to the wooden floor.

"Mr. Masters, you restrained yourself very well." She laughed, taking his hands into her gloved ones, amusement making her eyes dance and sparkle like the jewelry at her ears and throat.

"Was it that obvious?"

"Only to me." She caught his rhythm, feeling his excitement. "And I'm very flattered. Again, thank you for the lovely gown and the accessories."

He wagged his head. "They do you a fine justice."

Pausing, she gave a brief curtsy as the music changed songs.

"Ready for some fun?" she asked, a wicked gleam in her eye.

"Naturally." Already more dancers were coming onto the floor. What could his little vixen have in mind now? That gleam intrigued him, setting his thoughts on fire.

"Hold on tight," she whispered, gliding across the floor, pulling him to the far corner where the light was dimmest. Closing her eyes and leaning into him, she concentrated on just the two of them and the music.

Ty felt her grow tense, gathering herself. His heart skipped a beat or two as he felt his feet coming off the floor. Tempted to look down, he forced himself to hold her alluring and wicked eyes instead. She actually levitated them off the bloody floor!

How far off they really were, he could only guess. A few inches? More?

"I just wanted to make sure this evening was unforgettable to you," she drawled softly, with that alluring smile, drawing him in closer, making him feel as if he were drowning.

"You have succeeded," he breathed, a bit undone by the fact there was no floor under their feet as they swayed to the music. He wouldn't look down. He wouldn't. Oh yes, she'd succeeded.

She purred low. "Want to kick it up a notch?" Her eyes lit up dangerously as her lips parted.

Tempted, he reconsidered. "No, this is fine. Unforgettable enough." What else could she do with her abilities? Impossible to say. Hard to resist. Her soft laugh into his shoulder teased him further. What a woman.

⁂

"So explain to me why you cannot stop the rain," Ty asked, staring at the steady downpour from under the shed row roof.

"I can, but only for a little while," she replied patiently. "Not enough to make any difference right now. I would rather wait and conserve it in case we need it during the race."

Ty shook his head. "A woman who can lift man and herself off the floor or bend time and the laws of visibility ought to be able to hold the rain at bay for a race."

"That same woman can also turn an irritating man into a toad, so watch it. Plus there is the ethics issue too," she warned, stepping away to check on Sky Hunter. His amused chuckle followed her.

She read his thoughts enough to know they were echoing her own.

The cloudy skies, cold rain and periodic thunder bursts reminded them both of that rainy thunderstorm they rode out together in the hay loft weeks ago. Memories, same but slightly different, seemed to have stayed with both of them, warming their hearts each time the sky rained or lightening flashed and thunder cracked. She was pleasantly surprised to see he still held such strong memories and willingly shared them with her. From Season's perspective, she still recalled sitting astride the hay bales, her fingers moving over Ty's damp body, feeling the damage beneath the skin, then when he ignited, growing hotter under her touch, in concert with the thunderous symphony outside the barn loft door. Whereas he dwelled more on her nearly see-through wet camisole. Ah, men.

Now, with the memories warming her soul, she moved off to check the horses, glad for the excuse to get away from Ty and the images his own mirrored memories shook inside her. Now wasn't the time to get distracted by one afternoon spent in a hay loft. Now was the Preakness, serious business, time to pay attention to matters at hand.

Sky Hunter had run well during his final early morning workout, playful and excited. Now, after a light breakfast, he was bored, watching the storms come and go from his stall, with Doodlebug next to him. Season watched him nibble at the pony's neck until he must have bit a little too hard. Doodlebug laced his ears back and bit back, sinking his teeth harmlessly into Sky Hunter's shoulder which was all the further the little pony could reach.

"Play nice, boys," Season admonished them. "Or else we'll have to separate you two."

Not that it was likely, since they still needed the docile pony to keep the big colt in line. What an odd match, she thought, watching the two resume their watching of the passing storm, their tails flickering at random flies. The tall, elegant black colt and the short, butter round pony that looked like a patchwork quilt of colors. Thoroughbred from historic bloodlines and mongrel from who knows where. Hot temper and placid calm. Best friends.

Eventually it was time to saddle up for the post parade. The band was playing *"Maryland, My Maryland,"* as Eddie climbed into the saddle. Ty had left for his box seat and Season was giving out last minute instructions.

"He has some real competition out there today. Both Sun Waltzer and High Ransom are out to win. They will probably try to push you out, away from the rail, working together just enough to keep you behind them. Don't push Hunter. But don't let him get so irritated he forgets he's racing and tries to run them down to kill again. No time for potato tricks today."

"Got it," Eddie smiled and saluted her. "Will do."

Tommy took the reins and led them away to the track.

Heart in her throat, Season moved over to her vantage point, where she could see every move of the race. Just in case special help was needed. Glancing up, she was glad the rain had at least abated for a little while, though the clouds still hung heavy and dark, ominous looking. The air sparked with electricity. Even the horses sensed it and pawed nervously.

Sky Hunter loaded into the fourth chute, next to High Ransom. Sun Waltzer was in the second chute. If they broke evenly, it was going to be a tight race.

At the bell, Sky Hunter and Sun Waltzer broke even, with High Ransom and the rest of the field right behind. High Ransom poured on the steam and soon all three were running evenly neck and neck.

Sky Hunter shook his head, ears back, not liking being in the center of the other two, and crowded so closely. Mud slapped him as his head bobbed in unison with the other two. The rest of the field fell behind by the first turn. Going into the second turn, Sun Waltzer and High Ransom pushed together, their jockeys doing exactly what Season had predicted, working together just enough to push Sky Hunter out and into third position. Hugging the rail, they were ensuring at least they would come in first and second place.

Season felt Sky Hunter and Eddie's frustration as they slowly were forced back, and then watched as Eddie turned Hunter wide to go around them. Hot anger raged from the black colt as he went wide around the third turn, with much more track to cover in a short distance.

Shaking his head defiantly, he dug in, giving it his all, building speed to catch the leaders as the final turn approached. The rest of the field fell back, unable to keep up with the powerful speeds of the three leaders. It was a true three horse race.

Plowing through the mud with long, smooth strides, Sky Hunter gave a tremendous surge as he banked out of the final turn and swung past the two leaders, pulling ahead now by a nose. Ears laced back, white lather flying off his dark coat, he drove faster, pounding harder, pulling further ahead, as if in contempt of the trick they had played on him.

A cold wind swirled around, howling over the track, pelting cold rain down on the horses. Lightening zig-zagged and thunder crashed overhead in unison as Sky Hunter swept under the wire first, claiming another victory by a horse length.

Two jewels of the coveted Triple Crown were now his! He'd taken the Preakness with grace and power.

Scanning the box seats, Season spied Ty as his friends congratulated him, pounding him on the back and throwing things in the air. Catching his eye from the box above, she nodded, striking then for the winner's circle.

"Wonderful job," she praised Eddie, catching the colt's reins, resting a palm on his sweaty shoulder. While smiling for the cameras and waving along with Eddie at the reporters, she mentally linked with Sky Hunter, checking for injuries, probing for pain of any kind.

"Ty Masters!" Someone yelled excitedly and the ranks parted as Ty joined them, standing proudly on the opposite side of his colt. Season had never seen him look so satisfied.

Ty vaguely answered a few questions, giving praise to Eddie, Season and the horse, even to his competitors on the track. Season was moved by his sudden humbleness. So out of character for him.

What a nice change though, she thought as a recalled comment of Moose's came back to her. A mighty man becoming a better man.

Then he announced without question it was time to return the colt to his stall and he thanked the reporters for their time. Nodding to Eddie, he fell into step with them. Season barely noticed someone slip a small note into his hand. Puzzlement washed over him as he discreetly read it. Leaning over, he touched Season's shoulder.

"Go on. I shall be there in a minute," he whispered.

"Everything okay?"

"I believe so."

A prick of worry stole over her, but she nodded and jiggled Sky Hunter's reins as Ty fell back, turning off in a different direction. Tommy met them half way to the stall with a message for Eddie. He had an important phone call and needed to take it now. It sounded urgent. Eddie turned apologetically to Season.

"Go on. If it's urgent, it can't wait," she waved him and Tommy off, that same prick of worry stealing over her.

"But what about him?" Eddie asked, motioning to the colt.

"I can still handle unsaddling and cooling a horse off," she said lightly. "Go on."

Watching them walk hastily off, she felt apprehensive as to why suddenly everyone was sent off by mysterious messages, but to be honest she was glad for the time alone with Sky Hunter. Doodlebug would be waiting for him and she could link with both horses and see if anything odd was going on with them. A new chance to make sure in her own mind that the colt was fine. He certainly was showing no signs of injury on his leg.

Reaching his stall, she removed his tack and wrapped a cooling blanket on him, then started the walk to cool him off fully. Perhaps there was nothing to worry about after all.

By the time she was brushing him out and he was playfully nipping with Doodlebug, Season was beginning to feel a little foolish for thinking there was trouble about. Suddenly, the pony threw his head up, snorting and stomping, startling both Season and Sky Hunter.

"Hey, you," she scolded, chills stealing over her as both horses spooked and snorted.

"Sorry to have startled you." A feminine voice purred.

Swinging around, every sense jumping to high alert, Season stared into the face of the woman from the security videos.

Mustering every ounce of calm she had within herself, she pasted on a polite smile, setting the brush aside. "How may I help you?"

"I came to offer my congratulations on such a fine run out there," she nodded over her shoulder, her floppy hat bobbing. "Your boss asked me to stop by and check him over, just to make sure he was suffering no ill effects from that nasty tendon injury earlier."

She was lying. Season could sense it coming off her like black smoke. She also had an accent much like Ty's, perhaps stronger though. She was pretty. But she was lying, and the horses did not like her.

Resting a palm on Doodlebug, she sensed all the fear one would show a known predator. There was no doubt, this was the woman who had hurt Winter's Dawn and tried to lay out Sky Hunter. Questions flew around her mind. Who was this person? What could she do about her knowledge? Where was Ty and the other men? Surely their mysterious messages were a rouse to get them away for her to 'innocently stop in' now. Anger seethed through Season and she quickly tamped it down, more for the horses' benefit.

How much time did she have? Was the woman dangerous? She seemed to have made a friend with Eddie, so why lure him and Tommy away with an urgent phone call?

"Well, I'm not sure what to think," she hesitated, stalling for time. "My boss did not say anything about wanting him checked out by anyone," It seemed odd to refer to Ty as her boss, yet that was clearly how this woman was presenting him.

Remembering their shared experiences recently, in a floor of memories, it rocked her to see just how far they had traveled from mere boss and employee. But she sensed she had to carry the ruse for the sake of the moment. Peering at the woman, eyeballing her metal clipboard, she continued stalling. "Did you say you were a veterinarian?" *What could she have inside that clipboard?*

The woman gave her a thin smile. "Yes, of course I did. And even if your boss failed to mention his request for my inspection to you, he did mention it to me." Clearly, that was the important fact here.

Season shifted from foot to foot, putting herself between the woman and the horses. She shook her head. "My boss has a nasty temper you know. If I allowed something without his direct orders, I could be in big trouble." Nonsense but it sure sounded good.

The woman gave a polite little huff, as if growing impatient. "You just trained the horse that won both the Derby and the Preakness," she pointed out "I seriously doubt he can be all that angry at you. Plus he did mention to me to come check the horse over," she emphasized the 'to me' part once more for Season's benefit.

"You don't know my boss," Season argued, giving a shrug, then stopping when she caught the escaped thought that the woman actually did know Ty. She knew Ty? From where? A glint passing over the woman's eyes confirmed she did indeed know Ty personally.

"He can be, well, really angry sometimes," Season faltered, making it up as she went along, still reeling that the woman knew Ty.

The woman did seem to believe that much, but was at a loss as to move forward into the stall. She looked over her shoulder, as if her time was almost up.

"If you are so willing to risk his anger, tell him I stopped by as he requested and you refused to let me examine his horse," she said, her voice cold and angry. "Then you shall experience his very real anger." Giving Season a haughty shrug, she swung around, slipping down the corridor and disappearing in the crowds of horses and people.

Letting out a low breath, Season sank to the hay at Doodlebug's feet, pulling his shaggy head into her arms.

"Season! What in the world?" Ty asked a few minutes later, bursting into the stall and slamming to a halt, staring at the odd scene.

"She was here, Ty. She came back, trying to get to Sky Hunter again. And she knows you," Season said heavily. "Not just of you, but she knows you personally."

Ty was fit to be tied. After hauling Season into his arms, he held her as she spilled out the whole story. By the time she was finishing up, Eddie and Tommy returned, offering apologies for running off on a wild goose chase. Dark glints shone in Ty's eyes by the time Eddie finished talking.

"Prepare the horses," he ordered, his tone sharp. "I shall contact Stan. We are leaving within the hour."

Taking Season into his arms one more time, he softened his tone a little. "Are you acceptable to oversee the preparations while I attend to a few errands?"

"Of course. I'm fine now." She waved his concern off. "I'm just a little shaken."

He hesitated, eyes running over her as if to convince himself. Nodding, he turned back to the men. "We depart within the hour. Make haste."

Ty returned within half that time, two-armed security guards in tow. Posting them at the stall doors, his tight-lipped orders were very clear: shoot to wound first, question them later. Having assured the horses were safe, they returned to the hotel to pack their belongings.

Season picked up the lovely blue gown with its satin bow and rosettes. Gliding her hand over the cool fabric, she lingered, her perfume still subtlety wafting up. Was it just last night she'd danced with Ty, impishly levitating him off the floor? So much had happened since then. She now had a Derby and Preakness winner on her resume. And another threat against him. By a woman who personally knew Ty.

Wiping away a gathering tear, she carefully packed up the gown in its protective case and placed the rest of her things in another bag.

Carrying her two bags, she went downstairs to wait with the others for Ty. She found him already arranging transportation to the racetrack and for someone from the rental agency to come pick up their rental vehicle. Watching him, she found it a bit fascinating to observe his decisive movements, his clipped tone, which bordered on commanding, and the expressions that said he expected no arguments. No wonder people called him The Master. Who would be foolish enough to try to destroy his horses?

A woman who hated him very much.

It wasn't until they were up in the air that Season turned to Ty.

"Do you know who she is?" she asked softly, full of curiosity.

"Perhaps."

"What does that mean?"

He sighed. "It means I think I might know who she is. Until we meet face to face, I can't be sure."

"So who do you think she is?"

"Someone I once knew."

Clearly, he was in no mood to share his suspicions so Season let the matter drop.

"He ran a fine race and he appears fine in the leg," she said after another extended period of awkward silence.

"He did. You should be very proud."

His quiet calm invited no more conversation so she turned her attentions to the horses instead. It was going to be a long flight back to Heritage. Ty returned his attentions back out the window, lost in a world of his own thoughts, a stillness settling over him and a reminiscent expression on his face. He kept his thoughts well-guarded so she was unable to catch any glimpses as to what was going on in his mind.

They returned home without incident or further conversation. They had a month before the Belmont, lots of time to come to terms with what happened after the race and to hopefully talk.

Oh yeah, there was still the matter of that pesky rodeo next week as well. Did Ty still intend to ride that vicious horse in light of the current problems with the vengeful woman from the tracks? Not that there was any evidence she would show up there too, but Season put nothing past anyone as determined as she appeared to be. Not that it mattered; it seemed the horse was crazy enough for both of them. Surely Ty would sit this year out, right?

Perhaps she could plead her case one more time, appealing to logic and current events and hope he realized this was a bad time to take extra risks. If that didn't work, there was always higher methods she could pull from. If she had to endure his mighty wrath later on, but at least he would be alive to shout out his anger.

⚜

Season couldn't believe she was doing this, riding in the pickup, wedged between Ty and Moose on the long seat as they bounded along the wash board road to town. More importantly she couldn't believe Ty still intended to ride that crazy horse. That fact made him just as irrational in her opinion. Maybe the two were made for each other. And lastly, she couldn't believe she hadn't given in to the temptation to leave him out of it until the event left town.

He had been adamant that she didn't interfere with her hocus pocus, threatening dire consequences if she even tried lifting a finger to him. True to Moose's prediction, he became like a lobo wolf, avoiding people as much as possible, suspicious of everything and everyone, even her and spending more and more time practice riding on those wretched bucking horses in the corral. Briefly, she considered rendering the horses ill or unable to work, then reconsidered, unable to bring harm to horses for doing what they were trained to do. It was the foolish humans to blame for their behavior, not the horses.

While she busied herself with Winter's Dawn's medical treatments and Sky Hunter's routine workouts to keep him in shape for the Belmont, Ty rode the bucking horses each day. Season stayed away, unable to see him snapping around on their backs like a wooden puppet and frequently sailing through the air, landing in a dusty cloud.

"Fool!" she'd said to herself more than once, watching the stop watch or the thoroughbreds, even the towering mountains, anything to take her mind off what she knew he was doing.

Suicide. Stupid fool. Stupid, stupid fool.

And now she was bouncing down the road beside him, too angry to even speak, at him, at herself and at everyone responsible for bringing that horrible event to town. Had it not been for Moose's pleadings and sage advice, she wouldn't have made the trip into town. Even now she hated herself for her weakness. She crossed her arms over her chest, huffed yet again, and considered what led her to accompany them on this wretched journey.

"It would mean a lot to me if you came along," Moose had said, capturing her in the kitchen a couple of nights before. "Do it for me, in spite of him."

Unable to refuse dear Moose, she thought hard of some valid reasons when he effectively turned off any excuses she could use.

"Stop running from what hurts you so bad and come watch the show, Missy. Maybe this year will be different than the rest and a few demons will finally be put to rest."

Unable to deny him, she wordlessly nodded. And now she was paying the price, riding along the rough dirt road, just wishing this miserable day would hurry up and get over with.

Arriving at the festival grounds, they parked and she climbed out as soon as she could, eager to escape Ty's broody silence. Heading off to find herself somewhere else, anywhere else, she was pulled up short by Ty's hand circling her arm.

"Let me go," she demanded sharply.

"Are you going to come watch the main event?"

Jerking her arm free, she stepped back. "Watch you try to kill yourself, you mean?" She glared at him. "After everything I told you about my cousin, even after I took you back to witness it, I can't believe you could even ask me such a question, Ty Masters."

"Then why did you come along today?"

"As a favor to Moose." She folded her arms across her chest again, noticing Moose had disappeared. Either he was very wise or a big coward.

Ty blew out a breath, regarding her. "Look. We have some time before ... Well, can we go somewhere to talk."

"Now you want to talk?" She laughed in his face. "That's good. You pick now to want a chat."

"Why not now?"

"Why not on the plane back from the Preakness? Why not the first night back home? Why not the last two weeks when I tried time and time again to get you to see reason. Why wait until now?"

He pulled off his hat, raked a hand through his hair and plopped the hat back on. "Season, there is something important I want to share with you."

She never blinked. "Then tell me now so I can leave."

He looked around the festival grounds, at the lights and rides and arena in the distance. "There," he pointed. "We can go there."

"The Ferris Wheel?" she asked, following his pointing finger. "Why do you want to go there?"

"You'll see." He tugged her arm, leaving her no choice but to follow. Wordlessly, she stood by as he paid for two tickets, then took a seat on the lowest car. The attendant secured the bar and soon they were lifting slowly into the sky.

"Not quite the same as levitating, but it's the best I can manage," Ty said with a smile as they came to the half way point.

She felt an involuntary grin pulling at her lips as the memory resurfaced. "If you wanted to levitate again, all you had to do was say something. It would have spared you the cost of the tickets."

He shook his head. "It isn't the tickets I'm worried about, sweet Season. I wanted to do this to have you all to myself for a little bit."

"Why? Right now, I'm not very happy with you."

"I noticed that."

"And it's a long way down."

"I noticed that too."

The Ferris wheel car reached the top and halted, leaving them swaying slightly.

"Fine. You have me trapped up here, all to yourself, with roughly an hour before you go try to kill yourself. So what's on your mind?"

He smiled at her sarcasm and sass, then he chuckled. "Ah, Season, you are seasoned all right. The kind that could burn a man's mouth and keep burning all the way down his throat."

She snorted, looking away out over the festival grounds.

Pulling one hand away from where she held them clenched on her lap, he swiveled the best he could to face her. "Season, I brought you up here to say I love you."

Her jaw dropped. The words she'd been waiting to hear for so long and he finally says them—here? And now? *Really?*

"I can't believe you just said that."

He looked genuinely puzzled, and perplexed. "Don't you want me to love you? Don't you have feelings for me?"

"Of course I do, but I wanted to hear you say that over candlelight with soft music, like a scene from a romance novel. Not here, surrounded by carnival music, games, and those bellowing bulls, just before you go get smashed up by some psycho horse," she gestured to the scenes below them. "Honestly, you're timing isn't the best. In fact, it's downright lousy."

He laughed.

"What's so darn funny?"

"Nothing is funny," he chortled. "Once again you are right and I have made a right royal mess of things." He reclaimed her hand. "Season, dear Season, you are so right. You deserved to hear the words of my heart in a setting as pure and beautiful as you. In a romantic place and a well thought out situation. I have been impetuous. Please forgive an old fool for impulsive thinking? Or perhaps for not thinking at all is a better description. But make no mistake, the words are still true. I do love you so much," he paused, holding her gaze.

"When you first came into my life, you turned everything upside down. I couldn't understand any of it. You baffled me then and you baffle me still. But you inspire me as well with your way. You are confident, so lovely, so sweet, and you care for everyone. You are the champion of everyone, gentle and tough. Season, I love how you confound me and leave me wanting more. I love you and want you as part of my life forever. Will you please forgive my poor timing and say you have strong feelings for me as well?"

She felt her anger melt away by degrees as he spoke, felt the earnestness and honestly in each word, and she knew he spoke the truth. He loved her. Suddenly her heart took wings and sang a song of bliss. Ty loved her!

Suddenly the towering heights of the Ferris wheel was too short to accommodate her lofty joyfulness. She wanted to be free to soar above the sky like the freest bird. Free to cry out her happiness at Ty's love.

"Yes!" she cried out, capturing his face in her hands. "I love you too! You drive me insane many times but I love you too, Mr. Masters."

He pulled her into his embrace, claiming her with a kiss, sizzling hot and full of desire. Warmth ignited with Season.

The sudden lurch of the Ferris wheel slammed them back both into the moment. They were coming down now, the ride over. As they landed and the attendant removed the safety bar, Ty took her hand.

"I know it's painful for you, but please come and watch me," he asked, his voice low. "It would mean so much to me and it might help you as well."

Hadn't Moose implied the same thing? About to resist, to say no, she felt herself giving in. Already feeling the tears trying to strangle her, she merely nodded a yes. He beamed a bright smile at her, warming her heart, making her glad for his sake she was agreeing. For her sake, she wished she could just die.

Half an hour later she was sitting in the hard-wooden stands, crowded by dozens upon dozens of excited spectators. As she watched the cowboys come rushing out of the gates on top of the bulky bulls, she wondered what she was doing here. Why had she agreed to sit through what she knew was coming? Because Ty had said he loved her. Considering he was going to risk his life in just a short while, that did sort of seem like a silly reason to endure what these rodeo sights and sounds were doing to her.

The manure, the bellowing and snorting, the clowns, all of it conjured up memories more potent than a witch's evil brew. How many times had she attended these same events to watch Scotty? Even now, she saw his smiling, youthful face in the face of every rider who exploded out of the swinging gates. No matter what his number was or who the loudspeaker announced his name as, it was always Scotty in her eyes.

And soon it would be Ty.

Squeezing her eyes closed, she concentrated on the beefy hand holding hers. Moose, bless his soul, had appointed himself her guardian once he spotted her approaching the stands with Ty. Ty handed her off to him, saying unnecessarily, "Take good care of her. She loves me."

"He finally said he loves me," she told Moose as they took their seats.

"Man has the worse timing," Moose mumbled, letting the matter drop as the next cowboy came out of the gate.

The excited pulse of the crowd picked up, building as the bull riding turned to bronc riding and the Grand Finale approached: Widow Maker. How many had signed up to try and ride the monster? Like sharks lurking in bloody waters, the crowd anxiously waited for the entrance of the famous horse. Anticipation filled the air with currents of electricity.

Season wanted to vomit. Her stomach rolled. Her palms were sweaty. Every second was sheer torture. She trembled despite the warmth of the day. Her head pounded. Her only relief was Moose's steady, quiet presence beside her on the hard bench. Digging her fingernails into his palm, she silently willed time to fly. Closing her eyes, she tried to block out the charged excitement in the air and the yelling of the riders as they came off their bucking broncs and all the horrible, familiar sounds that resonated through her soul.

Suddenly a hushed quiet fell over the crowd, electricity sizzling now, an expectant pause as all eyes turned to the number one gate. Angry squeals and hammerings could be heard coming from behind the high fence. Season reluctantly opened her eyes, drawing in a deep breath. This had to be him.

The gate swung open and the ugliest horse Season had ever seen burst out of the chute like a fish leaping across the surface of a lake, trying to rid himself of the fisherman's lure. On his back clung a young, hot headed fool who lasted under two seconds before Widow Maker sent him sailing. He landed hard in the arena dirt and the ugly horse whipped around, ears laced back. Fortunately, the lad was close enough to the gate and he crawled hastily under the slats to safety, his eyes huge as saucers.

With an odd sort of fascination, Season watched as four pick up riders came pouring in to rope Widow Maker to prepare him for the next rider. The horse was an alabaster, the color of pale, late October moon light. His nose was big and roman, he had huge round eyes, rimmed in red and feathered feet big enough to belong on a draft horse, long mule ears and an arched back. His hips protruded out at uneven angles. Every flaw a horse could have seemed to be on Widow Maker. He couldn't look less like a stately thoroughbred then a toy poodle could look like a St. Bernard.

Snorting, squealing and fighting like an unbroken stallion, he was eventually forced back into the chute. The gate closed and only the angry sounds of squealing and pounding hooves and shouting men could be heard beyond the high slated fence. Seconds later the gate swung open and Widow Maker shot out again, Ty bobbing on his back.

Season's heart slowed down and she felt her sandpaper dry mouth drop as she sat, helpless and horrified, on the edge of the bench, watching Ty's body snapping and bending on the equine lightning bolt. His hat fell off and went rolling across the arena. Like a true bolt of lightning, Widow Maker had years of experience and an uncanny ability to twist his big ugly body into different directions at once. He seemed to know every trick and method.

No wonder the crowds loved to see him perform. No wonder so many riders were hurt or killed by him. He was a true master bucking bronc. One born and bred for the task.

Ty's face was fixed like stone, his sole concentration on matching every twisting and plunging move of the beast beneath him. Season felt the shared hatred of both man and beast, honed by years of personal battle. She could sense their mutual hostility even from her distance in the stands.

How long did it last? It was over so quick yet it seemed to last forever. Unable to blink, Season watched Ty's body being wildly tossed about, her eyes locked on his tightly drawn face as he was whipped around the area floor. She hurt, her body aching, feeling the hard jars as the horse went up and back down again time and time again. She could feel Ty's energy slowly draining away. He wouldn't last much longer. A few more of those bone rattling landings and he would be done. Each time the big horse catapulted himself into the air, twisted around in mid leap and landed on stiff legs, her own body felt it would snap in two. How much harder it had to be on Ty's.

Enraged, Widow Maker screamed, defiant and determined to unseat his rider.

Season forced herself to draw a shallow breath, unable to suck in any more.

She felt it more than saw it, before the crowd ever spotted it. Widow Maker's hind end went up, he twisted savagely in midair, managing a second buck while still in the air, before spinning around yet again and landing hard, almost falling to his knees. Ty's head snapped back, then forward, then back and forward again in rapid succession. As the horse finally landed, pitching violently forward, Season heard the words echoing in her mind: *Help me, Season!*

She felt Ty losing his grip on the horse and decided it was time to end this horrible battle.

Reaching out, she pulled up a handful of air, sending it out to pool under Ty as he slid off the horse, settling him gently onto the dirt floor where he lay still. Seeing his opponent finally down, Widow Maker turned savagely to the fallen man, rolling his red eyes, nostrils flaring and teeth bared wide. Pick up men rushed in, spurring their ponies fast, but Season knew they would be too late.

Selecting the most vulnerable place on a horse, she visualized the beating heart, deep inside his massive chest. Hot blood poured through the valves, fueling his desire to kill. Feeling each heartbeat, Season balled her fists, applying firm, steady pressure to him, aware his huge feet were reaching for Ty's still form, rising up to smash him. The crowd gave a collective gasp, only now realizing the danger.

In desperation, she pressed her eyes shut, clutching her fists tight, and squeezing steady pressure around the horse's heart until it exploded within him.

She felt the burst and then nothing more as the great horse collapsed in a heap scant inches from Ty. The pick-up men reached them and one cautiously approached the horse. Another rider gave a thumbs up sign as he leaned over Ty and the crowd went wild, cheering and clapping each other. Season went limp and weak all over, suddenly breathless. She sagged against Moose's shoulder.

Well done, Seasoned Salt, came a whisper in the wind, tickling Season's ear, followed by a familiar laugh.

"Scotty?" she whispered softly.

The gentle caress felt tender and loving against her cheek and she brushed aside her sudden tears. "Good bye, Scotty," she whispered back, knowing the bad memories of his ride were leaving her for good finally. The soft touch over her shoulders revitalized her, giving her strength.

Good bye, Seasoned Salt. I love you.

"Well, shall we go?" Moose asked, breaking into her thoughts.

Startled, she blinked at him. He nodded down to the arena where Ty was being placed on a stretcher and carefully carried away. "Reckon you might want to be with him. Figure he might have some questions for you."

Oh yes, he would want to know how the horse suddenly dropped dead and he should have someone with him right now. And he had told her he loved her. How could she forget that?

"Come with me, please, Moose," she requested, climbing to her feet.

Going down the steps, her gaze fell on the pale moonlight colored body of Widow Maker. She felt guilty at the killing of any horse, but in this case, she felt justified. Ty would have been his next victim if she hadn't intervened. As it was now, it was doubtful anyone would think it was anything more than a coincidence of a heart attack in an aged horse from strenuous activity.

❧ 17 ❧

Ty slowly came to a hazy sense of wakefulness, every fiber of his body ached and throbbed. From a distance he heard a man's voice and a woman's, both sounding oddly familiar. Gradually, he became aware he was lying on a hard bed. Not able to quite open his eyes yet, he focused on listening to the voices around him. They called him by name. He knew them. Season and Moose.

Fragmented memories came back, in bits and pieces. He was supposed to ride the Widow Maker soon and Season had been all up in arms about it. Had she put him under some kind of spell to make him miss the event? That would probably explain why he felt so badly. If so, he was going to murder her, hocus pocus powers or not. Or had Moose cunningly slipped some tranquilizer into his food or drink? It would be a very bold move and one the old cook would soon regret.

The voices grew louder, ringing in his head, talking directly to him now, instead of just in the distance, urging him to open his eyes or say something. His tongue felt too heavy to speak. Did something terrible happen to him? Pushing the clouds of haze away, he tried to grab the scattered memories.

He'd arrived at the festival grounds. Pangs shot through him as he recalled his bold declaration of love to Season atop the Ferris wheel. And he had ridden Widow Maker. He recalled it now, at least most of it. It had been a horrible, bitter battle. One he thought he had won. Except why was he lying here now, feeling like the losing end of a bad fight?

"Ty, look at me," Season persisted, leaning over him. He smelled her hibiscus and citrusy scent, tickling his nose like a puffy feather. Her soft hand squeezed his. She wasn't being very gentle.

Summing up great strength, he pried one eye open, blinking and gasping against the strong light.

"Ty! Thank God!" she exclaimed, holding a hand to her mouth, looking worried. "We were beginning to think something serious happened to you."

We? He moved his open eye around the room and spotted Moose's huge form standing in the corner, also looking worried, plus a stranger who could only be a doctor across from Season, studying him with a dedicated look of concern.

"What happened?" he asked, glad he could get the words out. They had to be over reacting. He'd fallen off that horse before.

Their collective worried looks deepened into exchanged glances of concern, then into frowns.

"Don't you remember?" Season slowly asked.

He tried to nod, giving up when it hurt too much. Forcing the other eye open, he cleared his throat before answering. "I rode Widow Maker. Just about had him to a stand-still this time. He was about done this time. Next time--"

"There won't be a next time, Mr. Masters, the horse is dead," the doctor declared, shining his light into Ty's eyes. "Our concern is brain damage to you right now. You were out for a little longer than we would normally like."

"Dead?" Ty turned his eyes to Season first, then to Moose, who both nodded in agreement. Season looked away just slightly at his lingering gaze. "No, my brain is fine," he assured the doctor, suspiciously sure there were a few pieces of the puzzle missing.

The doctor set his light aside. "Tell me what you remember, starting with today's date."

If he failed the test, he would end up in the hospital, so he dutifully answered every question with as much detail as he could recall, feeling pleased to see the surprised expressions on their faces by the time he was finished. Apparently, he was pretty close. He also liked the bit of blush that flared in Season's cheeks when he explained about their ride up in the Ferris wheel.

"So I can go then?" he asked the doctor, starting to get up, having had enough of lying about. He wanted to know what happened to the horse.

"Not so fast," the doctor began.

Looking quickly at the doctor, Season reached out and placed her palm on Ty's stomach. About to resist her, warmth spread over his belly, radiating through him like sweet comfort. Despite his best efforts, he felt a yawn coming on and darkness enveloping him.

᭳᭰᭳

Once he was asleep, Season pulled her hand back, hoping the doctor wouldn't connect her action with Ty's sudden nap. "So, can we take him home now?" she asked him. "He seemed cognitive, didn't he?"

Still checking Ty over, the doctor finally gave a shrug. "I don't see why not. He should sleep the rest of the day and night, I imagine. Keep him warm and quiet, but check on him once in a while. If he hasn't come around fully by tomorrow morning, get him to the hospital for some better brain scans."

"Great. Thank you, doctor," Season turned to Moose.

"Remind me to never upset you, Missy. And if the Master was smart, he would learn that lesson quicker than later."

Once more she noticed the knowledge of the intuitive cook and was glad they were allies.

᭳᭰᭳

"Come on, Ty, try a little broth please."

The voice persisted, begging him. He felt warm liquid touching his lips, passing into his mouth. Swallowing, he grimaced. He hated chicken broth.

"Good, a little more."

Nearly gagging on the ghastly stuff, he forced his eyes open, wondering who was making him drink it. Season. Of course. She sat on the edge of the bed, a huge cup cradled in her hands. Could she have found a larger mug?

215

"Hello there," she said, wearing the biggest smile. "How are you doing?"

Good question. He mentally took stock, his mind going back to another time she was at his bedside and he was lying and looking up at her. It seemed like very recently. Slowly, the pieces floated into place and the whole picture swam into focus.

"What day is it?" he asked, looking around. He was in his bedroom this time, not the cot at the festival.

Concern lined her eyes. "Don't you remember?"

He shook his head impatiently. "How long since I rode Widow Maker? Was it today?" Daylight shone through his windows.

Her concern faded and she set the mug aside. "Yesterday was the ride. It's now the morning after. About nine thirty."

"I see." He was glad to see the mug with the atrocious broth set away. "And you nursed me all night long?"

She shrugged. "More or less. I checked on you, waking you enough to get some broth into you once in a while."

He suspected there was more to it but let it go for now. He had more important questions to ask. Pushing himself up into the pillows, he noticed he was dressed in clean pajamas. A quick image flashed through his mind of her levitating him horizontal in the air and changing his clothes. Knowing it was possible, he shook the thought away, hoping he was wrong and his clean attire was compliments of Moose and not her.

"What did you do to Widow Maker, Season? Yesterday the doctor said he was dead."

"What makes you think I had anything to do with his death?" she asked evasively, pushing a strand of hair out of her eyes. Dead giveaway.

Capturing her hand, he studied her. "Because you thought it was either him or me? Am I right?"

Startled, she gasped. He smiled at her response. "You aren't the only one who can read minds. Occasionally I get a lucky guess in there too."

She twirled the hair around with her other hand. "He had thrown you. You were unconscious. He turned on you," she said, shivering a little. "If I had not done something, he would have ground you into the dirt. I can tell when a horse intends to kill."

"What did you do to him? You were up in the stands."

"I, uh, I ... I made his heart explode."

About to ask how, he reconsidered. Some things were best left unanswered, especially with Season. The fact was clear, though, she acted to save his life.

"Then it seems I owe you my life."

She shook her head, emotions strong on her face.

"I also recall when I landed, it was the softest landing I ever had. Like a soft pillow of clouds catching me." He lifted an eyebrow, stretching one arm over his head. "More of your doing?"

She nodded and shrugged. "Earth, air, fire, and water. The four elements of nature."

"Of course." He dimly recalled reading druids had power over the elements of nature and life. And could, when challenged, take life away as easily as they could save it. He believed it now.

"Somehow, Season Moriarty, I have a feeling I shall always be looking up to you," he said impetuously, sensing for the first time the magnitude of the woman he was in love with.

"Nonsense. That's just because you're lying in bed right now. You'll be up soon enough and back to towering over me again."

"No, this isn't a matter of location, my dear, sweet Season." He took both her hands in his, bringing her closer to him. "This is a matter of how big you are inside. It scares me a little sometimes," he admitted softly, positioning her for a kiss. "No matter how much taller I am, I shall always look up to you."

⚜

After a warm shower and one of Moose's delicious hot meals, Ty felt great. A bit sore, but still quite good. Stepping off the front porch steps, he stood in the yard, hands in his pockets, content to just soak in the sunshine and observe the day going on around him. In the paddocks horses frisked and grazed. Workers moving horses from place to place stopped to congratulate him on a wonderful ride.

He noticed the looks of relief on all their faces, no doubt thankful the horse was dead and the yearly battle was finished for good. He'd never stopped to consider how his personal feelings for the brute might have affected his employees until Season first mentioned it and now he could see it for himself. He'd mistakenly thought it was sufficient just because he had plans in place in case anything bad happened to him. He hadn't stopped to consider the feelings of the people who worked for him. Until now. What else had he never seen before?

Going down to the track, he watched Eddie and Season run Sky Hunter around, pitting him against Richmond, his promising up and coming youngster and one of the young mares.

Seeing Ty approach, Season greeted him with a big smile, then waved the three riders in.

"That's enough for the moment," she said as they stopped in front of them.

They offered Ty their congratulations and walked the horses away. Season sat down, patting the spot next to her. "Ty, I need to ask you a serious question. Does the name Victoria mean anything to you?"

He couldn't stop the bolt of surprise that knifed through him at the name.

"Why?" he asked around a growing knot of pensive dread. He thought he would never hear that name again.

"Last night, when I was in your room, you moaned in your sleep a few times. You said the name Victoria. Who is she, Ty?"

"Someone I once knew," he replied stoically. "What else did I say?"

"Nothing, just the name, as if it hurt you terribly to mention it."

No wonder it had hurt him. At least he hadn't become a blubbering baby in front of Season.

"You somehow rendered me unconscious again after the doctor's examination, didn't you? Surely that hocus pocus would make one speak gibberish."

She noticed the hint of accusation in his tone and moved back a little, startled.

"So what if I did?" she countered. "The doctor said to keep you quiet and still. It was the only way I could think of to do that. It was either that or a stay in the hospital under drugs. What I did would never cause you to talk in your sleep. You must already have that habit and have certain thoughts or emotions at that level of consciousness to come out. Just like anyone else. You were not talking gibberish, you were very clear. So who is Victoria?"

"Someone I once knew," Ty repeated dryly, climbing to his feet. "I thank you for what you have done, what you thought was in my best care. But please forget about her and don't mention her again."

Hunching his back, he walked away, hands stuffed in his pockets, head bowed in thought. Thoughts he kept carefully blocked from her access.

⚂

The next day the local newspaper arrived, with the festival covered on the entire front and second page of the Local Community News section. One front page photo showed Ty riding high atop Widow Maker's arching back beneath a caption reading: *Long Feud Ends Between Horse and Local Man. Checkmate* The article went on to explain the long personal feud between the two, how the battle had raged, and finally ended when the mighty horse suffered a fatal heart attack mere seconds after throwing Ty. It further explained Ty recovered without incident.

Season read it and wanted to vomit. Instead she made a copy and added it to her album, pressed between pages with Scotty's many clippings and the photo of her and Ty dancing on moon beams at the Gala Ball in Kentucky. Caressing her cousin's photos, she was pleased to find it did not hurt anymore. Touching her fingertips to Ty's photos, she was even more amazed to feel bewilderment.

⚂

The plane touched down in New York and bright sunshine greeted them as they unloaded the two horses. Armed guards, hired to protect Sky Hunter and Doodlebug, waited with the rental van. Ty was taking absolutely no chances this time. In gruff, clipped tones, he greeted the guards, shaking hands briefly before outlining his expectations for them.

He was the heavy favorite to win the final race of the season, the Belmont Stakes. If he won, Ty would make a lot of money and Sky Hunter would earn the coveted Triple Crown.

And it would validate her as a trainer of reputation and prove her early words to Ty about being sure he was capable of winning the Crown. So much was riding on this one race, no wonder Ty was taking no chances with that crazy woman showing up again. If and when she did, he planned on being prepared. There were to be no fancy gala balls at this race, no elaborate dinners, and no real time to prepare. The race was tomorrow afternoon. Did Sky Hunter really have what it took to do it a third time? Would his leg hold up to the long distance and pressures?

❦

"Are you ready?" Ty asked, his voice low at her ear. "We should take our places now."

Wordlessly Season nodded. She had done all she could, it was up to Eddie and Sky Hunter now.

Sky Hunter was fifth in the chute, next to his rival, High Ransom, and three down from his other rival Sun Waltzer. Would they attempt another trick like the last race? Eddie would be ready if they tried.

The buzzer sounded and Sky Hunter leaped out with a terrific bound, taking an early lead, High Ransom pressed close at his side. Eddie rode low over his neck, giving him lots of rein. Shy Hunter stretched his neck out, roaring on, as if defying even the wind to outrun him. He seemed to be floating along just above the track surface, not even touching the ground. High Ransom matched his long strides. Sun Waltzer put up a good fight initially, staying close on their flanks.

Seconds ticked by, and Sun Waltzer fell behind. The others in the field also crumbled by the second turn. Only High Ransom remained a threat. Picking up momentum, flying through the air, Sky Hunter ran, as if teasing his opponent, toying with him, like he was enjoying the challenge.

Humming along, banking into the turns, Sky Hunter moved fast down the stretch, High Ransom hanging on like a persistent bug.

It was over so soon, Season somehow felt cheated in the end. She had wanted to watch her horse run like that forever, free and proud. Bounding forward at the last turn, dropping his head and digging in hard, he pulled ahead of High Ransom and took the win by three lengths.

Ty's hand covered Season's and he smiled so warmly at her. "Great job. You just trained a Triple Crown winner."

His words flowed over her like warm honey as she watched Eddie trying to rein Sky Hunter in. He wanted to keep running, his own race not yet done.

"I think they shall be expecting us down at the winner's circle. If Eddie can stop him." Ty chuckled at the scene below. Tommy, on Doodlebug, dashed out to try and help, the pony's little legs nothing compared to Sky Hunter's lengthy strides.

Finally, Sky Hunter slowed down and walked to the circle, Doodlebug still next to him. Ty held Season to his side as cameras snapped and reporters asked questions. Ty handled them with practiced ease, his speech perfect. The crowd loved him, hanging on every word he said. Season was beginning to see why fans were so infatuated with the mystery around the man. His horse just won the Triple Crown and all he would say is he was a great colt, and he had a wonderful trainer, and a great support team. No inflated ego here, just a satisfied man.

In the background the announcer was reading over Sky Hunter's previous races and the records he had set. Not bad for a horse one man thought should be black listed last year and destroyed. Oddly, she found herself wondering if Ty's old trainer had followed Sky Hunter's racing starts and had bet on him for the Belmont Stakes today. He could even be in the stands. She scanned the crowd, wondering if she could pick him out.

Finally, they escaped the cameras and reporters, needing to take care of the colt. Tommy hot walked him and Season carefully watched every step he took, looking for any telltale signs of wear on that front leg.

"He appears sound enough," Ty remarked, coming up behind her and resting one hand on her shoulder, the touch soft and inviting. "Can I bring you anything? You have been with him all day long."

She closed her eyes, considering the offer. "Something to eat. Anything." She turned to look at him. He was smiling. "I'm starving," she added, realizing all she'd eaten was a banana that morning. Even Eddie had finally gone off to grab something since the guards were still posted nearby.

Nodding, Ty checked with Tommy for his request and winked at Season. "I shall make a burger run and be right back."

Watching him go, she wondered what their future held. Now that the threat of Widow Maker was gone and Sky Hunter's future secure. Wait, what was that? Had the colt just stumbled on that leg?

"Tommy, wait! Lead him another three steps, slowly," she said, leaning forward, eyes glued to that front leg. Not again.

Dread settled over her. He was favoring it. Taking the colt's lead rope, she sighed deeply. "Go call for the vet. I'll put him up in his stall. Give me Doodlebug's rope too." Hopefully it was nothing serious and just the ground.

"Here we go again," Tommy sighed as well, his face glum as he headed across the field.

"Oh, Hunter boy, what happened? You were doing so great," she cried, leading him into his stall and kneeling at his front leg, resting her palms over his tendon. It felt slightly warm, but she didn't feel any pain from the horse. Had she mistook just a normal misstep for an injury? Something on the ground? Doubts clouded her mind and she wished Ty would hurry back, her hunger forgotten now.

A rap at the wooden door caught Season's attention. A woman peeked her head over the door.

"So he pulled up lame again? What a shame." She clucked her tongue and pulled the door open.

"Your valet came and got me, saying the colt was limping again. He stopped off somewhere behind me, saying he'll be just a second."

Something inside Season went into high alert. But this wasn't the same woman as before. This woman had long straight hair loosely tied up in a wind-blown bun. She looked older than the imposter vet. And no floppy hat or heavy metal clipboard this time. Her eyes were a different color as well.

"Hello, I'm Kimberly. Doctor Kimberly Smith. I work here at the park." She extended her hand to Season, her eyes steady on the black colt.

Taking her hand, Season noticed her nervousness at the brief touch, heard a faint accent in her voice and tried very hard not to notice how the horses were acting. Doodlebug was pressed against the far wall of the large stall and Sky Hunter shook his head up and down, snorting.

She may not be the same woman as before, at least not look like her, but Season wasn't letting her near the horses until Ty returned.

"He is a nervous sort, isn't he?" the doctor asked, nodding to the colt, taking one step closer.

"Yes, he is." Season stepped between, resting a palm on the colt's shoulder. "It's been a real challenge for us whenever he races."

"I can only imagine," the woman agreed, her eyes narrowing as she noticed Season's intercession. "Look, I'm only here to help the poor guy. The guards let me by," she pointed out, hands held half way up in the air.

That was a good point, adding to Season's conflict. If the guards felt she was no threat, why did she? Why did the horses?

"Look, why don't you get him out, walk him around a bit and let me see him move?"

It was a reasonable request Season thought, a place to start. Hopefully by then Ty or the others would be back. Wordlessly, she nodded, reaching for the lead rope, noticing how Sky Hunter laced his ears back. Something wasn't right.

About to back the colt up, a cold voice stopped her, sending shivers along her spine with their venom.

"So the spider has spun another web."

Turning, she saw Ty, framed in the doorway, arms crossed, and the fiercest expression on his face. Ominous thunderclouds swirled around him. Following his dark stare, she saw the vet swirl, fire in her eyes.

"Hello, Tyrone," she said coolly, all traces of congenial friendliness gone.

"What are you doing here, Victoria?" he demanded curtly, hostility heavy in his tone, his eyes shooting daggers.

Victoria? Season gasped. Doctor Kimberly was Victoria, the one Ty moaned about in his sleep and refused to talk about? Intense emotions pouring off them both swirled around her, too much and too fast to take it all in. Hugging Sky Hunter, she pushed him further back in the stall.

"Is it not obvious, Tyrone?" Kimberly/Victoria purred smoothly. "You left me. I'm here to exact my revenge on the one thing you cared for more than me. Them! Him!" she spat, flinging her fingers at the horses. "The spawn of your treasured mare and stallion!"

Like a cornered rattlesnake, she was ready to strike. Just as angry, Ty took one step closer, ready to throttle her barehanded, eyes just as cold and deadly. Murder rolled off both of them. Insanity filled the air. Sky Hunter half reared as high as the stall would allow, snorting, pushing Season aside.

"Ty! Wait!" Season cried. "Officers, in here!" she yelled out. Where the heck were those armed guards?

Bursting upon the scene, one grabbed Ty and looked uncertainly at the women.

"Unhand me, you fool!" Ty bellowed, pushing the guard away, who hit the wall with a thud, narrowly missing the pony.

"Her!" Season pointed, holding the scared colt. "It's been her all along."

Hissing, spitting like a wildcat, Victoria ducked, making a break for the crack of daylight between the men. Spreading one hand out, Season sent a cloud of smoke at Victoria, momentarily blinding her. Ty's hand snaked out and caught her by the collar of her doctor's coat. The guards each grabbed one of her arms, halting her escape. Her messy bun toppled to the ground, revealing a head of short black hair. Coughing on the smoke cloud, she whirled to face Ty, her expression purely venomous.

A wig. Season stared at the wig, momentary stunned. Victoria shouted vile curses at Ty, twisting in the grip of the men. Too much for Sky Hunter, he screamed, rearing up, pawing the walls, squashing the pony in the corner, who protested loudly. He tried spinning in a circle, looking to escape the frenzy.

Oh mercy, someone was going to get killed. They needed to get out of the stall.

"Outside," Ty commanded, ushering them all away from Season and the horses. Once free of the confines of the stall area, Season could still hear the loud voices and the sounds of a struggle. Blocking it out, she weaved her hand through Sky Hunter's mane, whispering soft cooing sounds near his cheek, the image of Victoria locked in her mind. The pure, black hate still filled the stall like stale, dirty smoke. Lifting her voice into a soft chant, she pulled Doodlebug's shaggy head into her free arm, holding his nose to her chest, consoling his sweet, bewildered soul as well. The woman's evil poison would never again touch these horses. Ty would see to that.

Soon the wail of police sirens filled the air. From her spot on the stall floor, she could see the blue flashing lights, but paid them no heed. Eventually Eddie and Tommy entered the stall, each reaching out to rub and pet a horse, full of questions for Season.

Wearily, she shook her head, too full of images and emotions to put what just happened into words. "Ask Ty," was all she could get out. The savage, almost primeval intensity of the last few minutes left her drained worse than any druid spell ever had. The shock of discovering the woman out to destroy Ty's horses was evidently his wife, acting out a diabolical scheme, left her hurting deep inside. The strong reactions from the horses and her efforts to calm them took their final toll on her.

Returning to the stall, Ty was once more in control of his emotions. Having seen his ex-wife hauled away in handcuffs did much to disarm his murderous intentions. Thank God for Season's quick response or he might have given in to the temptations quickly filling his head. Now that he knew who the culprit was, and that she was safely under arrest, he could fully press every charge he could think of against her and make sure she never hurt anyone else again. Level headed again, he could go check on his horses.

Eddie and Tommy met him just outside.

"The horses are okay, Boss," they told him. "But Season is a little shook up."

New concerns rose up within him, making his heart skip a few beats. Season shook up? She was his rock in every crisis. She landed crashing airplanes without being shook up. Gave life and took life without batting an eye. She faced him square, battling for everyone she felt who needed a champion without a tremble. Why now?

Kneeling beside her in the straw, he touched her shoulder, shocked to find her shaking.

"Season, honey?" He felt at a loss for words. Her shaking scared him. "What bothers you?"

She cracked a shallow grin, not looking at him. "So that was the Victoria you wouldn't talk about? Guess you did know her after all." Her words came slow. Unnaturally slow for her.

He rocked back on his heels. "Yes. We were married when I lived in England. It ended badly."

"So I gathered." She gave a tiny laugh as she looked down at the straw between her feet. "Anything else you haven't mentioned to me?"

Actually, there was a lot, but this was neither the time nor place. She seemed so fragile right now, not a sight he was accustomed to seeing on her. He fought against the waves of powerlessness.

"Can you stand?" he asked her when she fell silent. Worry crowded him.

She nodded and prepared to lift herself up. Then he recalled she hadn't eaten all day and no doubt the food he had went to collect was lost somewhere on the ground. Standing up, he reached out and scooped her light weight into her arms, realizing she made no moves to resist him. He felt surprised by her lack of fiery protest. His mouth went dry.

"This time, sweet Season, it's my turn to take care of you."

She murmured and closed her eyes, bringing her arms around his neck in a tight clasp. By the time he left the stall, her head rested contentedly against his chest, nestled in the crook of his shoulder, and he found he liked it there.

"Take care of the horses. See the guards stay overnight. We leave in the morning," he instructed Eddie and Tommy.

"Is she going to be all right?" Eddie asked, concern on his face.

"I'm taking her to the hotel. Come along once all is attended to here."

⁂

S he hadn't unpacked her bath oils yet. Ty looked at the bag's contents, not sure what she put in her bath, but understood they helped her a lot. Feeling like a dirty stalker, he rooted around the bottles, reading labels and uncapping lids for quick smells to try to determine what would help her the best. She lay quietly on the bed where he placed her. Cold fear sliced over him. What if she were truly somehow wrecked from this ordeal? He had no idea what could happen to druids and the fae but everyone had their limits. She always assured him she was human and as a human, she might have just had too much tossed at her today.

Running the bath water, he added what seemed like the right mixtures of ingredients. It sure smelled good and turned the water creamy. He felt a little like a wizard preparing a potion. Going back to the bed, he pulled her pants and blouse off, sucked in a deep breath and took the rest off. She never protested once. More prickles of worry stole over him, almost overriding the unexpected pleasure of seeing her naked.

He would have felt much better if she had.

Carrying her to the bathtub, he tested the water temperature before sliding her in and kneeling beside it.

"Season, this would be much more enjoyable if you were actually partaking it with me," he pleaded, drawing the wash cloth over her soft shoulders.

She lay as if in a trance. He'd checked before and could find no injuries and her breathing was fine. She just seemed incredibly exhausted.

"Season, my dear sweet Season. I don't know what else to do," he said. Having bathed her all over, he knelt beside her as the water slowly cooled,

226

feeling at a total loss. He pulled the plug, lifted her up and dried her off. Carrying her back to the bed, he guided a lacy white gown over her head and draped her between the sheets. The doorbell rang. Giving a guilty start, he crossed over to the door, cracking it open. Dinner had arrived. Hers and his.

"Season, your dinner is here," he announced, wheeling the cart into her bedroom. "I selected something easy to get down."

Taking a seat beside her, he held her head and gently spooned the food in, recalling not very long ago she'd done the same for him with the broth. Finished, he settled her back, took up his own meal and ate, watching for any signs of change, hoping for some spark of his fiery Season to return to the still form.

Sometime in the night, he heard a soft moan. Jumping, he sat bolt upright, not remembering when he'd dozed off in the chair he had dragged up by her bed.

"Season! Talk to me, please," he implored, resting both hands on her arm.

"I'm tired," she said softy, batting her eyes. "How did we get here?"

"I brought you here." Feeling guilty at the slivers of pleasure, he told her of the bath and serving her dinner and now it was many hours after the Belmont win.

"So you got to turn the tables on me, huh?" she said after he finished, a ghost of a smile on her lips. "What was that horrible food?"

"Some sort of porridge. Oatmeal maybe?" He shrugged. "I requested bland porridge."

She wrinkled her nose. "Yuck. I hate any kind of porridge or oatmeal."

He chuckled heartily. "I detest chicken broth."

They shared a lingering laugh, that connection again. Then Ty sobered, the worry returning to his eyes.

"I don't understand what happened to you. Why could you not simply fix yourself like you fix everyone else?"

"In a way I did. All those negative emotions and evilness and intense wickedness just drained me. I had no strength. And to find out she was your ex-wife. What a shock to find out who was really after the horses. And when the horses themselves acted out so strongly, it was just all too much for me to take in at once. It took a lot of energy to calm the horses. I was depleted and needed some time to withdraw into myself. That time in what you called a trance was what I needed to put things right again."

"You scared me to death," Ty moved his fingers through her silky hair. "I thought I was going to lose you."

"No, I'm fine now. Just hungry. And tired."

"What would you like to eat?" Ty asked, reaching for the phone at her bedside.

"Anything but that oatmeal stuff," she said with a smile. "Sit with me, talk to me," she requested, patting the spot next to her. "Explain it to me while we wait."

Lying down next to her, fingers entwined in her wavy hair again, her hand resting on his chest, he took a moment to savor the sharing of one bed with her. The idea took life of its own in his mind.

❄ 18 ❄

"We met while we were both in University in London," Ty started. "To a young lad of nineteen, she seemed like the perfect woman."

One arm arched over his neck, his fingers were curled into the strands of Season's hair. With his other hand, he laced his fingers around hers. Her free hand rested, curled on his chest, rising and lowering with each breath he took.

"She was worldly, experienced, older than I, and spoke of grand things. She wanted splendid things. I fell hard and fast for her charms," he said, apologetic.

"How long did it last?"

"Not so very long. Three years while in school. After graduation, we married and she instantly became the next in line of the Masters dynasty. I never figured it out until much later that she was only after my money and fame."

"She called you Tyrone."

He groaned. "My full name. I hate it terribly."

"I'll remember that. So what happened?"

"The more time I spent at the races and with the horses, trying to build a name for myself outside of the Masters specialties, and especially when I bought Black Warrior's dame and started racing her and later him, she started seeing other men."

Season cringed, hating the pain she felt coming from him. But he was too far into it to stop now.

"So as I built up a list of wins with Jinx and then her colt, she built up a list of wins with the men. Eventually I found out and we fought. Horrible fights. Our love soon turned to cold resentment. Once she learned I had arranged it so she would never see a penny of the Masters inheritance or my money, the decision to divorce was mutual and immediate. Our marriage had lasted only five years. I left for America with Black Warrior the day it became official."

"I don't get why she came here now. That was a long time ago."

He shook his head. "I can only make a few educated guesses. I had learned she had remarried a number of times. Independently wealthy men with few family connections. The husbands seemed to die under mysterious circumstances, yet she was never brought to charges. A year or so later, she would remarry, always richer than before. She was selective of whom she married."

"I suppose she always harbored a large amount of resentment for you," Season guessed. "You alone defied her, embarrassed her. Left her with nothing."

Again, he nodded. "Over the years that resentment grew to a consuming hatred. And as my horses' fame grew, and Sky Hunter's reputation spread internationally, she learned of it all. She learned just enough about horses to pose as a vet and devised this clever plan to ruin him and any other horse she could get to and effectively ruin me. At least ruin the one thing she felt I valued more than her. She even had the costumes, wigs, colored eye contacts, and make up to change her look. Very well thought out I must say."

"When did you know it was her after the horses?"

"I didn't at first," he confessed. "Not until I saw her today. But seeing the film footage opened a door to my past and started a seed growing. And she started invading my dreams and thoughts where you should have been instead."

Season blushed under the suggestion. "What's going to happen to her now?"

"She is going to spend a very long time in prison. They can deal with her.

She might have succeeded in her plot had you been a puppet she could easily manipulate. She was always a genius at twisting people into doing what she wanted. Now, I want nothing else to ever do with her again."

Season drew circles over his chest with her fingertip. He'd painted such a vivid picture, exposing his thoughts to her. He was holding nothing back now. Even the fears he felt for when she first entered her self-repair rest were still a part of him, hours later. Still shaking him internally.

"What do you want, Ty?"

Burrowing his nose in her silky hair, he replied. "You, only you. I want to lie in bed with you like this every day, every night, and every morning. I want to feel you next to me, a part of me forever. All your strength and humor and sass and every part of you that makes you special and wonderful." He kissed the top of her head. "Season, I should have been honest with you in the beginning, when I first started to think about her. Forgive me?"

"Nothing to forgive. You just said you were not sure it was her until today."

"She is forever out of our lives, I promise you that. Now, sweet Season, what do you want?"

"You, Mr. Tyrone Masters, forever and always." The door chimed, heralding the arrival of room service. "And some food."

ॐ

The reporters caught them at the stables the next morning, begging for interviews about the races and, even better, the threats against them that lead to a woman being arrested. Was it really his wife? Ty brushed them effectively off with single word replies.

Season felt fine after a couple good meals and nice long rest. Anxious to see Sky Hunter, she was glad to see he was fine, with no signs of lameness on his leg. Apparently, his misstep yesterday after the race was just something along the path.

Hours later, they returned to the secluded peace of Heritage. Leaning against the fence post, watching Sky Hunter glory in his freedom making huge laps around the paddock, Season wrapped her arms around herself, enjoying the warm late afternoon sunshine and the pleasure of having trained a Triple Crown winner.

Hearing a rustling behind her, she closed her eyes. Ty slipped his arms around her shoulders, pulling her tight, and his chin on top of her head. His breath felt warm as she inhaled coffee and musk.

"He's earned a few hours of this," Season said, nodding to the horse, savoring the sensations of Ty next to her.

"Indeed, he has," Ty murmured.

"So now what?"

"A bit of a rest. More races later on. Stud service," Ty listed, his fingertips drumming along Season's arm as he counted. "He will stay busy."

She smiled. "No, I meant now what for us? You and me."

Spinning her around, he searched her face. "What is your desire?"

She took a long time answering, moving her gaze out to the horse, around the property, to the sun slowly setting over the towering mountains before coming back to rest on Ty's anxious face.

"I want to fall asleep next to you every night and wake up next to you every morning. I want to make babies, lots of babies, with you and watch them grow into men as fine as their father."

A broad smile broke out on his face. "And women as fine as their mother," he countered, bringing her into a secure embrace, lowering his lips for a hungry kiss.

As their lips touched a groan escaped Ty and he flinched painfully.

"What happened?" Season asked, alarmed.

"Just a twinge. Pulled muscle from a few days ago I believe," Ty said, rubbing his side.

Instantly Season's fingers were there, reaching under his rough shirt, going over him from side to side, making clucking noises with her tongue as she felt the hot inflammation.

"I know just the right thing for that." She took his arm and gently dragged him toward the house. "Come with me."

"I bet you do." With a wide grin on his face, he allowed himself to be led, and they entered the living room. Unbuttoning his shirt, she tossed it on the floor.

"Lie down there, on your stomach." She pointed to the sofa. "I'll be right back." When she returned with her lotions, she saw his boots were off as well, placed at the end of the sofa, with his shirt lying on top. His arms were folded under his chin and she could sense the questions in his silent waiting.

"Just relax. This will make you feel better," Season promised, straddling his hips and squeezing some lotion into her palms. Rubbing her hands together, she gently warmed the lotion, moving over his skin in wide circles, looking for the spots of inflammation.

Closing his eyes, sighing deeply, Ty surrendered himself to her ministrations. Fleetingly, he wondered if this was how the horses felt when she massaged them.

The clock on the wall ticked rhythmically, the setting sun cast long shadows through the room and a candle flickered next to the sofa, smelling of vanilla and lavender.

Season worked her fingers slowly along, enjoying the happy sensations she felt within herself and sensed coming from Ty. Occasionally he flinched when she touched the tender spots, probably the strained muscles left over from his ride on Widow Maker. She considered building a fire in the fireplace, but was reluctant to stop kneading. Perhaps later.

Closing her eyes, she concentrated on the rhythmic pulsing of her fingers gliding over Ty's skin, searching for sore areas. Gradually she became aware of the soft snore filling the room.

Pausing, she tilted her head, a smile on her face. He'd fallen asleep. Easing off him, she picked up the blanket lying nearby and draped it over his bare back and shoulders, letting her fingers linger at his neck. Finally, pressing two fingers to her lips and then to the side of his neck, she gave him a kiss. Turning to leave, she decided to light a fire after all, to ward off any late night chills. Then, blowing out the candle, she left the room, ready to go upstairs to bed herself.

❈

Season had drifted off into a restless sleep, full of images of Ty and her, when she heard the first terror stricken scream. Happy pictures of she and Ty instantly vanished as her sleepy mind registered the sound. Sitting up, glancing out the curtains, now parted to let the moonlight in, she saw the glowing red flames leaping into the sky. Smelling the burning wood, hearing more terrified screaming, she gasped. One of the barns was on fire!

Feeling a slam of fear to her chest, fear from the horses imprisoned within the barn, she tossed back the covers, hastily pulled her slippers on and raced downstairs. Out the front door, straight to the stallion barn she ran, yelling as she went, sending out a rally call for help.

A terrible shriek urged her faster, followed by the angry roar of the flames.

Throwing open the heavy door, she felt the intense blast of escaping heat, fanning her face. Momentarily stunned by the fear of the confined stallions, she knew she had only one choice—free the horses before they burned and suffered a horrible death. Drawing in a deep breath, she pulled the collar of her nightshirt around her nose and throat and plunged headlong into the smoky inferno, hoping there was help somewhere behind her.

Time stood still. Smoke blinded her. She felt the heat burning her exposed skin. The floor was tortuously hot under her thin slippers. Already her lungs wanted air. Around her flames greedily licked the dry barn walls, the timbers creaking and groaning.

Another scream blocked out her worries. Trapped, the stallions screamed, stomped and reared, battering at their stall doors in frenzied fear, demanding release.

Reaching the first stall, she threw open the latch, the metal bolt burning her fingers. Inside, the horse neighed anxiously. Cooing to him, she grabbed his halter and pulled him from the stall. In the corridor, she pointed him in the direction of the doorway and slapped him hard on the rump, sending him through the smoky darkness.

One by one, she pulled the hot latches on the doors, releasing the horses and sighing with relief as they bolted to freedom. Bold Raven, Black Warrior, Richmond, Blackhawk, Sabre, Ruffian and Sky Hunter, all escaping the scorching heat and smothering smoke and hungry flames. Cinders and embers flew up from their steel shoes as they raced away to fresh air.

The roar was deafening, tears flowed down Season's cheeks, her throat burned. Each new cough or gag felt like fire in her throat. Only two stalls left to go. Doodlebug and a retired stud called Phantom. She freed Phantom and turned for the last stall, hearing the timbers cracking above her. She heard shouting voices outside, telling her help had arrived. Only Doodlebug remained to be freed. His anxious whinnies drew her to his stall.

A sudden and load crack caught her attention. She looked up, dread in her heart. A support beam above them splintered and was poised to drop right on them, blocking their escape.

Coughing, having come too far to stop now, knowing she could never leave the delightful pony doomed to a living death to save herself, Season blocked out the burning heat from the floorboards and the pain to her feet. She gritted her teeth and touched the burning brass bolt, her finger stiff with pain from multiple burns. Cinders rained down around her as she forced the latch. Reaching for his halter, she tried to calm him, closing her eyes momentarily, letting him know they were safe.

Sensing his fragile and wary trust, she started moving toward freedom. The support beam snapped and plunged before them, causing Doodlebug to shy violently, snorting. Season spread her hand out wide, fingers splayed to the beam. Instantly water shot out, dousing some of the flames.

Next, she blew a breath at the remaining flames, making the flames turn and began feeding on the already burned wood. Knowing she had only a precious few seconds, Season tugged Doodlebug toward the makeshift escape path.

Staggering, coughing, almost falling, she felt the pony carry her along the corridor. Things grew misty as her eyes burned with smoke. Finally, gasping, trying to draw in a clean breath, her chest pounding, she saw the doorway up ahead. Weaving her fingers into the pony's mane, she mentally urged him on as darkness swam around her.

※

Ty tossed where he lay, in his mind he saw Season twirling around in a long white gown. Pure white with a long train and a flowing veil over her face. A wedding gown. He saw himself standing nervously at an altar, dressed in a formal tuxedo, cummerbund and bow tie. A set of golden rings burned his left hand as he watched her flit and dart along the long corridor.

He burned with yearning for her. Desires and passions ignited within him, kissing flames to life in his soul. He was scorching for her, he was on fire. He was full of fire, he was ...

"Fire!" A shout rang out. "Fire!"

Startled awake, Ty slammed bolt upright, blinking. He was on the sofa in the living room, covered with a light blanket. Dragging a hand through his hair, he stared at the small fire going in the fireplace, trying to put it all together. His shirt was off.

"Fire! Barn's on fire!" A shout echoed.

Fully awake now, Ty pulled on his boots and was half way out the door before he had his shirt on. Dodging panicked horses and screaming people, he tried to count running bodies. It was impossible.

"Is everyone accounted for?" he asked, yelling to be heard over the noises, as he stopped near the stallion barn. The heat was intense even from his safe distance.

"All the horses are out but Doodlebug," came the answer. The man jerked a thumb to the crumbling barn. "Season's in there, still trying to get him out."

Ty went cold. Season? Gazing in horror at the consumed barn, he tried to inhale. He couldn't. Fear curled around his chest and squeezed him tight. His Season was in there? He'd never felt so utterly powerless in his life. He felt as stiff and cold as a dead tree trunk.

A terrible rumble rooted him to the spot as he watched half the roof cave in, flames and black smoke billowing up.

"Season!" Leaping forward, he felt hands trying to stop him, heard voices calling to him. Moose's beefy hand made a grab at him. Slapping them all aside, he blindly ran for the remains of the barn, ignoring the sickening heat and flames. His Season was still inside.

Through the black of the smoke and the roar of the fire, he heard a clop of hooves as the pony raced by him, almost slamming him to the ground as he swept by.

"Season!" Ty shouted, almost gagging on the thick black smoke. And he was just barely inside. What chance did she have?

Sick, heart dropping, he stumbled another step, hearing more beams collapsing further inside. He had to know.

A form rose up out of the dark smoke, as if by magic and fell into his arms. She looked at him, dazed, through red rimmed eyes, her face black and her breathing hard and raspy.

"Ty?" she whispered once, fainting away.

Cradling her close, he carried her away from the inferno, barely noticing the fire engines as they blared into the yard.

All he knew was he held Season in his arms and he wasn't ever going to let her go. Savoring every ragged breath she took, he watched her, his own heart in his throat.

A pair of firefighters came over, forcing her from his grip enough to apply oxygen to her. Within minutes she roused enough to blink up at Ty, her eyes still welling tears.

"Ty? Where have you been?" she asked, her voice hoarse. She coughed once and winced.

"Where have I been?" he repeated incredulously, suddenly overcome by the silliest feeling of joy. "Right here with you, my love, wondering why you stayed inside so long," He gently held her burned fingertips and chided over her burnt slippers. "You are scorched all over. Even your lovely hair is singed," he said softly, touching a fingertip to her hair.

"Had to get Doodlebug out," she said, coughing again. "Remember?"

Seeing the confusion in his eyes, she smiled. "Everyone needs someone at some point. He plans ahead to that day. Always has."

A slow smile crept over his face, remembering that argument they had over the silly pony very early on in their relationship. He knew now how badly he needed Season in his life. How much richer she made him. And wiser, though he tended to fight her along the way. Ashamed now, he vowed to make it up to her.

"I thought I had lost you forever," he admitted, barely able to keep the sobs from his voice.

She shook her head. "Earth, air, water and fire. Remember? I had a little help. Just enough."

Pulling her into a hug, he let the sobs come. Sobs of relief she would be all right. "Marry me?"

❧ 19 ❧

The flames were licking up the walls, eating and devouring the dry wood like an angry monster. The heat was scorching, intense and relentless. Smoke curled around him like black phantoms, laughing at his feeble attempts to draw a breath. Waving his arms at the smoke, he tried to escape the maelstrom he was caught in. For every foot he gained, the heat and flames and smoke intensified as if to add insult to him. Burning hot cinders fell down like rain showers, slapping him with stinging bites.

Somehow, he had to escape.

Up ahead, coughing and staggering, he saw a light. Faint, but light. Hope in the utter darkness. Half falling to his knees, he coughed and gagged more, rubbing his stinging eyes, and then forced himself up, hurling himself toward the faint glow of light.

Closer now, he saw it was a robed figure. A figure in white, standing in stark contrast to the inferno blazing around them. Oblivious to the nightmare he was standing in.

"Who are you?" he asked, his voice raspy, wondering why he was stopping. Should he not be racing for the escape?

"An angel come to save you." The robed figure stretched out a pale, slender hand toward him.

Eagerly, he accepted. With his last ragged breath, he realized who the robed figure was. Season.

J olting up, dragging in a breath, wiping the sweat away, Ty looked around the darkness. He was in his bedchamber. Everything was fine. The clock on the dresser read 3:43.

He raked a hand through his hair, sucking in another breath. Beside him, he felt a stirring.

"Another dream, honey?"

"Yes. The fire one again."

His wife, Season, now five months pregnant, sat up next to him, turning on the lamp. "That's what, three times in two months? Why the fire scene I wonder," she mused, rubbing his shoulder.

"Wish I knew. Wish those doctors knew," he muttered, leaning into her tender touch. He loved her massages.

"Give them time. They might figure it out," Season suggested. "Or the dreams may stop on their own."

"Can't you make them stop?"

"I can knock you out again," she suggested with a smile. "But I can't stop your dreaming. Sorry."

"Worthless druid," he muttered again, this time with a smile. It was a familiar joke of theirs, now that they were married. And what a wonderful wedding it had been a year ago. Moose gave the bride away and it had been a lovely marriage since that day. Except for the nightmares that haunted his sleep from time to time.

"So how are you doing, darling?" he turned to rest a hand on her belly, swelling with child. Children. Twins. One of each she promised him before the ultrasound proved it.

"I'm fine. They're fine."

"Uh, Season? What are the chances they could have your abilities?"

"Pretty good I would say. They will need training in how to use their gifts properly." She traced tiny circles around his chest. "I love the thought of bringing heirs to the Masters legacy into this world and watching them grow, both as normal children and as ones equipped with their unique abilities."

"And we shall call the boy Scotty."

She smiled. "I like the sound of that, Scott Masters. I was thinking of maybe Esmeralda for the little girl. Essie would be a neat nickname. Or Merle."

"Season?"

"I'm fine, just thinking of the babies. Names and things like that," she said.

"I was thinking more of racing. Now that Winter's Dawn is sound again, she needs to get back into form. She put on weight while she was recovering."

"She's like me. Fat," Season laughed, rubbing her belly.

"She does not carry two foals in her belly. She is simply fat," Ty pointed out. "And Richmond and even young Sabre are doing well as starters. Soon it will be time to think of breeding the stallions and the new foals to come. There are pedigrees to examine and ..."

⁕

"Yes, of course, dear." Season smiled into the semi darkness, listening to her husband ramble on about his plans for the coming year with the horses. All the while she knew he was trying to keep his mind off the upcoming delivery of the twins. He was so anxious for them to be born, but already admitted to her he was scared to death of their actual delivery. Worse than any mare who delivered, he'd once confessed, even Cloudy Lass with all her problems.

"But darling, have you forgotten who exactly will be there for their delivery?" she'd chided him gently. "It will be all right."

"My wife with her hocus pocus, who handles every emergency with grace and bravery," he said, cupping her chin with his hand. Love sparkled in his eyes, making her heart leap with love. "A true hero, I shall always look up to you. Our children couldn't ask for a finer mother."

"Or father," she added. "And all the rest of the children to come along." She was convinced his nightmares were a result of his concern with her and the upcoming birth of the twins. The fire nightmare seemed to dominate merely because of its timing of a little over a year ago when a wire short circuited in their stallion barn and it caught fire. And it was the scariest time because he really thought he'd lost the one who meant the most to him.

In efforts to help ease his worries, she'd rested her palm over his, on her bare belly, letting him feel the healthy kicks coming from within. She had shared visions of their future with him. One that looked like a holiday photograph, with her and him looking gray and old near the fireplace, surrounded by several children, the twins first and future children. The twins had their spouses and one cradled a baby. Everyone was happy and healthy.

The other vision was the future of Heritage Farms, with multiple winners, multiple track records and famous offspring of Sky Hunter and other legendary racers. Their children one day would take over the daily running of the farm and training of the horses, allowing she and Ty to travel and enjoy their retirement.

Yet even with the gifts from the Sight, Ty's anxiety remained, so Season just decided to ride out his nightmares until the twins were safely born, suspecting they would end then. In the meantime, a little more intense love making to keep his active mind busy was always helpful. More passionate lovemaking with her husband was her preferred method to curb the dreams, giving him better ones instead. Each night, before they fell asleep, they sent each other loving whispers in the dark of their bedroom, wrapped in happiness and joy.

※

THANK YOU FOR READING

※

Did you enjoy this book?

We invite you to leave a review at your favorite book site, such as Goodreads, Amazon, Barnes & Noble, etc.

DID YOU KNOW THAT LEAVING A REVIEW...

- Helps other readers find books they may enjoy.
- Gives you a chance to let your voice be heard.
- Gives authors recognition for their hard work.
- Doesn't have to be long. A sentence or two about why you liked the book will do.

Eager to hear what's next for Ryan Jo Summers?

Join her mailing list!

www.ryanjosummers.com/contact.html

※

Don't miss out on your next favorite book!

※

Join the Satin Romance mailing list
www.satinromance.com/mail.html

Subscriber Perks Include:

- First peeks at upcoming releases.
- Exclusive giveaways.
- News of book sales and freebies right in your inbox.
- And more!

ABOUT THE AUTHOR

Ryan Jo Summers is an author who writes across the genres. She pens romance novels blending elements of Inspirational, suspense, mystery, paranormal and time travel in any combination. She covers non-fiction as well as fictional short stories and poetry.

In her spare time, she likes to hang out with her pets, go to the nearby forest and river or gather with friends. She enjoys chess, Mah Jongg, and word-find puzzles, and houseplants. She also likes to cook, creating new recipes from old favorites. If she has any time left over, she paints ceramics and acrylics on canvas. She makes her home in a century old cottage in the beautiful mountains of Western North Carolina.

Visit Ryan Jo at her website to sign up for updates on her writing!

Website: www.ryanjosummers.com
Blog: summersrye.wordpress.com
Facebook: www.facebook.com/RyanJoSummersAuthor

ALSO BY RYAN JO SUMMERS

WITH SATIN ROMANCE

Glimpse Eternity

It Happened at the Park

Coffeecake Chaos in Food & Romance Go Together Vol. 1

www.ingramcontent.com/pod-product-compliance
Lightning Source LLC
Chambersburg PA
CBHW050505260626
47157CB00004B/1200